PRAISE FOR *POSTC*

MW00331284

"In *Postcards from Wonderlan* brings us a heroine to cheer for. The touching journey of Rose Margolin whose life is turned upside down and inside out when she comes face to face with 1920s bootleggers and mob bosses is one readers won't likely forget. Definitely one for my keeper shelf."
—**KAREN WHITE**, New York Times Bestselling Author

"Rona Simmons has created a world replete with tortured characters, broken hearts, betrayal, crime and passion. Set against the gritty backdrop of Revere Beach in 1921, this story grabbed me by the throat and transported me, along with characters I both loved and hated, taking us all on a journey of ruin and redemption that doesn't conclude until the last, satisfying page. Stunning!"
—**KIMBERLY BROCK**, Georgia Author of the Year 2013

"*Postcards from Wonderland* offers gritty views of the Roaring Twenties, with an innocent young woman, Rose, increasingly victimized by the schemes of her mobster-wannabe husband. Replete with historical details and crackling emotion, this tragic story will linger with you."
—**GEORGE WEINSTEIN**, author of *The Caretaker,*
The Five Destinies of Carlos Moreno, and *Hardscrabble Road*

"In *Postcards from Wonderland*, Rona Simmons does a memorable job of capturing the long-disappeared days of Revere's Shirley Avenue neighborhood. Among a swirl of intrigue linked to the Jewish Mob, and the glitz and fun of the beach amusements, she plants Rose Margolin, the essence of a strong, loving, female character. Rose's difficult marriage draws her into an impossible situation, but with fine detail and smooth prose, Simmons manages to mix grit and tenderness, violence and love, and she makes the reader follow Rose, and root for her, to the final page."
—**ROLAND MERULLO**, Bestselling author of
The Return and *Revere Beach Boulevard*

POSTCARDS *from* WONDERLAND

POSTCARDS *from* WONDERLAND

a novel by

Rona Simmons

Deeds Publishing | Atlanta

Published by Deeds Publishing, Marietta, GA
www.deedspublishing.com

Cover design and text layout by Mark Babcock

Library of Congress Cataloging-in-Publications Data is available upon request.

ISBN 978-1-941165-64-5

Books are available in quantity for promotional or premium use. For information, write Deeds Publishing, PO Box 682212, Marietta, GA 30068 or info@deedspublishing.com.

10 9 8 7 6 5 4 3 2 1

Contents

* * *

For Harold Simmons, my father, also known to me over the years as Major then Lt. Colonel Simmons, Psaighe Simmons, T.O.M., and, of course, Dad.

Love's Journey

Love's Journey, Fatal Wedding, Theatre, Wonderland, Revere Beach, Mass.

*Love's Journey is the name of the amusement
pictured above at the left. It was one of the favorite
"rides" in the spectacular Revere Beach Wonderland
amusement park from the time the park opened in 1906
until it closed in 1911. Like other tunnels of love of
its day, the themed ride offered young couples a rare
escape from chaperones and disapproving eyes. Whether
by intent or design, in what is a touch of irony, the
developers placed the attraction adjacent to Fatal
Wedding, another of the park's popular amusements.*

Isador

THE TRUCK SAT IN THE ALLEY, LIGHTS OUT, ITS TAILPIPE BELCH-ing a cloud of black exhaust into the air. On Dana Street with a clear view of the alley, Isador Margolin paced a few steps one way then turned and retraced his steps. He stole a glance at the truck then looked away. Sakowitz's instructions had been clear. "Stay on your side of the alley by Olford's. Act like you live down the block or something. Maybe you've gone out for a smoke, or maybe you're meeting someone. Relax. And, whatever you do, don't pace up and down like a jack rabbit."

Isador halted in mid-step and flattened his body against the storefront. *Jesus. Suppose Sakowitz had been watching.* Isador's stomach churned.

"Keep a sharp eye out, Margolin. You've got Dana from North Shore to Garfield. Stover has the other side of the alley. You whistle if anyone shows up. And I mean anyone!" Sakowitz had said.

He'd asked a few questions, but Sakowitz had glared at him without saying a word and then stubbed out his cigarette in the ashtray on his desk, grinding the remains of the butt into a fine pulp until Isador had given up and walked away. Stover had filled in a few details. Mosko, Stover's boss, or was it Stover's boss's boss, was taking delivery of a shipment of bootleg liquor from a warehouse off Dana Street.

"Got it. Sounds pretty simple," Isador had said.

"Well, it is and it isn't. The shipment's not for Mosko. It's for a gang on the south side."

"So, we're supposed to keep our eyes peeled for the gang members?"

"Yeah. And the cops."

Isador's fingers twitched. He rubbed his thumb against his forefinger, back and forth, around and around, as if he were rolling a cigarette. Maybe a whole pack. He wanted one badly, but couldn't risk bringing attention to himself or the activity in the alley behind him by striking a match in the dark.

Isador stepped out from the night shadows, swung his head to the left, and squinted into the dark. Nothing. Same for the right. He stuffed his hands deep inside his jacket and wiped the sweat from his palms. He stepped back, becoming the wall again. A tune played in his head, and he hummed along under his breath. The first bars of the opening scene of *Pagliacci*. Last week, after reading a library book about the opera, he'd bought a recording and played it over and over until he'd driven his wife, Rose, half crazy. Even so, he'd already forgotten the next few notes. He laughed. *Rose probably knows the rest.*

By now, though, she was fast asleep. He'd thought about telling her what he was up to and the extra money he'd bring home, but decided it was best just to say he had to work late. She'd be upset at even a mention of Mosko's "enterprise." That was Stover's term and one Isador wanted to remember. Then when he learned there might be cops involved, telling Rose was out of the question.

A short high-pitched tone interrupted his thoughts. Stover's whistle. The signal. Isador shut his eyes, trying to remember what Sakowitz had said to do next.

In the alley, crates tumbled to the ground, wood splintered, and glass broke. A chorus of shouts, voices overlapping, the words fast and unintelligible. The truck roared to life. Its tires screeched as it sped away. Footsteps slapped the pavement and faded into the night.

For one small second, there was absolute silence. Then a blinding flash of headlights came from the vehicle parked at the corner of Dana and North Shore, the vehicle he'd thought vacant until that moment. Four uniformed men jumped from the car, guns drawn. Revere Police.

Three officers ran into the alley, whistles blaring. The fourth halted a few yards away from Isador and pointed his revolver at Isador's chest. "Hands up," he said.

Two more police cars rushed into the street. One blocked the alley beside Isador, making escape impossible.

"I said, put your hands up."

Isador pulled his sweaty hands from his pockets and raised them above his head. A breeze from the ocean blew cool against his palms. It was the first bit of fresh air he'd felt all day. Isador closed his eyes and took a deep breath.

The police blotter for May 13, 1921 noted the unusual demeanor of one of the two men apprehended during the hijacking. The man had a smile on his face.

After an hour or so of questioning at the Boulevard Police Station, Isador walked home. They'd offered to drive him, but Isador had refused. Said he wanted the fresh air, though, truthfully, he thought the sooner he escaped the company of the cops the better. They made him uneasy. It wasn't far anyway. Unconcerned about attracting attention on his way home, he lit a cigarette and ambled up Boulevard, paralleling the beach. He crossed over the boardwalk and strode out onto the rocks lining the shore to where he had a view of the beach uncluttered by the string of amusement arcades, ice cream stands, and dance halls, all silent now. While the waves rolled in and out under a thin curve of the moon, he finished his cigarette and stamped it out on the ground.

Isador pulled the cuff of his sleeve back to check the time. Two in the morning. He turned his back to the ocean and started inland, past the rows of stores in the mostly commercial area and then into the neighborhoods, less dense, but darker with only a stray light here and there as a guide. For the most part the streets were empty, but he had to keep an eye peeled to avoid tripping on the uneven sidewalk or bumping into an empty fruit stand outside a grocer, or worse, slipping on the residue of yesterday's litter beside the fish monger. He hated the smells of the working class neighborhood where he lived. He'd have to work a lot more nights with Mosko's group to afford a place near Brookline. That was his dream.

Pagliacci. He hummed aloud, slightly off key, remembering what had escaped him earlier. Tonight had gone well, he thought, despite the cops' interference. As far as he knew, he'd been the only one caught, and then he'd been released.

He'd done as he was told, said he'd been out for a smoke and that he'd stopped and was huddling against the wall of Olford's Hardware to light a cigarette when the commotion started. They'd searched him, examined the contents of his pockets, and confiscated the revolver stuffed in the back of his trousers. They'd offered him a cigarette, making nice. Then they pressed him, asking the same questions two or three times. Isador repeated his story, out for a smoke, lighting a cigarette, beside Olford's. And then, they let him go. Just like

Sakowitz had said. "Easy peasy. You'll be home before the little wife turns over in the rack."

And Sakowitz was right about Rose, too. Inside his three room apartment, Isador leaned against the bedroom's door-frame and listened. Rose's slow and even breaths finished with that familiar little wheeze at the end, an unending source of his good-natured teasing. He smiled. Careful not to make the mattress buck and heave, he inched into bed and nestled beside his wife.

In the morning, the light crept across the floor, over his discarded shirt and trousers and along the side of the bed until it filled the small room. Isador stirred. He turned over and sidled close to Rose. Sometime during the night, he'd stolen the sheet and left her only the cover of her nightgown—a silky thing, one she'd worn during their honeymoon; though the color of pearls at the time, it had acquired a beige cast. But then, nothing was as white as her skin. With the tips of his fingers, he traced the outline of her body, from her thigh, along her buttocks and hip to her waist, and then to her breast. She moved, but did not waken.

Isador crept from the bed. In the living room, he fumbled beneath the phonograph for his recording of *Pagliacci*. He kept the volume low and returned to bed, humming softly into his wife's ear and breathing in the scent of lavender.

Rose woke and raised an arm behind her to cup him around the head, drawing him closer. He climbed over her body and placed his knees astride her hips. As he bent to kiss her, a commotion erupted outside, a hammering noise, as if someone were trying to break down their door. Isador jumped to his feet. "Well, all I can say is that's goddamn bad timing."

Rose flinched.

"Sorry," he said. "Stay right where you are. I'll be back in a minute." Isador slid his feet into his bed slippers and started toward the door. The pounding resumed. "Coming. Coming."

Two uniformed men stood in the hallway. Their badges bore the words Boston Police. Neither wore a smile.

"Yes?" Isador asked. His voice wavered. He cleared his throat and drew his fingers through his hair.

"Margolin? Isador Margolin?"

"Yes. That's me."

"We need you to come with us to the station."

Isador glanced back toward the open door to his bedroom. A bitter taste filled his mouth. "I think there's been a mistake," he said, measuring his words and keeping his voice low. "I've already been to the police station, the one on Boulevard. I was there last night, ah, earlier this morning, that is. It's all been cleared up."

"We can ask you nice and polite, Mr. Margolin, or we can make it easy on ourselves and arrest you right now. Which way do you want it?"

"Isa, who is it?" Rose stood in the bedroom doorway, her blonde hair tousled and loose over her shoulders. She'd pulled a robe over her nightgown and was fumbling for the belt. The light from the bedroom cast her in silhouette, the curves of her hips and breasts as visible to Isador and the two men in the doorway as if she were naked.

"Rose, go back to bed."

"Sorry, ma'am. We didn't mean to wake you," the older of the two officers said.

"I need to go with these two to the station," Isador said.

"To the station? What for?"

Isador stepped toward Rose. The younger officer followed close behind.

"Honey, go back to bed. I'm going to get dressed and go with them."

Isador took another step to come between Rose and the officers. Aftershave with the scent of bay, wood, and leather swarmed over Isador. He put a hand on Rose's shoulder and urged her back toward the bedroom. The scent persisted. Though Isador turned and glared at the officer, the man stuck to him like a shadow.

Rose sat on the edge of the bed. She tugged her robe around her and folded her arms across her chest. "But, I don't understand. What can they possibly want with you?"

Isador plucked his clothes from the floor. "Don't worry," he said. "It's all a big mistake." He stuffed one arm into his rumpled shirt. "I'll be back soon. You'll see."

Isador bundled the rest of his clothes under his arm and retreated, closing the door to the bedroom behind him. He'd finish dressing in the living room so that Rose would not have to witness the indignities to come. The lack of privacy as he shed his pajama trousers. The rude pat-down to check for a concealed weapon. The humiliation of handcuffs locking around his wrists.

Rose

ISADOR HAD SAID EVERYTHING WAS GOING TO BE FINE. HE'D SAID there'd been a mistake, that she should go back to bed, and that he'd be home soon. But Rose did not go back to bed. She sat on the sofa in the sparsely furnished living room. On the far wall, above the bookcase where Isador kept his National Geographic magazines and his box of postcards from around the world, a clock ticked off the minutes.

An hour passed. Then two.

"You worry too much." That was what Isador would say if he were here. She did. She knew she did. "Don't be in such a hurry," he'd said, his words echoing in the empty room and her head. She had given it a go, moving at a slower pace for a few days, but the hours passed so quickly she had to race to complete the things she'd put off after "savoring the moment" with him.

Still, she admitted, he'd opened her eyes.

When they'd met two years ago, the only life she could have imagined was meeting and marrying a fine young man, a clerk, a doctor, or perhaps a rabbi, like her sister Esther, and, of course, having a handful of children to raise. "And cook and sew and clean for," Isador reminded her when she'd shared her thoughts. "There's plenty of time for that. Don't you want to see the world? Go on an adventure? Maybe even do something a bit dangerous?"

Rose didn't know about the dangerous part, but she could

see his point of view. She'd never been farther than Boston. And, she confessed to him, as close as she'd come to an adventure was riding the Over the Top roller coaster at the beach one summer.

Isador had put his hands on his hips, thrown his head back, and had a long laugh at her expense. Then, noticing the frown on her face, he'd apologized, taken her hands in his, and told her about the sights he'd seen during his time in the navy and how he imagined traveling the world with her.

Rose had tried to explain her excitement to her parents and her sisters. But not one of the Forman's understood, not even Esther.

"But why would you want to leave Revere?" her sister had asked.

Rose had opened her mouth to reply and, though she'd memorized a few of Isador's phrases, when the words came from her lips, they did not ring true. They lacked his conviction and his passion.

Rose paced back and forth across the living room, twelve steps from the bureau to the wall and twelve steps back. After countless repetitions, she fled to the kitchen and peered down at the street. Nothing but the usual Saturday morning traffic. People going about their business. Men. Women. Husbands. Wives. Children. Not one of them worried about a husband or father the police had taken away at dawn.

A small tin star, a memento from happier times, rested on the window sill beside her elbow. Rose grabbed the star and threw it across the room. It ricocheted and tumbled out of reach beneath the icebox. "Oh. No." Rose grabbed a fly swatter and nudged the star into the open, a cobweb clinging to one of the arms. She brushed the web away and held the star to the light.

A shadow of a smile formed on her lips.

Rose and Isador had found the star on the beach one Sunday last year, in the summer of 1920. She'd come close to cutting her foot on it, half-buried as it was in the sand.

"Take off your shoes," Isador had said. "And your stockings. Come on, you've got to feel the sand between your toes."

She hesitated, wondering if anyone were watching, but she'd done as he asked and walked along the beach with him, hand in hand and barefoot.

"Now, close your eyes. Imagine we're walking along a beach in...let me think...Japan."

Rose closed her eyes and saw herself surrounded by throngs of people. Small people, Isador had said—though at a hair over six feet, most people were small to him—dressed in exotic garb and all speaking at once in a language that sounded like music.

"And, there in the distance is Mount Fuji, snow draping its sides, even in the middle of summer."

Rose opened her eyes and peered at Isador. He plowed ahead, chin elevated, eyes closed, his head back as if to inhale the crisp air on the far peak. She laughed and halted.

"You're supposed to have your eyes closed," Isador said.

"How do you know Mount Fuji has snow in the middle of summer? Have you been there?"

"Well. No. I haven't, but I've read about it, and I've seen pictures of it. And I want you to see it with me one day."

Rose chuckled. "I'll add Japan to my list then, but mind you Mr. Margolin, the list is getting to be a very long one.

We haven't even gotten so far as—Ouch!" She jumped and hopped on one foot before falling into Isador's arms.

"What happened?"

"I stepped on something. Something sharp."

"Let me see." Isador stooped and took Rose's foot in his hand, holding it as if it were a bird with a broken wing. He tilted his head one way and then the other and then he planted a kiss on her toes. "No damage done, thankfully."

Rose braced herself against Isador's shoulder and rubbed her toes with her free hand while he dug in the sand.

"Here it is." Isador held the object he'd pulled from the sand.

"What is it?"

"I'm not sure. It's a star, or at least it was a star once." Isador fumbled with the misshapen metal trinket. He pried and pushed until he flattened the star's four surviving points into their original position. Then he stooped and washed the star in the foam of a receding wave. "I think it's something washed up from Wonderland. The amusement park that used to be up at the north end of the beach. Remember? There were hundreds of these attached to the ceiling in Love's Journey, my favorite ride. I think I have a postcard of it in my collection at home."

"Of course I remember Wonderland. But who, pray tell, were you riding Love's Journey with?"

"It had to have been you," Isador said.

"Wonderland closed years before we met. In 1911 or 1912, I think."

"Well, so there you have it. I can't remember ever being with anyone but you."

"Ha!" Rose gave Isador a playful push. "And now, before

any other mementos of our early days sneak up on us, I think I'll put my shoes back on." She didn't notice, but Isador had tucked the star into his coat pocket. Later, he placed it on the kitchen window sill where it had been ever since.

Rose held the star to her heart.

She threw her hands in the air. Another two hours had passed. Rose saw no alternative but to go search for Isador herself. She'd decided against asking her neighbors for help. Isador would be incensed if she confided in or mentioned the word police to anyone. Running home to her parents was out of the question as well. She hadn't seen or spoken to them in months and would do anything to avoid giving them the satisfaction of learning that Isador was in some sort of trouble.

Rose dressed and took one last look in the mirror. Worry lines were plainly visible on her forehead. She could abide the tiny creases at the edge of her eyes, but not the telltale signs of lifelong worry like the creases on her mother's forehead. She forced a smile and looked again. They were gone. If only she could as easily remove the knot in her stomach. Rose dabbed a bit of lipstick on her lips and pinched her cheeks. She tried to smile again, but her lower lip quivered.

It was a ten minute walk from her apartment at 51 Nahant Avenue to Revere's Boulevard Police Station. Rose climbed the stairs and pushed through the heavy wooden doors into the lobby where a stream of uniformed officers and other offi-cial-looking men came and went. The petite, attractive blonde would have drawn attention anywhere, even were she not the only woman in the room and not dressed in a peach-colored sheath that glowed like a sunrise in the drab interior of the police station. Though several men looked her way, their eyes lingering a bit longer than normal, not one stopped to offer help. She exhaled audibly and approached a man seated beside the door. He shrugged his shoulders and said he had no knowledge of anything to do with a Mr. Margolin or, for that matter, any incidents from the night before. He referred her to the Suffolk County Jail across the river in Boston, but didn't bother to check a register or make a phone call. Outside, Rose stopped an officer and asked for directions to the jail. He was kind enough to write down the route, a combination of taxis, buses, and streetcars.

After a tortuous, hour-long journey, Rose arrived. She flooded the first person she encountered with questions. He looked up from his paper and simply jutted his chin toward a counter on his left.

Behind the counter, a uniformed official stooped to speak through an opening in the glass partition, "No visitors today, ma'am."

"Please, you have to help me. The police took my husband away last night and I haven't heard a word from him since."

The official opened a register on the other side of the counter and flipped back a few pages. "What's the name?"

"Margolin. Isador Margolin."

Rose craned her neck to read what she could see of the ledger. Friday, May 13 was printed at the top of the page and indented below the date was a column of a dozen or more names. The officer turned the page. Saturday, May 14. Another column of names, Leyden, Lovaglio, MacDonald, Margolin.

Rose spotted Isador's name. "There he is. Margolin. What does it say?"

The officer tilted the ledger and leaned closer to read the entry. "Armed robbery."

"Come again?" Rose gripped the counter for support. For an instant, the light grew dim and everything around her blurred.

"Ma'am?" he asked.

Rose took a deep breath and blinked. Her eyes wandered over the officer's shoulder, trying to focus. She saw a framed photograph of Boston's mayor, a row of clipboards tacked to the wall, a file cabinet, a key in its lock. And then, in front of her, on the counter, the ledger bearing Isador's name. "That's not possible," Rose said. "There's been some mistake. Tell him Mrs. Margolin is here to see him. Rose Margolin."

"I'm sorry, Mrs. Margolin. No visitors."

"But, you don't understand—"

"You'll have to come back after he's seen his lawyer." He closed the ledger as if to emphasize his point.

"His lawyer? What lawyer?" she asked, her voice cracking. Rose blinked furiously to hold back tears that had welled in the corners of her eyes, but a single tear broke through and left a trail in the powder on her cheek.

The officer sighed. He thumbed through a card file, plucked one card from the middle, squinted at it, and scrawled something on a piece of paper. He shoved the paper through the opening in the glass.

Rose stared at the words on the page, Gerald Kilcourse, Number 5-A, Orr Square.

Number 5 faced the ocean. Bolted to the door were three copper plaques, discolored by years of exposure to the salty air. Mr. Gerald C. Kilcourse the topmost plaque read. And in smaller print below his name, Attorney and Counsellor-at-Law. Rose knocked and waited. Nothing. She tried the brass handle. The door opened to a short hallway with three doors set on the right hand side. The first was ajar and a light shone through its fogged glass panel. Rose tapped twice on the glass before entering.

Instead of a reception area with comfortable seating and framed artwork, as she imagined an attorney's office would look, two desks faced her, each piled high with towers of ledgers, notepads, and thick file folders. All threatened to topple to the floor with the slightest vibration or puff of air. Behind the desks, a wooden table held black metal card files perched one atop the other. A framed diploma, a dozen official-looking certificates with ornate script, and a large calendar covered every inch of wall space.

"Mr. Kilcourse?"

A man's voice shouted from behind a half-open door against the far wall, "Sorry, I'm closed for the day."

Undaunted, Rose advanced to the door. "Mr. Kilcourse, I wonder if I might trouble you for a moment of your time."

A squat man, fifties, spectacles pushed to his forehead, sat behind a desk stacked as high and in the same degree of disarray as those in the lobby.

"I've just come from the county jail. It's of utmost importance."

The attorney betrayed no emotion at either her level of concern or her mention of the jail; but he studied her from head to toe and back again. "Ahem. Well. Perhaps I can spare you a few minutes. Come in." He rose and motioned to a chair across from his desk, oblivious to the small stack of files on its seat.

Rose ignored his invitation. "My name is Rose Margolin."

"Ah! Mrs. Margolin. Yes. I've been called to represent your husband."

"Oh, thank God. Then, you know what's happened to him. I've been—"

"Please, Mrs. Margolin, as yet I know very little. Only what you probably already know."

"I don't know a thing. Just that there's been a mistake. Isador's never done anything wrong."

"Your husband, ah, Mr. Margolin may well be innocent, but he was apprehended at the scene of a hijacking."

Splotches of color formed in front of Rose's eyes. She slumped into the chair across from Mr. Kilcourse's desk, flattening the files. "But it's a mistake."

"Yes. Most of my clients say the same. And, I'll certainly argue that. But, we'll have to see if the court agrees."

During the hearing the following week, Rose sat in the space reserved for family and visitors, behind and to the right of her husband and separated by an aisle and a bannister. Had the matter not been so serious, Rose would have laughed aloud, the whole episode just one more of Isador's dreams gone terribly wrong. Instead, throughout the proceeding, she sat upright, her feet planted together on the floor, her hands clasped in her lap.

The state's representative presented the evidence against Isador and called three police officers to testify. Gerald Kilcourse made one or two brief comments. In less than an hour, Judge Albert Bell, his head barely visible over the elevated desk, rapped his gavel and sentenced Isador to six months in the Suffolk County Jail.

Isador's eyes bulged from his head. He jumped to his feet and opened his mouth to speak. "But, your honor—"

At the unexpected outburst, the judge raised himself in his chair and peered across the courtroom. His unruly brows knit together and creased his forehead. He rapped the gavel a second time, louder, silencing Isador and everyone else in the room. Isador blinked several times in quick succession and then let his jaw go slack.

"Next case," Judge Bell said.

Rose came to her feet. At the same time, two Suffolk County deputies stepped forward, grabbed Isador above each elbow, and escorted him out of the room. He was gone, swept behind a heavy wooden door and into whatever nightmare lay beyond, without so much as a turn of the head or nod her way.

The next courtroom audience entered and scrambled for the few empty chairs behind the rail. "Ma'am," someone said. "Ma'am. Is this chair free?"

Rose stared at the woman, wondering who she was and what she wanted.

"Ma'am?"

Rose hurried from the room. The rap of the gavel had turned her life upside down. One minute, she'd been a young newly-married woman of twenty-three, setting up home and making plans for the future. The next, she was alone, her hopes drowned, her plans interrupted, and all of her husband's dreams dashed.

For weeks after the sentencing, Rose rushed past her neighbors with nothing more than a nod to their "Hello's" and "How are you's." But, they grew bolder, gathering at her building's entry and peppering her with questions each time she came and went.

"I haven't seen Isador around lately. Is he due back soon?"

"Is everything all right?"

Rose knew they would have seen the report in the *Globe* within days of the hearing and would have read that Isador Margolin, the gentleman in 51-3B Nahant Avenue, was found guilty of participating in a hijacking and possession of a fire-arm. But, they thirsted for details the papers omitted, details to fuel the never-ending gossip that swept through the streets. She read their thoughts in their eyes. Isador Margolin. Their upstairs neighbor. A felon.

Jacob

Jacob Moll spotted Earl seconds before his Aunt Gladys shouted from their kitchen window three floors above the street, "Jacob. Inside. Now." Jacob squinted and brought a hand to his forehead as a shield against the sun's glare, catching sight of the tip of Aunt Gladys's gray head before she retreated.

Wallace Baker, a pushcart vendor, and his customer David Freda saw Earl, too. They faced each other across the cart, parked a short distance from where Jacob stood. David's jaws moved up and down and his arms flailed in the air, his words lost to Jacob, drowned in the everyday din of the Revere neighborhood. Then the air that had blown steadily off the ocean all morning calmed. David's arms dropped to his side. They turned their heads in unison, eyed Earl, and glanced away.

Earl would have been hard for anyone to miss. Despite the heat wave baking the town, Earl wore the same outerwear he wore throughout the year: a long raincoat, a felt fedora, and leather gloves—all black as coal. He paused under an awning at the corner of Shirley and Nahant. Standing with his back to the storefront's door, his broad shoulders obscured the words **MENARD'S MILLINERY** stenciled in large block letters on the glass. But Earl wasn't shopping nor had he stopped to take advantage of the shade. He retrieved a small notebook from his coat pocket and stood, head bowed, the notebook close to his eyes. After flipping through several pages, he snapped the notebook shut, raised his chin, and took a step forward on Nahant.

"Jacob," Aunt Gladys shouted again. A chorus of other women's voices ensued, calling their children inside. A moment ago, one neighbor had gossiped with another across their porticos. Now the sidewalks, stoops, porch steps, and entryways were bare. A moment ago, Jacob had swung his stick, sailing Sid's ball in a long sweeping arc until it veered to the right and crossed the designated foul line. Now the boys' makeshift field lay vacant and the rubber ball unclaimed in the gutter a yard from where Earl stood.

Sidney Gaeta had told Jacob about Earl. Jacob's friend was always reading stories in the newspaper about gangsters, local Boston criminals or those from New York, Detroit, or Chicago. He'd even adopted a street name of his own, Lefty, though he was right handed. Now he refused to answer to anything else.

From Sid/Lefty, Jacob learned Earl's street name, Earl the Ear, and that his real name wasn't Earl. It was Samuel. "Of course," Sid said, "no one ever calls him by his gangster name unless they're looking for trouble. They call him Mr. Bloom." Jacob figured out on his own why they'd given Earl the moniker. It wasn't hard to guess. The man's right ear was enlarged, misshapen, and missing its lobe.

The disfigurement made the thug a subject of endless speculation among Jacob and his friends. Just that morning, when they'd gathered for a game of stickball, Walt Abrams and Michael Thorpe—both thirteen, two years older than Jacob—had argued about Earl. "My father says Earl got shot in the war," Walt said. "He says Earl's a hero. He fought off eight

German soldiers. Singlehanded. But one of the Germans had time to get off a shot and it nicked the side of Earl's head and took half his ear with it." Sometimes when Walt told the story, it was twelve or thirteen Germans.

"Did not," Michael said.

"Did too."

"Did not," Michael countered again. "I saw him when he came back from the war. He was fine. He got shot over on Walnut a year ago."

Michael had been there when it happened, or at least Michael claimed he had.

"Tell us again what happened," Sid/Lefty said.

Jacob groaned and dropped his head between his hands while four or five other boys from the neighborhood closed ranks around Michael.

"A shot ricocheted off the side of the building. And then, blood started spewing everywhere." Michael paused and demonstrated for effect by flicking open his fist beside his right ear. "Blood spurted out the hole where his ear had been and ran down the side of his head. It ran down his neck and under his collar. He bled all over his shirt and coat. Then he covered his ear with his hand to try to stop the bleeding. But he couldn't stop it and it ran between his fingers in long red strings."

Long red strings. Jacob raised his head at the gruesome detail, a recent embellishment. He wondered if anyone else had noticed. One of the younger boys listening to the latest rendition covered his eyes while the others sat motionless, their eyes as wide as half dollars.

Michael continued, "He staggered around, about to collapse in the street when two men came out of the warehouse and hauled him away." According to his story, after the men disappeared with Earl, Michael crept from his hiding place to look at the blood on the sidewalk. "I saw it with my own two eyes," he said. "There's still a black spot on the street where it happened. Nothing can erase it. Nothing."

Last spring, Jacob had stood over the spot with Michael. Though he'd chosen not to dispute his friend's claim, Jacob had thought the stain looked more like dried paint than blood.

"Jacob!" Aunt Gladys called again.

"Coming!" he shouted. Jacob slid behind the entry door to his building where, through the rectangle of glass set in the door, he'd have a view of Earl as he passed. In the shadows, Jacob crouched, his hands on his knees, ready to sprint up the stairs to safety if Earl turned in his direction.

But Earl kept to the opposite side of Nahant Avenue and advanced at a deliberate pace, his shoulders squared, his gaze fixed forward, a demeanor at odds with the jaunty angle of his fedora. Earl halted outside number 51 and tilted his head back, scanning the upper windows.

Unable to tear his eyes away, Jacob watched Earl enter the building and climb the stairs until the soles of Earl's two-tone Oxfords turned from the first landing to climb the next flight. Then Jacob pivoted and took the steps in his own building by twos. He sprinted to the third floor and paused outside his apartment to check Earl's progress.

Jacob's building, number 50, was a mirror image of the one across the street. Both were three stories, brick sided, with four apartments on each floor, two facing the street in the front and two over an alley in the back. The stairwell and hallway divided the apartments, A and C on the left and B and D on the right. Each of the Nahant-facing apartments had two windows on the front, one in the kitchen and one in what most residents used as a living room, both directly across the street from their twins. A smaller window, common to the buildings, sat on each landing to allow a modicum of light and air to enter.

Jacob stood well to one side of the third floor landing window. He clamped his eyes shut and held his breath, straining to hear sounds from building 51. He counted to ten before risking a glance across the street. Earl stood on the landing opposite. He looked right then left—the bad ear to Jacob, grotesque even at this distance. Jacob crossed his fingers. *Please. Please not Mrs. Margolin.* But that is exactly where Earl headed. He took a few steps forward and disappeared through the open door of Mrs. Margolin's apartment.

Like Mrs. Margolin and most of the other residents on Nahant, no one ever locked or closed their doors in the summer, hoping what little air moved outside would find its way through the hallway and into their rooms. As he sped through the open door to his own apartment, Jacob stumbled on the iron doorstop, toppling it over with a thud.

"Jacob, is that you?" Aunt Gladys called from the kitchen. Jacob winced. "Yes, ma'am."

"Don't dawdle in the street when I call you," his aunt said, filling the frame of the alcove that separated the kitchen from the living room. She wiped her hands on a dish towel tucked under her apron's belt, each hand as red and swollen as his father's after a full day's work on the docks.

"Yes, ma'am. I was just going to put away my stick," Jacob answered. He held up his prized stick, one his father had made for him, as evidence.

"You come in here when you're done."

"Yes, ma'am," Jacob said. He waited until she turned her back. Then, on the run, he skidded across the bare floor into the room he shared with his cousins Ralph and Leila Cohen at the front of the flat. The room was empty.

Through the double hung window facing 51-3B Nahant, Jacob saw his friend Mrs. Margolin in her kitchen, her hand at her heart. Jacob waved his arms above his head, making circles, each one wider than before. Still, Mrs. Margolin did not turn or give any indication she'd seen him. And then, a gloved hand lowered her kitchen window and drew the shade.

Jacob clenched his fists. *I wish my father were home.* He imagined his father racing across the street and up the stairs to Mrs. Margolin's apartment, pounding on the door, and demanding to know what Earl was doing there and what business he had with Mrs. Margolin. Jacob hurried to the kitchen. "Aunt Gladys," he said, "did you see Mr. Bloom go—"

"Sit down at the table. This minute."

"But, Mr. Bloom, Earl the—"

Gladys remained beside the sink but spun around at Jacob's continued protests and gave him one of her looks, full on, her eyelids lowered so that only the dark irises were visible as they bored into his.

She'd been at the window, too. She must have seen Earl with Mrs. Margolin.

"But, it's Mrs. Margolin—"

Gladys slammed a wooden spoon on the counter. "Mrs. Margolin this. Mrs. Margolin that. It's always Mrs. Margolin with you. You heard what I said, young man. Sit. That man's business is his own business. You mind yours."

Jacob turned to the table where Ralph and Leila sat with

heads bowed over their soup. Neither looked up. He took his customary place beside Leila.

Gladys ladled soup into a bowl and set it in front of him. Then, without another word, she returned to her vantage point at the sink.

Jacob looked at his bowl, over to the alcove, to the front door, and back at his bowl. He hazarded a glance at Gladys. She was at the sink, facing the kitchen window opposite, the one with the drawn shade, out of his line of sight. Gladys raised the edge of her blue and white striped apron and wiped a line of sweat from the folds on the side of her neck. The air was thick and still.

Jacob picked up his spoon.

Rose

"YOU HARDLY KNOW HIM," ROSE'S MOTHER HAD SAID.

"Who are his people?" her father had asked.

Against the advice of her parents, Leo and Lillian Forman, and despite their last ditch effort to involve their Rabbi, Rose married Isador in the summer of 1919. The day after the wedding, Leo had all but ceased speaking to his daughter.

Esther was the only one of Rose's five sisters to refrain from voicing an opinion about Isador. Today, a little more than two years later, she was the only member of the family Rose saw on a regular basis. Rose suspected Esther shared some of what she gleaned during her visits to the Margolin household with their eldest sister, Sarah. In turn, she assumed, Sarah passed the information on to Leo and Lillian—with whom Sarah lived—and later to their sisters Ruth, Judith, and Leah and their spouses. By now, the entire family believed their predictions had come true. They'd called Isador a talker, a dreamer, and said he would never amount to much.

Rose had tried to mend her relationship with Leo, once begging her mother to intercede on her behalf. Lillian offered Rose little hope but somehow persuaded Leo to take their son-in-law into the Forman family business as an apprentice. She'd told Rose it was on a trial basis, though Rose chose not to pass that detail to Isador. She believed once her father had a chance to get to know Isador, to see how smart he was, how willing he was to work, Leo would welcome him into the business and, someday, into the family. And she believed, he then might repatriate Rose.

The job lasted six months. To be honest, Rose was surprised it lasted that long. Isador complained from the first day about Leo's rude manner. If anything went wrong, anything at all, he said Leo found a way to pin the blame on him.

One night toward the end, when Isador walked through the door after work, Rose had known something was wrong. Maybe it was the weight of his steps on the climb to their apartment or the droop of his eyelids or his long face. Before sitting down to dinner, Isador recounted the events of his day. "Today, I picked up a bolt of fabric from the stock room and carried it to the cutters without noticing the stain on the bottom, maybe from a leak in the roof, who knows. But, you know what your father said? Huh? He says, 'Look here, you've ruined the entire bolt!' He said that. Those exact words. In front of everyone.

"Leo shouted at me until his face turned red as a beet. I thought he was going to have a heart attack and collapse on the floor."

Rose bit her tongue and let him continue.

"'Look here. And here. And here.'" Isador mimicked her father's old-world accent and gestured from one side of the table to the other as if the bolt lay between them. "'You can't clean it. You can't salvage it. It's useless. Ruined! Finished!'" Isador repeated the words "ruined" and "finished" and pounded his fist on the table, rattling the dishes and utensils. "Then you know what?"

Rose shook her head.

"He throws his hands in the air and stalks off. Everyone was watching—the cutters, the pressers. Everyone. They all stared at me," Isador paused, "I'll tell you what's *ruined*. I'll tell you what's *finished*. I'm finished. I quit."

"Oh, Isador. I knew something like this would happen."

"What do you mean, you knew? How could you know?"

"I know my father. He has a very short temper. And he wants everything done his way or not at all."

"Well, he won't have it his way where I'm concerned."

"Come, eat your dinner. I'm sure things will look better in the morning."

"Damn right they will. I won't be going back there. I'll get another job."

Rose changed the subject.

Weeks passed. Isador left each morning to search for work, returning late and empty-handed. Rose had no idea how he spent the day, but the scowl on his face deterred her from asking questions. Then in March 1920 after two months without work, Isador surprised her with good news. He'd taken a job at Logrin's on Shirley Avenue, a few blocks from home.

"At Logrin's? Logrin's Green Grocer? Doing what?"

"Oh, this and that. I guess managing the stock, handling orders, deliveries. I don't know exactly what yet."

"Manage? But what..." Rose began. She halted, changing her mind. "That's wonderful, Isador. I'm so happy."

With the passing of time, Rose couldn't recall whether she'd been truly happy at that moment or in the months afterward. True, Isador had a job and she no longer worried about the rent, but he was often irritable. When she quizzed him, all Isador said was that he was bored; there wasn't much for him to do. He complained that the owner, Jack Logrin, was narrow-minded, old world, parochial—dragging out the same words he'd used to describe Leo when he'd started at Forman & Forman Tailors. He began to talk about helping Logrin open a store at the other end of the beach. One he could manage.

Then earlier this year, Isador's outlook improved. He stood taller and his eyes had a gleam Rose hadn't seen for months. The drawback, one she accepted willingly in exchange for his more agreeable state of mind, was that he sometimes worked nights.

Once, Rose had asked what Mr. Logrin needed him for at night and whether the other employees had to work overtime as well. Isador exploded. "I'm not just another one of the employees," he'd said. "I have plans to grow the business, even to take old man Logrin's place one day."

Rose had taken Isador at his word, but she worried that he worked too hard and about the effect it would have on him if things did not work out as he planned. One evening, she'd packed a dinner for him and walked to Logrin's as a surprise. She'd found the store dark and the door locked. Puzzled, Rose turned around and went home to wait. Isador arrived home at ten that night. Rose sat with him at the kitchen table while he ate and listened intently as he told her about his day and his plans. He said nothing about where he'd gone after the store had closed. Rose chose not to ask.

Rose expected to grow accustomed to being without Isador. Instead, her loneliness grew more profound and she developed a lingering state of depression. This morning, when she woke she could not take her eyes from the vacant spot beside her in the bed and, at breakfast, from the single place setting on the table. Tears welled in her eyes and she surrendered herself to them as she had yesterday and the day before and as far back as she could remember.

At dinner time, Rose stood transfixed, one hand on the cupboard door, her eyes staring blankly at the two cans of tomato soup on the shelf. If Sarah had been there, she'd have said that Rose was lost in thought and that nothing good would happen if she didn't pay more attention to what was going on around her. Sarah was right. And at this moment, if anything, Rose was buried deeper in her thoughts than usual.

She turned away from the cupboard and toward the ray of light angling in through the window.

Life for everyone below passed as though nothing had changed. Across the street, two of her neighbors were engaged in their customary Saturday afternoon exchange of neighborhood gossip, whether today's news or a rehash of news from the previous week or the week before that. Sooner or later, Rose knew, they'd arrive at their favorite topic, their grandchildren, one recounting for the one hundredth time how well her grandson had fared at Harvard while the other gave updates on her granddaughter's plan to marry a young man in a rabbinical studies program.

A few yards further on, Harvey Fecitt swept the sidewalk in front of his dry goods store, a task he did every day at exactly the same time.

And, from the voices in the street, Rose knew the boys in the neighborhood were in the midst of another afternoon game of stickball. Rose watched a ball rise along a wide arc over the street. She leaned forward and craned her neck and saw her young neighbor, Jacob, pedal his feet backward, further and further down the block until the ball descended and landed squarely in his hands. Before her recent misfortune,

Rose would have stuck her head out the window and cheered him on. Of all the young boys on Nahant, she favored Jacob. He had manners, saying "Yes ma'am" or "No ma'am" when she asked him a question; and he was always willing to do small tasks or run an errand for her if she so much as hinted at needing something.

Jacob took his turn at the plate, a manhole cover in the middle of the street. The ball careened again into the air before falling and coming to a stop in the gutter.

Rose turned away from the window and gazed at the open cupboard until her neck grew stiff. The two cans of soup stared back. She had to eat, despite not having an appetite. Rose grabbed one of the cans and reached for a can opener.

Had Rose not dropped the can opener, the streetcar on Shirley Avenue not braked sharply as it approached the corner, and her downstairs neighbor, Pauline Seidman, not chosen to raise the volume on her phonograph that very moment, Rose might have heard Earl enter and close the door. She might have heard him come into the kitchen and lower the window.

Sarah was right as always. Rose heard nothing until something shattered on the floor behind her. She spun on her heel and saw the shape of a man silhouetted in front of the window. In his hand, he held one of her china plates. A blush of pink flowers on bone white china peeked from beneath the thumb of his glove. The plate was one of four she'd received as a wedding gift. One of four, if she counted the plate in pieces on the floor.

Rose reared back against the counter and clutched her hand to her chest. She opened her mouth wide, as if she intended to scream, but struggled to find a breath. She gasped for air and swallowed hard. "Please." For a moment the man did nothing and she wondered if he'd heard her soft-spoken plea or if she'd said anything at all. Then he released his hold on the plate and the dish fell, splintering, and adding to the scatter of shards on the floor.

Downstairs, Pauline raised the volume on the phonograph again and sang along. The music reverberated through the floor.

"Do you know who I am?" he asked, his raspy voice cutting through the soprano harmony downstairs.

"No." Rose moved her head from side to side in an exaggerated sweeping motion. "No, I don't. What do you want?"

The man looked around the kitchen. He looped his thumb around a drawer pull and yanked the drawer into the air. Cutlery spilled to the floor.

"What do you want? Why are you doing this?" A lump filled her throat and her eyes stung, but she blinked back her tears and tried to make sense of the chaos in her kitchen and the odd sight of leather gloves in the middle of summer.

The man grabbed her arm. He shoved her ahead of him and toward the back of the flat, her feet skimming across the floor. In the bedroom, Isador's bedroom, their bedroom, he slammed her against the wall, and pinned her there with one hand around her neck. "Does the name Mosko mean anything to you?"

"No. I don't know anyone named Mosko. Please, I've done nothing."

"Your husband."

"Isador? My husband? He hasn't done anything. He's never mentioned anyone named Mosko."

"Oh, he knows Mr. Mosko."

"No, he's never mentioned—"

"He knows him, little lady. I can assure you. And Mr. Mosko has a message for him. Mr. Mosko wants to tell him to be very careful while he's away."

"I don't know what you mean. Careful? Careful of what? Is he in danger?"

"Yeah. You could say that." The man tightened his grip around her neck and inched his arm higher until only the tips of her toes touched the floor. There was a click. The sound of metal on metal. He brandished a knife in front of her face and placed the tip to her cheek. She felt faint.

The next thing she knew, he'd flung her across the bed and caught the edge of her collar as he'd done so, ripping her blouse, exposing the pale lace trim of her camisole and beneath it the ivory white skin on her breast. As he climbed on to the bed, it groaned under his weight. A gloved hand covered her mouth. Rose grabbed for air to form a scream, but the glove stifled the sound. For a moment, he was still, and then she heard him take a series of short breaths. She wrestled, trying to free herself from his grasp—succeeding only in having him bear down harder. He placed one knee on each side of her hips and slid his free hand from her waist to her half-exposed breast. Then he withdrew both hands and fumbled to loosen his trousers.

An acrid taste filled Rose's mouth. She stifled the urge to be sick and turned to face the wall, fixing her eyes on a tiny blemish in the plaster, a mark she remembered having made when she tried to hang a wedding photograph.

He pressed his body pressed heavily against hers. She stopped fighting and let the strains of the melody on the phonograph downstairs play in her head.

When he was through, the bed jostled, tossing Rose as if she rode a small craft through a storm out on the ocean. She knew he stood over her because her face was in the shadow he cast with the open window behind him. She kept her eyes on the mark on the wall.

"Yeah. Isador is in danger. But you can tell him what he needs to do if he intends to walk out of County."

Rose heard muffled noises above her head. She closed her eyes to avoid the sight of him as he fastened his pants, straightened his trousers, and buttoned his coat. When he spoke again, his voice was faint. He had moved away, perhaps as far as the door, yet without a sound of his steps on the floor. "He's never to mention the name Mosko. To anyone. He needs to know that. Mr. Mosko has friends. Friends over in Boston. Friends inside County, if you understand what I'm saying." He paused, but Rose did not turn to face him. She made no move at all. "Your husband doesn't want to have a visit from one of Mosko's friends," he said, picking up again. "You give your husband Mr. Mosko's message. He plays his cards right, he'll be home again soon."

A tear in the corner of Rose's eye trickled through her lashes and trailed across her cheek before it melted into the sheet.

"You follow me?"

Rose nodded her head without lifting it from the bed, without looking at the man, without losing sight of the mark on the wall. She lay as he had left her, until the latch on the front door clicked.

Earl

ON THE GROUND FLOOR LANDING OF 51 NAHANT, EARL PAUSED to check his reflection in the glass of the entryway door. He grabbed the knot of his tie with one hand and pulled on the tail with the other, settling the perfect four-in-hand beneath his collar. He exited, and after a quick but unnecessary glance in both directions, stepped onto the sidewalk.

The streets were quiet, normal for the places Earl traveled. Then from somewhere above and behind his right shoulder came the sound of wood grating on wood, someone had cracked a window or dragged a chair across a floor. Earl cocked his good ear toward the sound and caught a movement out of the corner of his eye. A figure in the window across the street. Sandy hair shorn straight across a freckled forehead. Earl watched the boy watch him until someone came from behind, placed a hand on the boy's shoulder, and tugged him from the window. A woman wearing a blue and white striped apron came into view. She lowered the window and drew the blind.

Earl strode up the block the way he'd come not half an hour ago. Once again, he paused at the corner and pulled his notepad from his pocket. Earl flipped it open, turned a few pages, and marked through the fourth item on his list, 51-3B. He made a mental note of the last unchecked item on his list and stuffed the notepad back into his jacket before heading east to Ocean Avenue.

Earl had been assigned five errands for the day: two "introductory visits" to new shopkeepers in the area, one a laundry and the other a dry goods store; two routine collections; and the Nahant visit. He had saved the routine collection at Greenfield Pharmacy for his last errand of the day, as the drug store was a block from his home. For once, the proprietor, Louis Greenfield, was prepared. Without Earl's having to ask for payment, the druggist dropped an envelope on the counter. Earl slid the envelope into his jacket. They exchanged no words, just a nod as Earl left.

It wasn't until he'd come through the door of his flat that the image of a woman flashed in his head. It was the Nahant woman. He shook his head, scattering the vision. Then he removed his hat, coat, and jacket, loosened his tie, and poured a drink.

Fifteen minutes later, Caroline burst through the doorway, her finer features on display. When she grabbed him around the waist and rubbed the nipples of her breasts against his chest, both the vision and the memory of 51-3B fell away. He grasped Caroline by the arm and drove her toward the bedroom.

With a start, Earl jolted awake. He punched his fists into his flattened and slightly damp pillow and rolled onto his back. Half an hour or so later, he was still awake, his eyes fixed on the ceiling. Earl stretched an arm over Caroline, fumbling in the dark for his alarm clock. It clattered to the floor.

"Goddamn it," he said.

"Same to you," Caroline said, her voice hoarse with gin.

"What time is it?"

"I have no idea." With one hand, she felt around the floor

beside and under the bed. "Jesus, it's three o'clock in the morning."

"Oof." Earl pressed his fingers into his temples to dull the pain that accompanied him every waking hour since the incident on Walnut.

Caroline turned toward him. She ran her fingers through the hairs on his chest and then walked them like a daddy-long-leg spider toward his groin. "Hungry for more?"

Earl swatted her hand. "Go back to sleep."

She groaned and rolled over, dragging the sheets with her. Earl waited until her breathing settled into a regular rhythm, in and out, steady, like the ripples of waves at low tide. Taking care not to jostle her again, he raised himself to a sitting position on the edge of the bed. He looked back at Caroline once before stepping through the trail of clothes she'd discarded last night: something satin-like near the foot of the bed, another two feet away her stockings, and further on a brassiere and panties. Near the door, a slip. A dress, flung over the arm of a chair.

"Earl, honey..."

"Go back to sleep. I'm getting up."

"It's too early. Come back to bed."

He pulled the bedroom door closed behind him and padded in the dark to the kitchen, a niche barely large enough to open the icebox and a cabinet drawer at the same time. On the counter, the still open bottle of gin stood alongside two empty shot glasses. Earl stuffed a cork into the throat of the bottle. He bent at the waist and opened the icebox, letting the chill air wash over him, hoping to clear his head. He slid a bottle of milk from the shelf and carried it to the living room where he settled into an easy chair. After a long draught of the cool liquid, Earl wiped his mouth with the back of his hand and set the bottle on the floor.

He had slept an hour, maybe two. Earl pinched the bridge of his nose between his thumb and forefinger and then rubbed his temples and the back of his neck. When he opened his eyes again, the Nahant woman was at his feet. She lay in a pool of moonlight on the rough wool rug, an arm as fresh and white as a Boston winter's first snow covered her eyes. He leaned forward to pull her arm away and look at her face and into her eyes. Earlier, they'd betrayed her show of calm when, at the sound of the dish smashing on the floor, she'd spun around and seen him, met his gaze, and guessed his intent.

She'd guessed wrong. He hadn't gone there to do what he did. It wasn't supposed to happen.

Colin Sakowitz had said, "Mosko wants the woman to know what her man has to do. *Capisce?*"

"*Capisce*," Earl had answered.

"Get over there and rustle up the place a bit. Smash a few things and explain the deal. He gets protection as long as he keeps his trap shut. Got it?"

"Got it." And he had, at the time. He couldn't explain why he'd done what he'd done, not then, not now. It wasn't supposed to happen.

Earl stretched forward, nearly coming out of his chair. His hand hovered over Rose Margolin. He tried to move a lock of hair from her shoulder, but found only wool strands in his fingers. Earl squeezed his eyes shut. She was still there when he opened them again. He rose and side-stepped his way from the room, taking care not to tread on her.

In the safety of his kitchen, he turned his back to the vision. He emptied the remains of yesterday's coffee in the sink, filled the pot with fresh grounds, and drummed his fingers on the counter as he waited. The liquid percolating into the glass bubble ran clear, then with a stain of brown, then darker, then rich black. The aroma alone soothed the tension in his body and the ache in the soft spot above his injured ear.

A shuffle of feet behind him. "Umm. Coffee sure smells good."

Earl swung his head around. *Caroline.* He breathed a sigh of relief but glanced behind her, scanning the rug on the living room floor.

Caroline followed his gaze and glanced over her shoulder. "Hey, baby. There's no one here. Just you and me." She ruffled her hair with one hand. "How about we take that coffee back to bed?"

Earl turned back to the counter and the coffee without a word.

Caroline snuggled close behind him and snaked her arms around his waist, clasping her hands in front of his belly. "I could make you some breakfast."

"Nah. I got to go." It was a lie. He was not due at Mosko's until nine. *That's one good thing about Caroline and women like her, you don't owe them the truth. Hell, you don't even owe them an explanation.*

"Okay, baby, whatever you say." She released her grasp and backed away. "Will I see you tonight?"

"I don't know. It depends." Another lie. Keeping his back to Caroline, Earl poured the steaming liquid into a single cup.

"Okey dokey, I can take a hint," she said as she shuffled back to the bedroom to dress and collect the five dollar fee from the night stand—the fee they'd settled on some weeks ago for her occasional visits.

Earl bent over his cup of coffee, inhaling deeply, listening. He heard the scrape of the front door as it passed over the loose floorboard beside the threshold.

"Ta ta, sugar! You know where you can find me," she said, punctuating her goodbye with a smack of her lips. A kiss blown across the room.

Earl listened for the scrape of the door closing. Nothing. *Goddamn it.* After giving Caroline time to reach the street, he padded to the front door, closed it, and padded back to the kitchen, giving a wide berth to the rug in the living room.

Only four men remained in line in Rosenberg's small office, all of them cohorts in Mosko's army of strong-arms, leg-breakers, and henchmen. Nicholas Rosenberg was one of Mosko's right hand men. There were three: Colin Sakowitz who handed out assignments, Nicholas Rosenberg who handled collections, and Jack Koiles who did everything else. Allen Foye faced Rosenberg at his desk. Gene Smilowe was next in line, then Earl, then Francis Toomey. Foye finished his business and turned to go, tipping his hat to Earl as he passed. Earl nodded and returned to his conversation with Gene. Earl and Gene had known each other for a long time and had partnered on several Mosko assignments. With his slight build, Gene was useless in a fist or knife fight, but anytime firearms were involved, which was often, Gene was the man Earl wanted by his side.

"Smilowe." Rosenberg called for the next in line without taking his eyes off his ledger.

Gene's business took no more than a minute or two. On

his way out, he clasped Earl's hand and gave it a firm shake. Earl stepped forward anticipating Rosenberg's call. From his pocket, he withdrew a cylinder of dollar bills bound together by a rubber band. It had a nice heft to it. Earl set the money on Rosenberg's desk along with a few slips of paper torn from his notepad—his errands, listed by nothing more than the street number, the amount collected written at the top of each page, and the extra errand "51-3B" noted at the bottom of yesterday's stub. Beside it, a check mark.

Without any sign of acknowledgment, Rosenberg set the list aside. He swiveled in his chair to a clear spot on the desk and removed the rubber band from the circle of bills. *Ten, twenty, thirty...*Earl counted with Rosenberg. *Four hundred.* Rosenberg swiveled back to the ledger splayed open between them and penciled a check mark in the column labeled 3 July. He raised his eyeshades to a perch near his hairline. "And the Margolin woman?" Rosenberg asked, wheezing before and after he spoke as if the counting had taxed him to the point of exhaustion.

"Taken care of," Earl said.

"Taken care of," Rosenberg repeated without inflection, a neutral tone somewhere between a question and a statement. He dropped his pencil to rescue the last of his cigarette from the ashtray. He took a drag, leaned back, and rocked in his chair, a squeak at each forward movement. "What did she say, exactly?" *Squeak.* Pause. *Squeak.*

Earl wondered what would satisfy Rosenberg. He took a chance. "She didn't say anything."

"Well, then." Rosenberg sat back, his face drawn into the shadows, the cigarette clamped between two fingers and growing shorter. Rosenberg coughed. He stubbed out the cigarette and pounded his chest with his fist. When the coughing fit passed, he sat forward in his chair, his elbows on the desk. "Well then, how can you be sure she understood?"

"I asked," Earl said. "I asked. She nodded. She was..." Earl paused, searching for the appropriate words, "too scared to speak."

"I suppose that's as good a sign as any." *Squeak* "You might want to follow up to be sure." *Squeak.*

"Follow up?" Earl dreaded the thought of returning to Nahant.

"Yeah. Check on the husband over in the joint. Check with Pete. He'll know whether or not things are copacetic."

Squeak.

On hearing Rosenberg's clarification, Earl breathed a sigh of relief. He hadn't seen Peter Wersted for close to ten years, not since he himself had spent three weeks in the county jail for lifting a wallet and a couple of bottles of whiskey from a saloon. Pete had sought him out, gotten to know him, and vouched for Earl when Mosko had asked. *Yeah, Pete probably has a whole clan of informants in the joint by now. He'd know if Margolin had veered from the script or given up any names. Thank God. Anything but go back to Nahant.*

"How much time does he have up there?" Earl asked.

"Oh, Margolin's not going anywhere, but the sooner you pay Pete a visit the better."

"Got involved in that hijacking in May on Dana Street, so I hear." Earl said, still fishing. The word on the street was the cops had broken up one of Mosko's deals and nabbed a few of his men. But the particulars were sketchy. Mosko called all the shots and kept the details to himself. "You only need to know what you need to know," Mosko had said to Earl more than once. But Earl disagreed. Information was the key to survival in his line of business. He made it his habit to poke his nose into every corner and root around until he found what he needed to know about the men he worked with: where they came from, who their friends were, how long they'd been in the business. Even when he'd gotten to know someone, Earl kept his guard up. He trusted no one but himself.

"That the one? Dana?" Earl asked, prodding, but trying to keep a tone of indifference in his voice. Rosenberg grunted. Earl interpreted the grunt as confirmation and pressed no further. He knew when to push and when to let up.

Squeak. "Here you go. Colin's list." Rosenberg slid a list of new assignments across the desk.

"Toomey," Rosenberg said, calling the next man forward.

Earl waited until he was on the street outside Rosenberg's office to check the list. Twenty items, each indicated by a street number, no street name, no store name, each a routine collection that Earl would enter in his notepad. Nothing out of the ordinary. He sighed.

Rose

After Earl Bloom left, Rose lay in bed, unmoving, her eyes glued to the mark on the wall. She had no idea how long she remained in that position, but when the light outside faded and turned muddy, she sat and rested her feet on the floor. Every inch of her body screamed in protest. Unwilling or unable to stand and put one foot in front of the other, Rose winced and lowered herself to the floor.

She crawled into the living room and across the floor to the bureau. She grabbed the top of the bureau and pulled herself up. Rose sighed in relief. The key to the front door, the key she'd never used, lay to one side of the top drawer. The door lock was rusty, but with a bit of pressure, the bolt slipped into position. Rose sighed again and slid to the floor. She crawled to the other side of the bureau and crouched in the small niche between the bureau and the window. There, she brought her knees to her chest and waited, praying silently, listening, and clenching the key in her fist.

Doors opened and closed. Neighbors coming home from synagogue. Pots and pans and dishes banged in one of the apartments below. Someone cleaning after dinner. Snippets of conversations wafted from the street. A young couple out for a stroll on a Saturday night. She must have dozed for some period, because the next time she opened her eyes, the room was dark, the surfaces and angles of the furniture barely discernible. From somewhere close by a baby cried and was hushed and blocks away the faint blare of a car's horn sounded. Normal everyday noises. Still, Rose cowered in her hiding place and listened for the other sounds. Sounds she had a name for now, sounds of fear: the soft slip of a shoe on a stair, a slow turn at the landing, a gloved hand on a door latch, a dish shattering on the floor.

Hours later, Rose's chin dropped to her chest and she slept propped against the wall, the key tucked away inside the pocket of her robe.

The living room windows faced east toward the beach, though a view of the ocean was obscured behind row upon row of two- and three-story houses, apartment buildings, and a series of blocks with shops and dwellings between Nahant and Boulevard. Even so, in the summer, long before the sun broke the horizon light bloomed in her windows.

The brightness nipped at her eyelids. Rose woke and raised her head. She was shocked to find herself on the floor in the corner of her living room and not in the comfort of her bed. As she pushed herself onto her knees, something brushed against her thigh. She pulled the front door key from her pocket and for a moment wondered why she had put it there. Then she gasped, drew the edges of her robe together, and scurried back into the corner.

Darkness returned. Rose's back, shoulders, arms, and legs ached from having sat in one position so long. She forced herself to stand and to walk to the kitchen. She dragged one of the two straight-backed chairs from the kitchen table to the front door and jammed it under the door's handle.

Rose made her way to the bathroom and stood in front of the porcelain sink, blinding in its whiteness. Rose let her robe fall to the floor. She removed her brassiere, the strap on one side torn but repairable. Her panties were somewhere on the bedroom floor—those she would discard. She drew a bath of hot water and lay nearly submerged, soaking. After the skin on her fingertips puckered and the ache in her muscles dulled, she scoured herself from head to toe.

She stepped from the tub and studied herself in the mirror over the sink. There were her eyes with lashes so light they made her eyes look bare and set too wide. Her nose. Her lips. Her chin. Her blond hair wet from the bath and slick around her head and neck. The woman in the mirror looked identical to the Rose Margolin of yesterday, from before the sound of the dish shattering. But unlike the Rose Margolin of yesterday, this woman was like one of the Hollywood movie sets she'd seen in a magazine, a house with a false front. A shell. Empty inside. On the other hand, deep inside her shell, there was something. A dark and hurtful thing. One she would never name, never mention.

Monday. Rose removed the chair from under the handle and unlocked the door. She shook her head in dismay at the futility of the defense. But she had no time to dwell on her thoughts. Esther was due any minute and Rose didn't want her sister to find the apartment locked and barricaded.

She'd double checked her effort to straighten up, but she scanned the apartment a third time. She'd tidied the kitchen, sweeping up the broken shards of china and collecting the scattered contents of the drawers. She'd straightened the rug in the small hallway from where it had slid and come to rest against the wall. She'd removed and changed the bedding and discarded the clothes she'd worn on Saturday.

"Rose," her sister called from the stairwell.

Rose dashed to the mirror, patted her hair in place, and ran her fingers across the front of her skirt, smoothing rumples only she could see. Evidence.

"Rose dear. My goodness, you're ready. What a surprise."

"I am."

"This makes a first! I thought I'd have to wait for sure."

"No. I was up early this morning."

"Did you get some sleep?"

"Some."

"Well, I'm sure you'll feel better when you see Isador."

Today would be Rose's first opportunity to see Isador since the sentencing. It was to have been a celebration of sorts. The Fourth of July, even in prison. But Rose was in no mood to celebrate. The visit had a new purpose. She'd have to pass Mosko's message to Isador, while keeping the circumstances from him. It would test every nerve in her body. Isador could not know.

"Rose?"

"Sorry Esther. I'm sure I will. I need to see him. I've got so many questions to ask."

Esther nudged Rose with her elbow. "Rose, have I lost you again?" The two were aboard the bus to town, seated side by side.

"Yes. Guilty," she said, cringing at her choice of words. "I was day dreaming. Tell me, what's going on at home."

Esther relayed the news of their siblings, keeping track by ticking each one off on her fingers, starting with Sarah, fourteen years older than Rose, almost a generation removed. She moved on to Ruth, Judith, and Leah, the three closest in age, born in quick succession, arriving a year apart. Esther had followed four years later.

Rose was the youngest of the six and had caught her parents by surprise. So unexpected that Leo and Lillian abandoned their practice of bestowing a time honored biblical name on their daughter. They'd settled for Rose.

In danger of drifting off again, Rose pinched the skin on the inside of her arm. Esther was going on about Rabbi Daniel, her husband. He was the same as always, still suffering from chilblains. They rode in silence for a few minutes. Esther resumed, "I'll be honest with you, I'm not surprised."

"Not surprised about what?"

"About Isador. I knew the first time I met him. I suppose we all knew, but you were so much in love you wouldn't listen. There I go." Esther said. "I told myself I wouldn't lecture you. Tell me what I can do to help."

"You're helping by going with me. I'm not sure I could have done it alone," Rose said. She gazed out the window at the unfamiliar neighborhoods as they passed and let Esther carry on a one way conversation for the rest of the journey, responding only with an occasional nod or half smile. When Charles Street came into view, a block ahead, Rose pulled the cord above the window to signal their stop.

The jail sat a half a block further on, but Esther hung back. "You go ahead. I'll wait for you here."

Rose glanced at the gray stone facade ahead, a turret capping the far corner. She turned back to Esther. "Are you sure you won't come in with me?"

Esther shook her head.

Rose counted her steps to the archway, remembering her

first brief and unsuccessful visit and unsure if she wanted to hurry or prolong the moment.

This time, she merely nodded at the seated guard before joining the queue of other visitors. Ahead of her, a woman she recognized from the bus spoke her name to the guard behind the glass and then passed through a door to the left. A second woman, her two small children clinging to the folds or her skirt, spoke her name. She disappeared through the same door. When her turn came, Rose stood on her tiptoes and gave the guard her name. He cupped his hand over his ear.

"Margolin," she repeated, more loudly and with a glance around the room.

The guard consulted a clipboard and nodded toward the door on her left. Fifteen minutes more passed as Rose penetrated the series of checkpoints, each with a dour-faced guard and a clipboard or ledger, each scrutinizing Rose from head to toe, until at last she stood in front of a room marked **VISITORS.**

Her eyes danced over the heads of the scores of women and children in the hallway. Some of the women held baskets in their laps, some sobbed quietly into handkerchiefs, some shushed their children. Rose worried that she was witnessing her future, that she would look just like them in the months ahead. Rose shut her eyes. She'd seen all she wanted to see of the coarse and broken crowd.

"Margolin."

Rose started. The guard was staring at her. "Margolin," he said again.

Isador

THE WEEKS AFTER HIS HEARING WERE A BLUR OF SMALL WINDOW-less rooms, dark corners, cigarette smoke, bright lights, and foul odors that grew worse and more penetrating each day. He saw Rose once before the hearing and hoped to have time alone with her afterward, but instead, the guards had whisked him away without a word. In a matter of hours, he was processed, transported, and assigned to a cell deep within the county jail. He wondered how he'd ever get word to Rose. A day or two later, Gerald Kilcourse appeared on his way to see another inmate, Isador a thing of the past, an old case, an unlikely source of revenue. Kilcourse promised to send word to Rose.

Isador had heard nothing more until this morning when the guard had stopped outside Isador's cell, glanced at the cell number, back to the clipboard in his hand, and over the rim of his eyeglasses at Isador. "Margolin, you've got a visitor. Twenty minutes."

Isador pushed his breakfast tray aside, his oatmeal—or what passed for oatmeal at Suffolk—half-finished. On the fifteen-inch-square table next to his cot lay inmate 26609's worldly possessions: a comb, a bar of soap, a toothbrush, a tin of tooth powder, and a roll of toilet paper. Isador rubbed his hand around his jaw with its growth of stubble. He'd missed his chance for a shave earlier Friday. He prayed for the chance to shower before ten.

In the visitor's room, he caught sight of Rose before she saw him. She sat straight backed, but her head drooped forward. Her hands, fingers spread wide, lay on the table before her, as if the table were a piano and she a pianist, pausing at the end of the music. Perhaps by keeping something familiar in sight, she thought she could block out her surroundings. He'd thought that too, at first.

"Rose," Isador said, astonished at how raspy his voice was, as if it had dried from lack of use.

"Isador!" Rose jumped from her chair and started around the table. A guard materialized from where he'd been standing against the wall.

"Sorry ma'am," he said, "you have to keep your seat and stay on your side of the table."

Rose's cheeks flushed. She retook her seat and placed her hands on the table as before.

Isador sat opposite. He brushed his fingers through his hair and placed his hands on the table across from hers, noting the grime beneath his nails and the iridescent gleam of hers, like the inside of an oyster shell.

"Oh, Isador. I've been so worried. I have so many questions that I don't know where to begin. I came as soon as I could after I found out when visitors were allowed. Esther came with me. I didn't know how—"

"It's okay," Isador said. "Slow down." He closed his eyes, tilted back his head, and inhaled deeply, taking in the scent of soap and fresh air, holding it in his lungs for as long as he could. "Just let me look at you for a minute. Wait. Don't turn away."

"Isador."

"I'm sorry. I know you have lots of questions. To tell you

the truth, so do I. I don't know what they've told you, but you have to believe me, this is all a big mistake. I'm innocent." He whispered the last comment and avoided a glance toward the guard who stood near enough to overhear their conversation. He imagined a smirk on the man's face.

"You have to tell them that," Rose said. "This isn't right. It can't be."

"I did Rose. I did. It's done. Now it's up to Mr. Kilcourse to get my sentence reviewed."

"He has to get you out of here."

"He's optimistic. But you know, I don't want to put all my eggs in his basket. I've been trying to find another way. I've been thinking things over and I've got some ideas. I just haven't been able to put them together the right way."

"Let me help."

"This is nothing for you to get involved with. I'll figure something out."

"But I want to. Tell me what happened."

Isador took her hand in his. "As I told everyone, I was just walking down the street, down Dana. I stopped to light a cigarette when all of a sudden the place lit up. Cars came out of nowhere. The police were yelling and flashing guns. People were running up and down the street. They scooped everyone up and I got caught in the middle of it all. You remember, they let me go, but then, when I suppose they couldn't find anyone else to blame, they came and arrested me. I'm telling you, I had nothing to do with it."

With his eyes again on the table and their intertwined fingers, he continued, "Of course, as you heard in court, they have a note they say ties me to the hijacking."

"Mr. Kilcourse said it was just a piece of paper with an address on it."

"And a time of day."

"It could mean anything. Someone could have planted it on you. I've heard of such things happening."

"And there's the weapon."

Out of the corner of his eye, Isador noticed the guard shift his weight from one foot to the other. "I...I don't think we should say any more. Talk to Mr. Kilcourse for me. See if he can think of anything. Let's talk about something else. Let's talk about you. About home. Are you doing okay? You look pale. You're not sick are you?"

"No. I'm fine, Isador. Fine. I'm worried about you."

"Me? I'll be fine."

"But are you safe in here?"

"Safe? Safe from what?" He pretended ignorance of the dangers inside the prison system and hoped Rose had no idea of how difficult life was inside. Rose looked away and took a breath. Her lips parted. She took another breath.

"What is it?"

"No one has asked you to say things have they? I mean, say things that would get you in more trouble. Somehow. I mean..."

"What are you talking about? Who would I say anything to?"

"You mustn't talk to them." Rose said. Her eyes flicked toward the guard. She lowered her voice and continued, "You must talk only to Mr. Kilcourse." Isador had to lean closer to hear her. "Only to him."

"I have no idea what you are talking about."

"I've heard about things. Things happen to people in...

here. Bad things." Rose's eyes shifted again toward the guard. "If there's something you need to say about anything or anyone involved in this situation, you say it to Mr. Kilcourse. Will you promise me that?"

Isador chuckled. He had no idea what ideas filled Rose's head.

"Don't laugh, Isador. There's nothing humorous here. Will you promise to do as I say?"

"Okay, okay, I promise."

"Swear it."

"I swear it."

Rose

ROSE TUCKED A STRAY HAIR UNDER HER CLOCHE. SHE TAPPED her knuckles on the door. There was no answer. She tried the handle but found Gerald Kilcourse's office door locked. Nevertheless, Rose thought she could hear a conversation inside. She'd wait a few minutes. She fished in her purse and found her compact. The walk in the warm morning air had left a shine on her nose and forehead. She dusted a fresh layer of powder here and there and refreshed her lipstick. Satisfied with her touch up, she snapped the clamshell closed.

From behind the glass, Rose heard the sound of something scraping across the floor. Something heavy. Rose pressed her ear against the door and detected a low rumbling noise followed by a series of bumps and a crash. No doubt, one of the towers of papers she'd seen on her last visit had spilled to the ground. She tapped the glass again, this time harder and faster.

The noise stopped. A moment later, through the fogged glass, she saw someone cross the room. The figure grew taller and more distinct as it approached the door. The door swung wide. A blonde, at least two heads taller than Rose, smiled. "Yes? May I help you," she asked.

"I'm Mrs. Margolin. I'm here to see Mr. Kilcourse."

"You're early! I'll let Mr. Kilcourse know you're here."

"Thank you," Rose said, though with his office only ten feet away and the door ajar, Mr. Kilcourse had to be well aware she'd arrived.

The receptionist turned and walked a few steps toward the private office. She halted once to stoop and roll her stocking in place. She disappeared inside the office, and though she'd lowered her voice, Rose overheard their conversation.

"It's your ten o'clock appointment, Gerry. A Mrs. Margolin. She's early."

Rose glanced at her watch. Nine thirty. She'd been so preoccupied; she'd never thought to look.

"Show her in, Mrs. Shulman. Show her in."

The woman reappeared, touched her fingers to the corners of her lips, and smiled again. "You may go in now." Rose sidled past the woman and entered Mr. Kilcourse's office.

"Ah! Mrs. Margolin. Delighted to see you again, of course, as always. Please come in and have a seat."

Rose scanned the room thinking she'd see a mound of files on the floor. But there was nothing out of order, or at least nothing more out of order than she remembered from her previous visit.

Mr. Kilcourse took her hand and squeezed it gently. Rose cringed but made no move until he withdrew his hand and waved her toward a chair, the same one she'd occupied during the previous visit. Rose perched on the chair's edge away from a tower of files on a nearby table. As he retook his seat behind his desk, Rose noticed it was bare. His notepads, pens, files, and telephone were gone. Rose looked at Mr. Kilcourse, at Mrs. Shulman who stood in the doorway, and again at Mr. Kilcourse.

"So. What brings you here today?"

Mrs. Shulman, the receptionist, or secretary, or whatever she was, stood in the doorway. Perhaps sensing Rose's discomfort, the attorney dismissed the woman, saying "Thank you, Mrs. Shulman. I'll call you if I need you."

When the receptionist had disappeared, Rose spoke. "What brings me here today? My husband, of course. I visited him yesterday. He mentioned you were working on an appeal."

"Indeed, I am." The attorney raised his hand as if to show her Isador's file but found his desk swept clean. A slight look of puzzlement crossed his face.

"Isador simply cannot spend another day in that place." Rose took a deep breath and fought back tears. "This has all been such a terrible, terrible mistake."

"Mistake, yes. Yes, that's it exactly. That's what I am working on."

"Oh, thank goodness. I wasn't sure if you even remembered who he was."

"Why, of course I remember. Just because his trial's over doesn't mean I'm through. He's still my client."

"I meant no offense. It's just that I'm so anxious to have him out of there. How long do you think an appeal will take?"

"Well, well, let's not get ahead of ourselves. I have quite a few things to investigate and people to see before we can even think of getting his conviction overturned."

"But he shouldn't have been convicted of anything. He was caught up in some...some robbery or something. He's innocent."

"Oh, of course, of course. I agree completely," he said without a trace of hypocrisy.

"Isador said it's all because of that silly piece of paper. How could a measly piece of paper be enough to put him in jail?"

"A piece of paper with the address, date, and time of the hijacking noted on it is not just a piece of paper," he said, making a point of waggling his eyebrows as he'd said the words "piece of paper."

Rose's eyes narrowed. She was conscious of her lips pressing together, her jaw clenching. In her lap, her fingers rubbed the metal clasp of her purse. "It's a note I gave him. I didn't think it was important. I thought he'd told you. I had asked him to go there to meet my sister."

"Yes, yes, of course you did. If it were only that simple, we might have been able to argue our case differently. But, then too, there was this matter of the gun."

"The gun. Yes."

"Mrs. Margolin, have you ever heard of Mr. Saul Mosko?"

The color drained from Rose's face, her already pale complexion turned chalk white. Her fingers tightened on the clasp. "I've heard of him."

"Excuse me, I did not hear you."

"I've heard of him," Rose repeated, louder, but without inflection. She glanced at the doorway and the still open door. Mrs. Shulman sat at her desk, in plain sight, ostensibly absorbed in a file open in front of her.

"It's okay, Mrs. Margolin. You may speak freely here. I've been hired to represent your husband and that duty continues until he serves his sentence or I secure his release. Everything we discuss is completely confidential, one-hundred percent. The same as any conversations I have with your husband."

"Hired by whom? How are we to pay for your services?"

"You needn't worry about that. Now, where were we? Ah, yes. So, you know of Mr. Mosko. Mr. Saul Mosko."

Rose nodded.

"And, you know your husband is working with Mr. Mosko?"

Rose's heart skipped another beat. Other than a brief flutter of lashes on one eyelid, however, she exhibited no outward sign. In mere seconds, the events of the last six months fell into place. Rose's plan changed. The "piece of paper" no longer mattered.

"If what you say is true, Mr. Kilcourse, that my husband is working for Mr. Mosko, as I suppose you are, then surely things can be worked out. He's a very influential man, so I've heard. I've read...well, it's in the newspapers every day. People in his employ are brought in one day and released the next."

"That's true, sometimes." Gerald Kilcourse linked his hands over his midsection and the straining buttons of his vest. He teetered back and forth in his chair.

Rose did not avert her eyes. "Well, then?"

"Unfortunately, now and then, the authorities decide to make an example. This little *incident*," Kilcourse said with his eyebrows once again twitching on his forehead, "involved some pretty big names. It seems Mr. Mosko picked on some powerful foes this time. If it weren't for the—"

"I can explain the gun," Rose said, staring into Mr. Kilcourse's eyes. "It's mine."

"Yours? Now, Mrs. Margolin, the gun—"

"It's mine."

Shooting the Chutes

COPYRIGHT 1907 BY H. L. ROBBINS BOSTON   SHOOTING THE CHUTES AT WONDERLAND, REVERE BEACH, MASS.

A lagoon meandered through the center of Wonder-land Park—a feature the designers incorporated into one of the popular rides, Shooting the Chutes. Riders in gondolas were hoisted high above the crowds and then released down a steep water slide and into the lagoon.

Isador

ONCE OUTSIDE THE DOUBLE DOORS AND THROUGH THE ARCHWAY of the Suffolk County Jail, Isador stopped to take a deep breath of air, air that for the first time in weeks did not feel as if it had been breathed by someone else. He spotted Rose walking toward him, her face obscured by a wide brimmed hat.

"Rose! Rose!" Isador waved his hat high in the air to catch her attention. He put the straw boater on his head, adjusted it, took it off, and put it back on, reveling in the luxury he'd once taken for granted. He nodded at the officer in the guard-house behind him, tipped his hat, his fingers hesitating on the brim for a breath longer than necessary, and sprinted away under the summer sun.

When he opened his arms, Rose rushed forward. He hugged her and despite her protest pulled her hat from her head. He pressed his nose against her hair and breathed the familiar scents of soap, lavender, and oatmeal and powder and blue sky and salt and ocean. Arching his back, he drew an arms-length away. Then he placed his knuckles under her chin and tilted her face to his.

Isador indulged in a long, passionate kiss. *The guards and passersby be damned.*

"Oh, Isa. I've missed you so much. I...Let's get away from here."

"I couldn't agree more. Let's go home." Though he didn't

care if anyone heard his next remark, out of respect for Rose, he lowered his voice and placed his lips near her ear. "I want to make love to you all afternoon. Maybe all night." He pulled her close and hugged her again, surprised at the resistance he felt in her shoulders. A stiffness he attributed to her discomfort at being near the jail.

"Hush."

"Why should I hush? I'm a free man again! I may announce it to the world."

"You'll do nothing of the sort. We're going to go home and lock the door and not answer it again, I don't care who comes knocking."

"Relax, Rose. Everything's going to be fine. You can see for yourself. Here I am. Free as a bird." Isador spread his arms wide and threw his head back. "I told you it was all a mistake."

"So you did. But right now, the first thing we need to do is get you out of those clothes. You need a long hot bath."

"Ah ha. So you *do* want to have me take off my clothes. Good."

"It's not what you think, Isa. I can smell this place on you. You need a good scrubbing."

"This any better?" Isador asked. He raised a hand and patted his hair, grinning at his reflection in the hallway mirror.

Rose glanced over her shoulder. "Much."

He sidled up behind her at the sink and slid his arms around her waist.

"Stop that. Let me finish or we'll never have dinner."

"Dinner can wait." Isador nuzzled his clean-shaven chin against the back of her neck.

"No, it can't. I've made you something special."

"I know what I want for dinner."

"Isa, sit down."

"Okay. Okay." He stepped aside, but instead of taking a seat at the kitchen table, he swung open one of the lower cabinet doors and, crouching, groped under the counter until his fingertips brushed against a slim glass bottle. Isador raised the flask in front of his face, waving it back and forth for Rose to see.

"What in the world? How long has that been there?"

"We should have a toast."

"Where did you get that?"

Isador jiggled the flask, letting the brown liquid slosh against the sides of the bottle. He removed the cork and held it to his nose, drawing the sharp scent into his lungs.

"You don't need to know."

"I think I do. In fact, there are quite a few things I need to know."

"Let's just say that Mr. Logrin kept a little stash at the store. He paid me once with a bottle in exchange for some extra work. I knew someday there would be a good occasion to celebrate."

"Mr. Logrin? I would never have thought he...Is it safe to drink?"

"Sure. Here's proof." Isador sipped from the flask. "Ah. Wonderful." Then he coughed and thumped his chest with his free hand. He coughed again, made a choking noise, and opened his eyes wide. He pounded the counter with his palm.

"Oh my God!" Rose's hands flew to her face and the lid of the saucepan she'd held a moment ago clattered to the ground. She ignored the lid and reached for Isador. As she did, Isador snatched her arm and pulled her to him. He tilted his head back and laughed.

Rose slapped his chest. "That's not funny, Isa. You know very well that people die from alcohol poisoning every day."

"Okay, okay. I'm sorry." He plucked two glasses from the shelf above the counter and poured two drinks.

Isador spent his first days of freedom at home, sleeping late and doing as little as possible during the day. He didn't think about work or mention going once. "It's a sort of vacation," he said to Rose when she asked his plans on Tuesday morning. Except for his year in the navy, he'd never hopped a bus or train or boat bound for some far off place, never spent the night in a hotel, never been away from home for an extended period. He didn't count the time he visited his aunt in the Berkshires when he was nine or ten, as he remembered little more than fishing in the lake with his father, the can full of worms, a mass of mud and slime, and how the one fish he'd caught flopped on the shore, opening and closing its mouth, gasping until his father whacked off its head.

"Besides," he said, "the world can wait another day." Before Rose had a chance to slip out of bed, he climbed atop her and made love to her.

When he began again, Rose protested, making soft noises in the back of her throat, but Isador continued. He raised himself, one hand on each side of her head. He had always liked to look at her while making love, but as she lay beneath him, she turned her head to the side and put the back of her hand over her eyes, something he'd never seen her do before.

Afterward, spent and still breathing hard, he stretched out beside his wife and let his eyes feast on her. Her hair, the curve of her nose, the soft lobes of her ears, her lips, and her skin. Rose indulged him, but when the sun passed above the window frame, she grabbed her robe from where it lay at the bottom of the bed and left the room without looking back.

The next morning, by the time he woke and rolled over, searching for her with his leg, he found only the wrinkled sheets. He bolted upright thinking he was back in his cell, remembering the dank smell from the cement floor and the odor of sweat and urine.

"Rose? Honey? Where are you?" Isador called, looking around their bedroom and cocking his head to see down the hall to the bathroom.

"Ah, so Sleeping Beauty has woken," Rose said from the hall. She wore her Tillinghast store clerk uniform, a starched white blouse and dark skirt. Isador hated the outfit, preferring to see her in pastels and silky fabrics. *Then again,* he thought, *maybe it was better she didn't attract unwanted attention at work.* There were too many men around the store for Isador's satisfaction.

"You're not going to work yet, are you?"

"Yes, I am. Someone has to make the rent," she said. Isador frowned and studied her face, relaxing only after she winked.

"I know, I know. I guess I've stayed away long enough. I'll go to see Mr. Logrin today. Find out where he needs me."

Rose came to the side of the bed to say goodbye. He slipped a hand under her skirt and ran it along the back of her calf, behind her knee and over the rolled top of her stocking, to her thigh and bare skin.

Rose swatted at his hand. "Behave." She smoothed her skirt and leaned over to kiss him on the forehead.

When the front door closed, Isador flopped back and pulled his pillow over his head, drowning out the light. He needed a few more minutes after all the sleep he'd lost at Suffolk. Quiet hours were anything but quiet there with inmates arguing or shouting or throwing things until the guards intervened.

The sound of breaking glass woke Isador. He opened one eye and pulled the pillow from his head. A woman's voice below his window. One of the Nahant matrons shouting. The commotion outside subsided, blending into the ever-present cacophony of sounds from nearby Shirley Avenue. Isador sighed. Without raising his head, he dragged the clock from Rose's bedside table across the bed and turned the face up. *Three twenty-five. Too late to go by Logrin's.*

There was a thud from the street, as if something had hit the wall below him. More shouts rang out, this time boys voices and a scramble of footsteps. Isador made it to the front room and looked out over the street. Below, the usual group of neighborhood boys enjoyed an afternoon game of stick-ball.

He'd go to Logrin's tomorrow. *Thursday. Plenty of time.* Isador thrashed through the closet for a pair of pants, a shirt, and his shoes. From the top shelf of the closet, he retrieved his well-worn official baseball mitt, one he'd had since his days in the navy when he played catch with a few guys from his department. He galloped down the stairs.

Isador blinked in the bright light of the outdoors and put a hand to his forehead to shield his eyes. Jacob Moll stood in the middle of the street, his hands on his knees, his eyes fixed on a spot down the block. A few houses away, also in the street, Michael Thorpe stood, knees bent, a stick in his hand. *Crack.* The ball soared toward Jacob. The boy edged backwards, his bare hands splayed against the sun, his eyes glued to the track of the ball. Isador traced the path, glancing at Jacob then back at the ball then back at Jacob.

"Jacob! Behind you." One more step and the boy would have collided with a parked vehicle.

As Jacob turned, he lost sight of the ball. Isador strode forward glove outstretched beneath the ball on its downward slope. He fielded the ball, plucked it from his mitt, and tossed it back to Walter Abrams at what he guessed was first base.

"Thanks, Mr. Margolin."

"Isador, Jacob. Isador."

"Thanks, Isador. You want to play?"

"I think I do, Jacob. I think I do. I'll take the outfield. You go on in for shortstop."

"Okay, Mr. Mar—Isador. I'm really glad to see you home."

"Me, too. Jacob. Glad to be home."

Whack. Another ball rose in the air and over Isador's head. He pedaled back in pursuit.

The game ended as dinner time approached. The boys dispersed to their homes. All but Jacob. He and Isador sat side by side on Isador's front steps, their feet extended in front of them, their bodies supported by their elbows on the steps behind them.

"It was back in 1917," Isador said. "The Babe only hit two home runs that year. One of them was at Fenway. I was there that day with my father. But when the Red Sox sold him off to the Yankees, I gave him up. Still, it was great to see him play."

"I'd give anything to—Look, here comes Mrs. Margolin." Isador waved.

"Is Mrs. Margolin okay?"

"Is she okay?" Isador turned back to Jacob. "Of course she's okay. Never better."

Rose came closer, nodding as she passed Philip Seidman, their first floor neighbor Eleanor's husband. Philip stopped in the middle of sweeping the sidewalk, nodded in return, and pivoted as she passed. Isador smiled to his wife and at Philip, who could not tear his eyes from Rose.

Isador spun back around to ask Jacob why he had been concerned about Rose, but the boy had disappeared.

On Thursday, Isador was ready to face Mr. Logrin. He dressed in his best summer suit and the black knit tie Rose had given him for their anniversary last year.

"So, what do you think?" Isador asked. He shuffled his feet in a mock soft shoe step. He struck a pose, one hand in the air, one toward the floor as if in mid-dance. "Ta da."

"You look very smart," Rose said. She snuggled a hat over her head, her blond hair wound into a knot and fastened at the nape of her neck. "The 'Bee's Knees'—that's what Jacob tells me everyone says now."

"Indeed."

"A bit overdressed, though, don't you think?"

"It would be for my old job, but not for my new one."

"New one?"

"Yes, I'm going to float some ideas past old Mr. Logrin. I had time to do some thinking in, ah—," he stopped, avoiding saying the word "jail", or referring to the place as Rose did, as "Suffolk." He'd promised himself never to mention the place again.

"And?"

"I'll tell you later, after I run it by Mr. Logrin. We might have some celebrating to do after dinner."

Isador and Rose left for work together, walking hand in

hand up Shirley Avenue to Thornton. There, a few doors out of sight of Logrin's, Rose offered Isador her cheek, with its dusting of peach powder. But, instead, he grabbed her around the waist and wrestled with her until she squirmed free. "Behave yourself, Isa, or I'll have to go home and fix my hair all over again."

Isador pecked her cheek and said, "See you later, dear." Then he swatted her on the buttocks.

"Isa!"

"Hello, Mr. Logrin," Isador said. "A fine Thursday, don't you think?"

Mr. Logrin looked up from behind the counter where he was poring over his accounts. "Well, well. So you're back."

"Yes, they finally saw the error of their ways and released me."

"I heard that. Yes, I did. Lester said he'd run into Rose and got the news you'd be here this week."

At the sound of his name, Mr. Logrin's handyman set aside his broom and waved from the back of the store.

"You don't look any worse for the wear," Logrin said, eyeing Isador's suit of clothes and his fashionable two-toned Oxfords. "But, you might want to hang your jacket back in the office. The cauliflower and broccoli need trimming and there are cartons of tomatoes waiting to be unpacked and stacked."

Isador hesitated.

"You are here to work, right?" Jack Logrin asked.

"Yes, but I'd like to talk to you for a minute. I have a few ideas to run by you."

The bells above the front door jangled.

"Good morning, Mr. Logrin." A woman's singsong voice.

"Why, hello Etta," Logrin said. "I've told you over and over. Please, just call me Jack. It's good to see you. What brings you out today?"

Etta Lemont, a widow, was one of Jack Logrin's favorite customers. He'd once confided in Isador that Mrs. Lemont was his leading prospect for the third Mrs. Logrin. Isador knew from Lester that the first Mrs. Logrin's had died ten years ago after a bout with the flu. Not two years later, he'd remarried, only to lose his second wife in an automobile accident right outside the store.

"I've got some fine apples, just in from Northboro," Mr. Logrin said. "Let me show you."

"Mr. Logrin?" Isador called, trying to draw the old man's attention.

"Later, Isador. The cauliflower. The broccoli. We can talk later." Jack Logrin closed his ledger book. He took Mrs. Lemont by the elbow and steered her toward the apples. He selected one from the top of the perfect pyramid and polished it in his apron. "Take a look at that, Etta, even smells like ginger. I just know these golden beauties would be perfect for one of your delicious pies." Logrin's eyebrows danced over his eyes. He held the apple to his nose. "Um, um. Good."

As he glanced back at Isador, Mr. Logrin's eyebrows flattened and drew together in one long dark line across his forehead. Isador slapped his hands against his thigh, spun on his heels, and headed for the storeroom, his fine straw boater and jacket in his hand.

Just after five, when the last customer had exited, Isador flipped the sign in the window from OPEN to CLOSED. He skipped to the store room, pulled his apron over his head, and hung it on a hook behind the door. He straightened his tie and smoothed his hair in place. As he stepped from the room, he noticed the stain on the cuff of his trousers, a half circle of dried tomato juice. He swore to himself as he plucked a bit of shriveled skin and a seed or two from the cuff.

He found Mr. Logrin as he had that morning, hunched over his ledger. "So, Mr. Logrin. As I said, if you have a minute, I'd like to talk about some of my ideas."

Mr. Logrin stabbed a finger on his ledger to mark his place.

"I've been thinking," Isador said. "Take a look around the store. What do you see?"

Mr. Logrin looked around without moving his finger from the mark.

"Leave the books alone for just a minute. Come here." Isador sauntered into the middle of the main aisle. He raised his arms, shoulder height, palms up, and swiveled to the right and then the left.

"I see a man standing in the middle of my store, that's what I see," Logrin said.

"Please. Mr. Logrin. Look again."

"I see dollars."

"Yes, dollars to be sure. But what else?"

"What more do I need to see?"

"Like how crowded the aisles are? Like how Mrs. Meltzer can barely make it to the bananas."

"Mrs. Meltzer can barely make it anywhere."

"Listen. What I'm trying to say is what if you could see more dollars? Twice the number of dollars!"

"And how would I do that, if, as you say, I'm already too crowded."

"But you could, that is, *we* could," Isador said, correcting himself. A tiny vessel pulsed above Jack Logrin's eyelid. *Slow down*, Isador said to himself. He took a deep breath before continuing, "With a second store. A second Logrin's."

"A second Logrin's?"

"You know that vacant storefront on Franklin, where Galea's used to be?"

"Isador, I don't think—"

"Hear me out, Mr. Logrin. Please. This is something I've been thinking about for some time now. It's not something I just dreamed up." In fact, he'd thought about it since the day he started working at Logrin's.

"Here, let me show you." Isador shepherded Mr. Logrin back to the counter. He pulled a folded sheet of paper from the pocket of his trousers and spread it on top the ledger, smoothing it with the heel of his hand. He pointed to the first line of figures. "Three thousand square feet. Exactly the same. And, see here," Isador dragged his finger down the page to another figure, "this is the number of residents in a three block area surrounding the storefront. I've estimated that's about the same as there are around here. Ernest Fazio's the owner. He's asking a hundred dollars a month, but I've talked to him and I think we can get him to take less. He's willing to give us a break." Isador paused and searched the old man's face for a reaction. Nothing. "I told Mr. Fazio you and I would come—"

"Isador," Logrin interrupted. "Look at me."

Isador looked up from his figures. It was his turn to mark his place with his finger on the sheet of paper.

"I'm seventy-two years old. And in case you hadn't noticed, I'm not in the best of health."

"All the more reason, Mr. Logrin. Here, look here. You said

dollars." Isador flipped the paper over to his calculations for sales and profit.

"I have all the dollars I need, right here. My life is winding down. I don't want more than I already have. I don't want to work harder than I already do."

"You wouldn't have to Mr. Logrin. See, that's the point. I'd manage—"

"Stop! I'm sorry, Isador. My answer is no."

Isador drummed his fingers on the counter. He grabbed the page of calculations, square feet and market size and rents and sales and profits, folded it over, and stuffed it in his pocket. He turned, retrieved his hat from where he'd left it atop a stack of potatoes, and left the store, slamming the door behind him. The bells jangled overhead.

Isador had stormed out of Logrin's without giving a thought to where he was going. His head pounded, his thoughts raced. He could not go home and face Rose. Not yet. Not until he had some idea of how he might approach Mr. Fazio himself. A bit farther east on Shirley Avenue, an awning shaded the sidewalk. White script against a maroon background. Kelly's, the awning said. Like everyone else in the neighborhood, including the beat cops, Isador knew a blind pig occupied the basement below Kelly's drugstore.

Inside, Isador settled on a stool, spreading his knees to keep from bumping the wall under the rough-hewn bar. To his right, four other men nursed their drinks. And across the room, underneath a chandelier, its globes occluded with the residue of years of cigarette and cigar smoke, another handful of men sat, talking in hushed tones.

"I'll have a pint," Isador said to the barkeep. He fished a

quarter from his pocket and flipped it onto the counter. After taking a sip of his pint, Isador retrieved the sheet of paper from his pocket. He folded it over several times and ripped the small square into strips, dumping the remains onto the counter. "Profit" the shred on top read, the other stubs indecipherable bits and pieces of his grand plan.

A man slid onto the stool next to him, removed his coat, folded it, tucked the arms to the inside, and placed it on the far stool. He set his fedora on top and turned to the barkeep. "Another round, here, Theo," he said, indicating Isador's near empty glass and his own vacant space on the counter. "Whatever he's having."

Isador recognized Earl the Ear at once. He nodded. "Make it a whiskey."

"Heard you were out," Earl said.

"Yeah."

"Goddamn Stover."

"What?"

"Joe Stover," Earl said in a low voice. He scanned the room. "He was supposed to have had the block watched. Said it was clean. We'd have called it off if we'd known."

Isador nodded. The two sat in silence while Theo set two glasses on the bar. He pulled a cork from the bottle in his hand, filled one glass for Earl and then another for Isador. Earl tossed a handful of coins on the counter and raised his glass, tipping it toward Isador.

"Cheers. This one's on Mosko," Earl said.

Isador grunted and took a gulp of the dark liquid, holding it on his tongue until his mouth burned.

"He wants to thank you," Earl said.

"Thank me?"

"Yeah. He knows you did the right thing."

"What's that?"

"Kept your trap shut."

"Oh."

"Yeah, while that stinking rat Stover blabbered like a baby."

Another grunt from Isador.

"306 Ocean. Monday. At noon," Earl said. He rose, tossed back his drink and placed another quarter on the counter. "Mr. Mosko would like to see you when you're ready for work. Assuming you're looking for work." Earl gathered his hat and coat and disappeared into the haze.

"306 Ocean," Isador repeated. Then to Theo, "One more." He slid a coin across the counter. With a pencil from his pocket, Isador scrawled the address on one of the shreds of paper from the pile. *306 Ocean,* he wrote. He added an exclamation point.

Rose

SHE'D NOTICED THE MAN THE MOMENT HE WALKED THROUGH the door. Most likely, everyone on the main floor had. He stood nearly as tall as Isador and had his same slender build, but he had an air about him, one that made you look and then kept you from looking away. He hesitated in the middle of the lobby, but somehow looked anything but ill at ease. Rose kept him in sight while trying to carry on a conversation with a customer. "Why yes, that looks lovely." Then, "I'm sorry? Oh, yes, it matches your shawl perfectly." And, "Try this one. Let me know what you think."

She had looked down for a second to find a hat pin and when she raised her head, the man had made a beeline to the men's department, a gaggle of men trailing in his wake. Moments later they returned, one of the followers toting three flat Tillinghast shirt boxes.

"Graceful" was the word Addie chose. Addie Azarian worked in ladies hosiery and joined Rose for lunch each day in the room reserved for employees in Tillinghast's basement. Addie nibbled a cucumber sandwich, squinting at the toast squares between bites. She picked up from where she'd left off, "Yes, graceful and slender, but not all elbows and knees like my Hugh. Him? No. Not at all. And did you notice his hands?"

"How could I not have?" Rose said. "He put both of his around mine and wouldn't let go, not until I told him my name."

"He asked for your name?"

"Yes, he did. What do you think he did that for?"

"I have no idea," Addie said. "He didn't have that much to say to me. Mostly he talked with the manager while I wrapped three pairs of our finest black silk stockings for him. Wrapped them in tissue and tied them with a red ribbon. He insisted on red." She eyed her sandwich again. A few crumbs clung to the edge of her mouth.

"I wonder who he was," Rose said. "Do you think he's a movie actor or something?" She propped her head on the heel of her hand, her elbow on the table, trying to picture the man's face again. All she remembered with any detail was the feel of his palms as they pressed against her hand.

"Movie actor?" Addie asked. "Seriously? You mean you don't know who he was?"

"No. Should I?"

"Maybe if you took time to read the paper you'd know about such things. He's a big cheese around here. He's always on the society pages. In fact," Addie leaned over the table and lowered her voice, "I think Mr. Mosko likes having his picture taken."

"Mr. Mos—" Rose's face drained of color.

"So, you do know him."

"No. Not really. It's just that, well, I mean, everyone knows *of* him."

"I thought you knew who he was. I thought everyone knew. He comes in every six months or so and spends a wad. I wonder who the stockings are for."

"I have no idea. Nor do I care. We should be getting back." Rose folded the uneaten half of her sandwich in a scrap of wax paper and tossed it in the bin on her way out.

On Saturday, Esther and Sarah came to Rose's apartment for dinner. They hadn't been inside for a minute before Isador made his excuses, mumbling something about a meeting with a Mr. Ernest Fazio. He'd mentioned the name once before, the day he'd come home from his disastrous proposition to Mr. Logrin. With Esther and Sarah present, Rose couldn't ask why or for how long he might be gone, but her mood brightened with the thought he was close to finding employment.

"Would you like some tea?" Rose asked.

"I'd love some," Esther said, plopping onto the couch.

"Sarah?"

"No, thank you."

Sarah stood at the window, about as far away as the small room allowed from where Isador had stood moments ago. When Rose returned with two cups of tea, Sarah was still there, peering at the street. She turned and surveyed the living room, her head back like a cat scenting the air. *She'll have a lot to tell the family at dinner,* Rose thought. *She'll comment how small and cluttered the rooms are, how meager the furnishings, and about the signs of wear on the sofa's arms and the edges of the footstool.* Rose had traipsed behind Isador all afternoon, collecting whatever he dropped or left in his wake, the morning's newspaper, his reading glasses, two pairs of shoes, a shirt needing mending, and bits of notepaper. Isador had a habit of scribbling notes on slips of papers and then forgetting where he laid them, once scolding Rose for having deliberately tossed his notes in the trash. He'd not apologized, even after she produced a shoebox full of notes she gathered and placed in his closet.

Rose gave a furtive glance around, checking to see she'd not overlooked something.

"So, what has Isador been doing since he left the tailoring business?" Sarah asked.

Sarah knew very well that Isador had taken a job at Logrin's. The offhand remark about the Forman family business Rose took as an attempt to spotlight one of her husband's failings.

"Last time we talked," Esther said, "you told me he was in line for a promotion, isn't that right?"

Relieved at Esther's comment, Rose continued the thread. "Well, he and Mr. Logrin have been talking, but I'm not sure they've come to an agreement. That's why he had to go see Mr. Fazio," Rose added, though she had only the faintest idea who Mr. Fazio was. "Tell me about the kids, Sarah. I haven't seen them in ages."

Sarah and Esther left at five. Rose expected Isador to walk through the door any minute, as if he had been watching from the corner. At six-thirty when he'd not shown, she tacked a note on the front door and walked to Logrin's. It was the only place she could think to look. She hoped he'd returned for one more go at convincing Mr. Logrin of his plans and that they might be mulling it over now.

When open for business, Mr. Logrin had a bin of produce outside the front door—apples, peaches, lettuce, whatever was fresh. Rose found the sidewalk empty. Still hoping against hope, she pressed her face against the front window. Inside, it was dark and still.

"They're closed. They've all gone home," a man's voice said.

Rose turned toward the sound.

"Oh, Mrs. Margolin, I didn't recognize you." A smile lit

Lester Tighe's face. He removed his cap from his head and held it in front of him with both hands.

"Hello, Mr. Tighe." He was clearly uncomfortable being addressed formally. He'd dropped his eyes and shuffled his feet.

"They've all gone home," he repeated. "Mr. Margolin didn't come in today."

"Yes, I know," she said. "Still, I thought I'd try to get here before closing. To pick up a few things." She pulled back her sleeve to check her watch. "I guess I lost track of time."

"I wish I could open the store for you," Lester said, scanning the ground.

"That's quite all right, Mr. Tighe. I'll see Mr. Logrin on Monday, I'm sure." Rose tapped her fingers against her thigh. "Anyway, Isador's probably back home and wondering where I am."

"I'm sure that's so."

"Thank you anyway. Bye-bye and please say hello to Josephine for me!" A forced lilt at the end of her sentence.

As she approached 51 Nahant, Rose glanced at the third floor windows. No lights. There was no sign of Isador anywhere. At nine, Rose ate a snack of soda crackers and peanut butter, and washed the meal down with a tall glass of milk. At ten, she went to bed.

A thump in the living room woke her. Rose drew the sheets into a knot at her neck, cocked her head, and listened for more sounds. Nothing. Then another thump. This time, a shoe tumbled across the floor and into her line of sight. A groan.

"Isador?" Rose called from the bed.

Another groan.

Rose grabbed her robe and ventured barefoot into the living room. Isador was prone on the couch, his tie loosened, his hat still clinging to his head. An undeniable stench told her what she already knew. He was drunk. She sat on the edge of the sofa, pulled off his hat, and tried to tuck a pillow under his head.

"How was your meeting with Mr. Fazio?" Rose asked.

"Fuck Fazio,"

"Isador!"

"Fuck Jack Logrin, too."

Isador

FOR EXACTLY TWO DAYS AND THREE AND ONE HALF HOURS, THE time between when Isador walked out of Logrin's until the time he met with Ernest Fazio, Isador had dreamt of nothing more than going into the green grocer trade and besting Logrin. With a little bit of backing from Fazio, of course. He thought of buying out Logrin when Margolin's Market became a success. Margolin's Market—the name he'd given his new venture. Fazio, as it turned out, had no interest in leasing the shop on Franklin to Isador without Mr. Logrin's involvement.

Isador hadn't devised a backup plan, but he knew he was not going to crawl back to Logrin's, no matter what. He didn't care if the old man retired, had a stroke or keeled over dead. And then, Earl Bloom had appeared at Kelly's with his invitation. 306 Ocean, he'd said. Noon.

Isador arrived ten minutes early and found Earl waiting outside, his back to the doors of the Crescent Beach Café, his arms folded across his chest.

Lunch out was a rare occurrence in Isador's life. Leo Forman had never allowed Isador, or anyone else in the shop, enough time to leave the premises at midday. Rose packed him a lunch and he ate with the other employees, though he usually sat apart. When he went to work at Logrin's, Rose simply continued her habit, and so Isador carried a sandwich with him each day: liverwurst on Mondays and Tuesdays, mashed, baked beans on Wednesdays and Thursdays, and salami—Isador and Rose joked that if necessary they would swear to Esther the salami was made of beef—on Fridays. Lately, out of work, he'd skipped lunch entirely.

Then again, Earl hadn't exactly said they were meeting for lunch. Nor had he indicated what type of work Mr. Mosko had for him. Isador had had only two prior encounters with the local gang. The first was an odd job he took after leaving Forman's. Men he guessed were tied to Mosko had arranged the job—men so far down the chain that the actual connection was hard to discern. And then, he'd done the second job, the one on Dana Street, the one that landed him in jail, a place he was not eager to see again. But they'd provided for him, arranged for Kilcourse and, true to their word, he was out in no time.

Isador wasn't certain what Kilcourse had actually done, whether he'd paid someone off or maneuvered the docket to schedule a review with a friendly judge. He'd never asked the details and that was probably best. Joe Stover was still languishing inside, and based on Earl's comments, Isador thought he'd be there for some time.

"Ready?" Earl asked.

"You bet," Isador said, noting Earl's perfect knot and starched collar underneath his coat and thinking the man had class despite his tough guy reputation.

"Here's the deal. We go in together. We wait inside the door. His table's at the back and he may have a guest. We wait until they're finished. I go back, alone, let him know you're here, and remind him who you are. You stay put till I call you."

"Simple enough."

"You're not carrying are you?"

"Carrying?"

"Mr. Mosko has two associates with him. One will frisk you. Don't even think of resisting. If you've got a piece, they'll take it. Hell, if you've got a piece, you're done for."

"No. No way. I'm clean."

"Okay. And you don't say anything—not a word. Nothing, unless he asks you a question. You don't breathe unless he says breathe. You don't sit unless he says sit. *Capisce?*"

"*Capisce*," Isador repeated and nodded. He liked the sound of the word.

Earl pushed the door open and the two entered along with a shaft of bright white light. Once the door swung closed, the light changed to gold with hues of orange and yellow, tinted and shaped by the hexagons of copper from the stained glass front windows.

His eyes still adjusting to the half-light, Isador nearly collided with Earl who had advanced no further than a step or two, just enough to allow the door to close. Earl removed his hat and stood to the side of the door. Isador stepped alongside Earl. He removed his hat and, like Earl, held it in front of him. He set his feet shoulder-width apart and squared his shoulders to the wall. *Like the navy. I can do this.*

Though he dared not turn his head, Isador surveyed the room from the corners of his eyes. A lone male figure wiped the bar with a cloth. He wiped the same spot over and over. The shelves behind him, which might have once held fifths of liquor, were empty. No one sat at the bar, not even for a cup of coffee. Then, Isador noticed that no one sat at any of the tables in the main dining room either.

A handful of men were at the back, seated around a circular table. At that distance, their conversation was nothing more than a murmur. A ceiling lamp cast a glow on the center of the table, and in the glow, smoke swirled, rising between the silhouettes of two men seated at the table, their backs to Isador. A single man sat opposite. Saul Mosko, Isador presumed. From where he stood, all Isador could see were the man's hands holding a knife and fork above the only plate of food on the table. He gestured with the utensils and then froze, poised as if he were an orchestra conductor who'd come to a pause in the piece of music. More murmuring. He lowered his hands and sliced something on his plate. As he leaned forward to take a piece of food from his fork, the top of his head pierced the circle of light. Black hair, glistening with pomade, parted down the middle as precisely as if he'd split the two sides with his knife. The head retreated into the shadow, denying Isador a view of the face.

Isador stole a quick glance at Earl. Standing side by side, he realized for the first time how much taller he was than Earl, though he lacked Earl's breadth and, he guessed, his strength. Isador took a deep breath and re-squared his shoulders. He raised his chin, hoping to add an inch or two to his six foot frame when viewed from the boss's perspective.

After several minutes passed, the two men who'd had their backs to Isador scooted their chairs from the table and rose. Mosko cut another piece of food. He did not rise or offer his hand. When they passed Earl and Isador, neither of the two men made eye contact. A shaft of light broke through the doorway, signaling their departure. Still, Earl did not move or say a word.

A motion in the shadows near Mosko's table. A man stepped away from the wall and circled the table. A bodyguard, Isador surmised. The man nodded and raised a hand, motioning them to come forward. Isador caught Earl's glance as he did. It said everything Isador needed to know. His irises, a pale blue earlier, were translucent, icy, freezing Isador in place. *I go back alone.* Earl's earlier instructions reverberated in Isador's head.

Earl crossed the floor of the luncheonette to where the guard stood. They exchanged words and Earl moved again only after the man nodded. Earl continued to the back of the room, passed to the far side of the table, and bent at the waist, his mouth above Mosko's ear.

Still in shadow, Mosko nodded. He dotted his mouth with a napkin, the white square gleaming in the light.

Earl lifted his hand toward Isador.

As Earl had warned, the "associate" blocked Isador's path to the table. "Raise your arms," he said in a low voice. Isador complied and stood still while the man patted his arms, sides, chest, and the back of his trousers. When he was done, the associate cocked his head and made a half step to the side to allow Isador to pass.

"Mr. Bloom tells me you have been of use to us in one of our recent business matters, Mr...."

Isador formed an M sound with his lips, but stopped short of saying his name. He did not have to look at Earl to feel the icy glare.

Earl answered for Isador, "Margolin."

"He tells me you proved you're a man who can be trusted," Mosko said. Isador noted the odd way he joined his words, saying *het-tells* and *whoc-can*.

Mr. Mosko's thin, almost delicate hands brought the

corners of the white linen napkin together and folded it twice, forming a neat triangle. He tucked it beside his plate and rested his hand on top. A gold signet ring on his third finger. His nails as smooth and perfectly shaped as a woman's.

"You are looking for work," he continued, *look-king*. It was a statement not a question. "We can use someone who understands our business. Someone who knows what to do and what to say. And, perhaps, what not to say."

Another statement. Isador said nothing. Beside him, Earl exhaled softly.

"We have a place, a place near Broadway. We need a manager. Someone we can trust." He paused, his fingers fidgeting over the top of his napkin on the table. He took his time before speaking again, but Isador, having heard the word "manager" was already thinking ahead. *Manager. That will show Logrin. And Fazio. Manager. Rose will be bowled over and Leo and the whole lot of Forman's will see how wrong they were about that understudy of a raincoat cutter.*

"Mr. Bloom will introduce you to Foye who will show you around. We may ask you to do other work later. You will do exactly as you are asked." Saul Mosko leaned into the light. "You follow me?"

Instead of an icy glare like Earl's, Isador saw a tiny reflection of the overhead bulb burning in each of the man's dark irises like two tiny suns. The hair on the back of Isador's neck bristled. He searched for his voice. "Yes," he croaked and then cleared his throat. "Thank you, Mr. Mosko. I won't disappoint you."

Saul Mosko sat back in his chair, returning to the shadows.

Earl wrapped a hand around Isador's arm and urged him

back toward the front door where another two men waited, their hats in their hands, their eyes averted.

"Wait a minute," Isador said, once they were outside. "I have to go back. He caught me off guard. I didn't think to ask where, or when to—"

"Eight o'clock tomorrow morning. 39 Cummings. It's above Murphy's."

"Cummings?"

"That's right. Unless you want to change your mind. You can do that right now, this minute. But not tomorrow."

"No. No. I'm good. 39 Cummings. Eight sharp."

At the sound of Rose fumbling with the front door, Isador leapt from the sofa. He twisted the doorknob and threw the door open. Rose jumped back and raised a hand to her heart.

"Oh, Isador! You scared me half to death."

"Come on in, Rose, come on in." He pulled her toward him and kissed her on the mouth.

"Wha—what's gotten into you?"

"Come in and take a seat. Right here." Isador waved his hand toward the sofa.

"Can I take my hat off?"

"Keep it on, we're going to have a toast and then we're going out for dinner. Maybe even dancing. How about a night at the Beachview?"

"The Beachview? My. What's the occasion?"

"I have a new job. But there's better news. Come. Sit." Isador skipped into the kitchen and returned with two glasses filled with a small amount of honey colored liquid.

"A toast."

"Goodness, how much of this do you have stashed away?"

"Never mind about that. Listen, beginning tomorrow morning at eight o'clock, yours truly—I, Mr. Isador Margolin—will report for duty as the new manager of a prosperous and growing business establishment on Cummings. To celebrate this momentous occasion, I propose a toast. Here's to the new manager and our future." Isador raised his glass, clicked it against Rose's, and downed the whiskey in a single swallow. "Drink up."

"To the new manager." Rose said and took a swallow. "Tell me..."

"It seems all my hard work and planning and my reputation for having a head for business have finally caught someone's attention."

"Fazio came through?"

"Ah, no. No. My boss, you don't know him, of course, but... Well, I'm sure you've heard of him. Saul Mosko. 'Mr. M' as I call him. It's one of his businesses."

"Mosko."

"Now, before you go jumping to conclusions, let me tell you. He's not at all like what you hear, the awful way they portray him in the newspapers. I had a chance to meet him today. He's actually very refined."

"What kind of business?"

"A speakeasy."

"Isador!"

"So what? If that's the job he needs, that's the job I'll do. You haven't forgotten how much he already did for us. Kilcourse and the rest. Besides, I'd sure rather be managing a place of my own than playing Logrin's delivery boy to a bunch of old biddies."

"Where is it?"

"On Cummings, just off Broadway."

"What kind of people go there?"

Meaning, Isador thought, was it safe and were the customers predominantly Irish, Italian, or Jews? The descendants and first generation immigrants lived side by side in most of Revere's neighborhoods—a synagogue on one block, a cathedral on the next, and on a third, a kosher meat market tucked beside an Italian-owned bakery. At times, disagreements in the close quarters erupted, some growing into outright skirmishes. And, to be sure, there were gangland killings, either the Irish against the Italians or both against the Jews, but Isador had not heard of any happening around Cummings.

"What's it called?" Rose continued, peppering him with questions.

"I'm not sure it has a name. Earl told me to meet him at the corner of Cummings and Broadway. The place is between a bank and a café named Murphy's."

"It doesn't have a name?"

"Not that I know of. But you've given me an idea. Maybe I'll give it a name. Something catchy. Let me think..." Isador paused tapping his finger to his chin. He looked back at Rose and noticed two thin lines dimpling the soft flesh between her eyebrows. "Now what are you worried about?" he asked.

"I just wish it weren't with a..."

"With a gang? Forget about that. There are dozens of speakeasies all over town. They're harmless."

"Anything involved with...well, you know. And a speakeasy is hardly harmless. Addie's cousin was killed in one in New York. She said—"

"Who's Addie?"

"Addie. Addie Azarian. You know, my friend at Tilling-hast's. Anyway, she said—"

"Rose, don't go spoiling this. It's a first step for me. I'll get the experience I need and then I can look for something better. Maybe we'll be able to afford something in Boston, maybe New York. Better yet, I might stay right here and buy out old man Logrin." Isador studied Rose's face, expressionless except for the lines between her brows. "Are you listening?"

"Yes. Of course. Logrin. Boston. New York."

Everyone referred to the speakeasy as Murphy's, though technically the joint had nothing to do with the café downstairs. Isador hadn't had a chance to give it a proper name, but he'd tried a few out in his head. He wanted something with a bit more *oomph*. The Ritz or the Orpheum or the Palace, names he'd jotted down from his collection of books and journals.

Isador yawned. Though he'd been working at the speakeasy for a little over a week, he hadn't adjusted to the odd hours. At Logrin's he'd worked from seven until six. Here he came in around four o'clock in the afternoon and stayed until well after midnight.

Three customers sat at one table, two more at the other end of the bar, and one in front of him. A slow evening. Edwin, John, and Alexander—or "Sandy" as the man had said to call him—at the table. Regulars. Roy and Jimmy at the far end of the bar, Aken on the stool closest to Isador. He'd taken Rose's advice. "People like it when you greet them by name. At least that's what we do at Tillinghast's." He was good with names and had known all of Logrin's regulars by name. Mrs. Hurley, who came in on Tuesdays and always left with a large bag of shredded cabbage, Mrs. Bidder, Bette Bidder, on Wednesdays—he couldn't forget her name or, for that matter, what she bought. Beets. Bette Bidder's beets. And on Thursdays...

A rapping sound at the far end of the bar broke his concentration. Roy waved his empty glass in the air.

"Right there," Isador said, grabbing the bottle of whiskey from under the counter. "Pretty quiet tonight, no?" He poured another whiskey for Roy and pocketed the two bits from the counter. "How about you, Jimmy, you ready?"

Jimmy knocked back his last sip, shook his head, and set the empty glass on the bar. "Nope, not for me tonight. Got to be getting back."

"That old lady of yours has a tight string on you," Roy said, grinning and raising his full glass to his lips.

"Fuck you," Jimmy said, though he meant it good-naturedly. He donned his hat and headed toward the exit. At the top of the stairwell, he stepped to the side to allow two customers to pass.

"Hello, Aken darling!"

At the sound of the woman's voice, all the men in the room turned their heads toward the entrance. Two women sashayed—that was the word that came to Isador's mind—across the room toward Aken. He rose from his stool to greet them. The brunette pressed her cheek against his then settled next to him on a stool. The blonde, who had held back, wrapped both her arms around Aken's neck and then pecked him on the cheek, making a deliberately loud smack as she did.

The volume of chatter grew sharply. Both women spoke at once, stopped, and started again. They laughed as if they'd been laughing all night at a party or some other speakeasy.

"Isador," Aken called, "can we get a few drinks here?"

Isador sauntered to where Aken sat, between the two women. "What can I bring you ladies?"

"Well," the blonde said, peering at Isador through thick lashes, "let me see." To Aken, she said, "What are you having, darling?" She snuggled close, her bare shoulder digging into his chest.

While she made up her mind, Isador turned his attention to the brunette.

"I'm still thinking," she said, her voice as silky and smooth as his best whiskey. "You must be new around here."

"I am."

"Make mine gin," the blonde said. She giggled and rubbed her nose against Aken's ear. Aken put his hand around her shoulder and turned her around to face Isador.

"This is Estelle, Isador," Aken volunteered. "Estelle, meet Isador, Murphy's new barkeep."

"Pleased to meet you," Isador said.

"And this is Estelle's little sister, Sylvia."

"Hello, little sister Sylvia," Isador said, lightheaded from the scent of the woman's perfume wafting toward him. Instead of shaking the hand she offered, Isador bowed his head and kissed her knuckles, gathering another whiff of her scent.

"Now, that's what I call a gentleman," Estelle said, her voice tinkling like glass.

"My pleasure," Isador said.

Sylvia nodded, smiled with her eyes, and pursed her lips, as if she were taking his measure.

"We haven't got all night, Sylvia," Estelle said.

"Surprise me, then," Sylvia said to Isador, her eyes still devouring him while she fingered the long chain of beads strung around her neck and dangling below her breasts.

Isador backed away a step or two, avoiding turning his head until he feared he might trip. After serving the trio their drinks, Isador left the bar to check on his other customers, though he never went more than a few seconds without eyeing Aken and his friends.

He had to ask Jimmy to repeat his order twice. "Gin, yes. You said gin. Indeed you did," Isador said and immediately lost his concentration. Down the bar, Sylvia placed a cigarette in a holder and bent close to Aken to accept a light. She drew in a long breath and turned to exhale, sending the smoke upward behind their heads. Her eyes found Isador and lingered on him, before she rejoined the conversation between Estelle and Aken.

At close to eleven o'clock, Aken, Estelle, and Sylvia rose from their seats at the bar. Aken hooked a hand underneath an elbow of each of his guests and guided them toward the door. Isador rubbed his palms on his pants. They tingled as if it were he and not Aken who held the soft skin in his hands. He nearly missed hearing Estelle's offer.

"Isador. Isador. Hello!" After a pause, she said, "Ah, I thought perhaps you'd gone deaf. Would you like to join us? There's a fine party at a friend's place. It's probably just getting revved up."

"I would love to, but I still have customers, and...well, you know, as the manager, I have to attend to them and close out later."

"Oh, pooh. You're no fun at all," Estelle said, waggling her fingers over her shoulder.

"Perhaps another night," Isador said.

"Next time, buddy," Aken said.

Estelle and Aken ducked into the stairwell. Sylvia, who'd said nothing, turned back for one more look.

Earl

EARL RAPPED HIS KNUCKLES ON THE DOORFRAME. HE'D COME into Murphy's without a sound, an hour before opening on a Wednesday, normally a slow day. The place was tidy, chairs squared against the tables, floors swept, clean glasses stacked on the shelves behind the bar.

"Hey there, Earl. I didn't hear you come in," Isador said, emerging from the storeroom at the far end of the room. "Have a seat. You're early, but you want a drink?"

"Nah, I've got to make my rounds."

"Rounds?"

"Yeah. You should come with me. Mosko said it'd be good for you to learn another side of the business. I'm just going down to Grand to collect from a few of our clients." Earl patted himself on the back for his use of his boss's term "clients."

Earl might not be able to afford to dress like him, but he could adopt some of his attributes. Like his speech, polite and precise. No slang. No swearing. Or his demeanor, the way he held his head. And the way he eyed people, always with the same blank expression, whether he was shaking hands or pulling the trigger—though he did less of that himself these days. It was only Mosko's eyes that changed, soft one minute and then so sharp they might pierce right through your soul the next.

"Collect? Well, sure," Isador said, glancing at the clock on the wall. "I guess I've got an hour or so." He slipped off his apron, folded it neatly, and placed it on the bar.

"Ready?" Earl fumbled with the flap on his pocket and turned to go. He listened for a sign of hesitation. "Ready?"

"Sure. Whatever you say."

"That's what I wanna—," Earl broke off, catching his lapse, "that's what I want to hear."

They walked together to Grand, Earl lengthening his stride to match Isador's step. "So," he said, "I've got two clients here and one around the corner. Stick close and keep your ears and eyes open. But don't say anything. I'll handle the talking."

Their first stop was Premier Watch and Clock Repair. The owner, Herb Shankle, was wrapping a package for a heavyset older woman when Earl and Isador walked through the door. The smile on Herb's face vanished and a vein in the side of his neck pulsed noticeably. Herb nodded and then returned his attention to the woman and her package.

Earl stepped behind the woman as if he were just another customer waiting to claim or drop off an item. On the counter, Herb maintained a display of mantel clocks, their pendulums synchronized—left, right, left—ticking in perfect unison. Earl tapped his foot in time to the beat.

"Th-there you go, Mrs. Simon. Th-thank you for coming by," Herb said.

"Thank you, Mr. Shankle," the woman said. "I'll be sure to let you know if it keeps good time. If not, I know Mr. Simon will be around directly."

"I'm sure he will, but I don't th-think he'll need t-to. It's right on the money. You can t-tell him I said so."

"I'll do that." She turned and waddled toward the door.

God, Earl thought. *Could you hurry it up? I don't have all night.*

Herb dashed from behind the counter to hold the front door for Mrs. Simon.

"Why thank you. That's so kind of you."

"Not at all," he said. He smiled and nodded and waited for her to pass. Once outside, she turned and waved. Herb nodded again, waggled his fingers, and smiled with a weak upturn of his lips. He fished a key from his pocket and locked the door from the inside.

"Hello, Mr. Bloom," he said. Herb withdrew a handkerchief from his pants pocket and patted his forehead.

When Earl worked collections with Elliot Kriger, he never had to do or say much. All it took was the sight of Kriger for the money to appear. Kriger's head was as big as a melon, his hands like steaks, his chest like an icebox. Lacking Kriger's size, Earl had developed his own technique. He would walk in with his hat on to show that he was in a hurry, that he had places to go. He would stand in plain sight in the middle of the room and say nothing. Not one word. And if he did have to speak, he started with a whisper. He liked giving the frantic little people time, listening to their ticks and stammers, observing their hand-wringing, their brow-wiping. He'd done it so often that he knew the precise sequence of mannerisms his clients exhibited as their discomfort grew. Herb, for instance, after the stammering and sweating and toweling off, would begin with excuses.

Herb licked his lips and swallowed, the tendon in his neck as busy as if it were a creature with its own beating heart. "I was so busy all day, you can't imagine."

Earl said nothing and continued to tap his foot. *Tick tock.*

"It was getting so late, I thought you might not come by." *Tick tock.*

"Don't I come by on the last day of the month, every month?" Earl asked, his voice a whisper.

"Y-yes you do. I guess I forgot what day it was."

"Mr. Shankle, is there something you want to tell me?" This time, Earl's voice was one notch higher than a whisper.

"I can give you everything I have in the cash register. It's yours." Herb's eyes were wide, his hands alive, dancing outside his pockets. "Yes. I can certainly do that, give you what little there is here."

Earl leaned over the counter and scooped the bills from the cash drawer.

"Five, ten, twenty..." Earl laid each bill face up on the counter, one on top of the other, corners squared. "Forty-five, fifty." Earl paused and made a show of looking at the floor to the right and left as if he might have dropped a note. "Fifty," he said under his breath. He waited.

"I know. I know. It's been very slow. T-terribly slow." Herb's head shook vigorously from side to side. "I think it's the heat. But I'll have the rest for you soon. Next week, I'm sure. You can count on that." His words came much too fast.

"Next week? Did you hear that, Isador? Herb says next week." Earl looked over his shoulder at Isador, paused, and turned back to Herb. In a raised voice, one decibel short of a shout, Earl said, "What...the...fuck...do...you...think...I...am? Do you think I'm a bank?"

Herb's hands halted their dance.

"You know what I oughta—ought to do?" Earl asked, whispering, again. "I ought to have this gentleman here," Earl thumbed his hand toward Isador, "beat you to a pulp. How would you like that?"

"Please," Herb said. "It's just—" Beads of sweat formed in

the crease across Herb's forehead, like a string of pearls, but Herb left his handkerchief in his pocket.

"Maybe you think this is Chanukah? That's it. You think it's Chanukah." Earl laughed, making no attempt to disguise the forced nature of his humor. "Well, I'll tell you something, Herb," in his low tone, drawing Herb close. Then loudly, "It's not Chanukah. It's not Christmas. It's August thirty-first and I need my goddamn money."

"You have everything I have, Mr. Bloom. You can see that for yourself." Herb pointed at the cash drawer. Only coins lay in their bins.

"Fifty then. Fine. But let me tell you this. You run one nickel short when I come back on Friday, and you'll find out why you want to pay me on time in the future. You follow me?"

"Yes. I'll have the rest by then. I promise."

"You're goddamn right, you will." Earl thumped his fist on the counter. He slipped the fifty dollars into his pocket. "Let's go," he said to Isador and spun on his heels.

At the front door, where Herb Shankle had placed a bowl of hard candy, Earl selected two yellow cellophane wrapped treats, butterscotch, his favorite. He tossed one to Isador. Then he turned the key Herb had left in the lock and walked out, leaving the door ajar. He did not look back but heard the door click shut and the lock turn once again.

"Did you take everything he had?" Isador asked.

"Damn right, I did. Herb has more money stashed somewhere in the back. You can count on that. Cockamamie story about the heat." Earl popped the candy into his mouth and tossed the wrapper on the ground. "Next stop, the grocer on the corner." Earl said as he sped ahead, forcing Isador to hustle forward.

"So, you've had a chance to check him out."

"Yes, sir."

"And you vouch for your new friend," Mosko said over the half open window of his automobile.

Earl nodded, "Yeah, er, yes, I think so."

"You think so."

"I mean, yes, sir, we can trust him. He's eager. Wants to get ahead. He'll be ready when you need him."

"Good."

Earl stood a few feet away from the black Buick. He knew better than to place his hands on the gleaming fender and leave his fingerprints.

"Someone new?" Mosko asked, jutting his chin toward the woman standing several steps away.

Earl looked over his shoulder at Emily. Mr. Mosko could not have missed her, nor was it likely anyone else on the block did. *She's a looker all right.* The fabric of her blouse puckered as it stretched over her breasts, screaming, "Look at me!" *Those two giant knockers catch everyone's attention, and she knows it.*

"Oh, I've been seeing her for a while."

"Here. Take this and treat her to a nice dinner. Make an impression. I want to see you settle down. Have a few kids." Mr. Mosko handed Earl a folded bill through the window.

"Thank you, Mr. Mosko. I'll do that. I'll take her up to the Beachview."

Saul Mosko tapped the back of the seat in front of him. His driver edged away from the curb and drove off.

"Who was that?" Emily asked.

"A friend."

"Some kind of fancy friend I'd say. Nice car."

"Yeah. What do you say we go dancing?"

"Well, now you're talking."

"Come here, girl." Earl drew Emily close and squeezed her buttocks.

"Woo. Cut that out!" Emily slapped him on the chest in mock protest. He squeezed her soft flesh again, knowing she liked it as much as he did.

On Shirley Avenue, they weaved left and right, threading their way through the Saturday night strollers who poured into the streets after Shabbat. Shops reopened to capture spur-of-the-moment purchases, an ice cream from the drugstore or a hot dog from a street vendor. Couples walked two abreast, most held hands. Young toughs, little more than boys, practiced being tough. They slouched on the stoops or lazed against lamp posts, feigning disinterest and bravado, hoping to attract the attention of a passing gang leader. Groups of girls, three, four, and in some cases five or six strong, linked arms and strolled in the street, their laughter rolling back to Earl and Emily.

Emily cozied up to Earl. She liked being seen with him, or at least, that's what Earl thought. She knew he worked for someone important which in her world made Earl important. She'd said that. Still, despite Mosko's encouragement, she wasn't someone he would settle down with. Settling down was far from his mind. *It would have to be someone like—*

"You sure are quiet tonight," Emily said. "Penny for your thoughts?"

"Just taking in the scenery."

The Beachview pavilion came into view. It sat at the end of the pier like a crown. Lights strung around the perimeter reflected in the water, doubling the effect.

"Earl! Earl!" From the far side of the avenue, Isador weaved his way through the crowd toward Earl and Emily. Earl saw that Isador had his wife with him. He breathed in and cleared his face of expression.

"Earl, I want you to meet someone. This is my wife, Rose."

Rose tipped her head, a half nod, and looked down, her hands fidgeting with the pleats of her skirt. Though the daylight was fading, he caught a flush of color at her throat.

"Rose, this is Earl. Earl Bloom, the man I told you about."

"Very nice to meet you, Mrs. Margolin," Earl said.

"Rose. You can call her Rose. Right, Rose?" Isador kept talking. Only Earl realized she'd not said a word nor lifted her eyes. "Looks like you're out for a nice stroll tonight," Isador continued.

"We're going dancing," Emily said and paused to look at Earl. "Isn't that right? And dinner after. I'm Emily." She stuck out her hand, waited, and then dropped it to her side. "Pleased to meet you."

"Well, we best be going," Isador said.

Earl tipped his head at Isador then at Rose, who had raised her head but looked past him, or maybe through him, as if he did not exist.

"Who was that?" Emily asked a second later. "Kind of got her nose in the air, that gal."

"Someone I work with. Come on, we'll be late." He grabbed Emily's arm above the elbow urging her forward, but turned his head in time to catch a glimpse of Rose before she and Isador faded into the crowd. Her hand was at her temple, shielding her eyes.

Isador

A BEAM OF LATE SUMMER SUNLIGHT STREAMED THROUGH THE windows in the Margolin's flat. Gold and already heavy with heat at seven in the morning, the light traveled the left side of Isador's head from his ear, across his cheek, and to his forehead, searing the back of the one eyelid not buried in his pillow.

Goddamn it. He threw the covers back and stumbled toward the window. He tugged the two sides of the draperies until they met. Still, the room glowed a yellow-gray. "Goddamn it," he said again, aloud this time. Rose had the luxury of going to bed and waking at what most people considered normal hours. He did not. To compensate, on most days, he tried to sleep until at least nine, often missing his wife or waking only when her lips brushed his cheek before she left for work.

Isador rolled onto his left side, away from the window, and sank back into the soft mattress. For double measure, he covered his head with Rose's pillow. But it was no use. The cacophony of sounds outside grew in volume with the temperature, a vendor barked a slow, repetitive jingle, horns tooted between the clip clop of hooves on the pavement, a newspaper boy shouted, "Five cents! Five cents!"

At nine-thirty by his watch on the bedside table, he eased out of bed and ambled to the kitchen. Rose had brewed coffee, but it had long since cooled. While he waited for another pot to brew, he pulled a bottle of milk from the icebox and took a long sip straight from the lip, knowing all the time Rose hated when he did that. He wiped his mouth with the back of his hand and the edge of the bottle with his forearm. On the kitchen table, Rose had left him the newspaper along with a banana and toast. *Good girl.*

Dressed only in his underwear and slippers, Isador took a seat. He flipped through the paper until he found the baseball scores. Footsteps in the living room caught his attention. Rose with a basket of groceries in each arm.

"Aren't you off to work?" Isador asked.

"Work? You silly man. It's Saturday. I went to Logrin's for some fresh vegetables. I wanted to make a pot of soup before you had to go." She set the groceries on the counter.

"I wish you wouldn't shop there. I'm through with Logrin, and you should be, too."

"I know. But when I'm in a hurry, well, he's so close. I thought I could dash over and be back before you got up." Rose came behind his chair and leaned over, wrapping her arms around his neck. "I didn't want to miss my time with you."

Isador closed his fingers around her arm, preventing her from pulling away. The scent of fresh scrubbed skin filled his nostrils and, as always, sent a twinge to his crotch. He stood and swept Rose off her feet.

"Isador, put me down. I have to put the groceries away."

"The groceries can wait."

"Put me down, you oaf!" she said, pounding playfully on his chest and shoulders.

Isador ignored Rose's protests and headed to the bedroom. He pushed the door open with his foot, crossed the room, and laid her on her back. He held her there with one of his hands on each of her shoulders and rubbed his unshaven chin against her neck. She squealed in response. He rose again and sat astride her while he tore at the dozen or more tiny blue buttons on her dress.

"My, you are impatient! Watch out or you'll tear—"

"I'll watch out when I see you naked."

"Isador!"

Two Saturdays had come and gone since Isador had seen Aken and his two lady friends. On each of those Saturdays, Isador had gone about his business at the speakeasy with one eye on the stairwell and an ear out for the sound of laughter. It was Saturday again. He hoped Aken would show, that Aken would bring Estelle, and that Estelle would bring Sylvia.

She'd been on his mind all day. While making love to Rose earlier, he'd had to catch himself. He'd come close to saying Sylvia's name, the S on his tongue, set to explode when he did. He'd swallowed the word, pushed it down his throat, and held it there until he was finished. While Rose stroked his back, he'd closed his eyes and imagined Sylvia's dark cherry ovals raking his skin. Harder, he had said, and Rose had dragged the rounded tips of her fingers along his spine.

Ten o'clock. The bar was crowded. Isador sauntered from one end of the floor to the other, stopping here and there to greet or wait on someone who had just arrived. Eleven o'clock. Still no Aken. Isador's pace slowed. He plodded as if he were walking on sand the tide had just bared. When a few latecomers took their seats at the far side of the room, Isador asked his helper, Carl, to spell him.

At eleven-thirty, laughter erupted in the stairwell. "Aken! Stop that! You're such a tease!" A flash of sequins and fringe.

Estelle entered, then Aken, and behind Aken, Sylvia. More laughter, to Isador's ears, blissful, joyous peals of laughter. Estelle nearly stumbled head first over a chair, though Aken caught her in time and helped her to a seat. Sylvia broke away from the two and came straight to the bar where Isador stood transfixed.

"Good evening, Isador. You're still here."

"Sylvia. You're back."

Isador had done his homework. In the intervening weeks since they'd met, he'd discovered that Sylvia was an actress and sometimes danced on stage. An advertisement in the newspaper listed her name along with several other women as one of the cast in a vaudeville act at the Grand Theater. The paper mentioned two shows on Saturday.

"What a day! What a night. I'm exhausted. Make me something," she said. "Something special."

"I have just the thing. Don't go anywhere."

"I have no intention of moving from this spot. Ever!"

Isador returned with a gin splashed with tonic water. "So, rough night?"

"Two shows today, two very long shows."

"The Grand, huh? I'd love to see one of your shows sometime. Maybe next week?"

"Maybe."

Across the room, Estelle squealed and then erupted into laughter. She sat on Aken's lap and tugged at his tie. Aken circled Estelle's buttocks with his right hand. He flexed his fingers, digging into the sequined sheath. Another squeal of delight.

"Those two have been very bad tonight," Sylvia said. "I have half a mind to let them make their own way home."

"You should, I'm sure they'll manage. What about you? Maybe you need some help getting home?"

"Maybe," Sylvia said. "First, I need to powder my nose." She scouted the room for a sign of washrooms. "Which way?"

"Let me show you," Isador said. He led Sylvia to the back of the speakeasy, down a hallway, and to the right. "That way," he said, pointing ahead. As Sylvia took a step forward, Isador placed his hand on the wall blocking her progress.

Sylvia pivoted and leaned against the wall. They stood face to face, not saying a word, each searching the other's eyes for a sign. Sylvia wrapped her fingers around Isador's tie and tugged, bringing his face down to hers. Isador drew a breath of the thick air in the hallway and held it as if he were about to dive headfirst into the ocean. He pressed his body against Sylvia's, pinning her to the wall, her breasts rising and falling against his chest, her hips cupped in his, her thighs warm where they met his, his erection undeniable, pressing against his trousers. He grabbed the back of her head with one hand and placed his lips over hers, his mouth open, her tongue finding his, searching.

Then, somewhere above him—or was it to the left or the right—came the sound of men shouting, a scuffle, chairs scraping the floor, glass breaking. The sounds made no sense. They were muffled and dull. Isador was drowning, his head deep beneath the water.

A woman's high pitched shriek.

At that, Isador tore himself from Sylvia, lifting his head, listening and gathering his wits. Something was wrong. He needed to go. He was the manager. It was his responsibility, but his feet hesitated as if they had a mind of their own, unwilling to move from the place in the hall.

Another shriek. Men's voices, speaking all at once.

Sylvia had not moved. She'd heard nothing or wanted to hear nothing. Isador summoned every muscle in his body and turned, leaving her slumped against the wall.

Inside, chaos reigned. Isador took in the scene with one long sweep across the room, noting overturned chairs and spilled drinks, patrons huddling in small groups, and women standing with their hands to their mouths.

Carl had his head propped in his hands over the bar, while Jimmy, one of the regulars, held a towel to Carl's forehead. Vince Dorfman, another customer, stood to the side, patting Carl's back.

"What happened?" Isador asked. He rushed behind the bar, broken glass crunching under his feet. He bobbed and swiveled to look behind Carl, seeing only a void where the cash drawer should be. Isador found the box upended on the floor, a few stray coins toppled aside in a puddle of liquid.

"You should have seen him, Isador," Vince said. "He tried to fend them off by himself. Refused to give them the money. They whacked him good, grabbed some cash, and ran."

"Carl!" Isador said, noticing for the first time the blood dripping from a gash on the side of his forehead.

"Didn't see what they hit him with," Jimmy said.

"Carl, are you okay?" Isador asked.

"Yeah. I'll be fine. My head hurts like hell, but I think it's okay."

"What happened? I...uh...I stepped to the back for a minute and then I...uh...I heard all this commotion and came running."

"They were in and out quick. Took all the cash," Carl said.

Isador's thoughts raced ahead, anticipating what he'd say to Earl. And worse, what Earl would say to Saul Mosko.

"Okay, okay," Isador said. A number of the speakeasy's patrons were on their feet, keeping their distance while gawking at the men around the bar. Some had left and more were crowded at the top of the stairs. "Everyone, please. Take your seats. We'll straighten up a bit and be back around to get your orders. The next one's on the house. Have a seat. Please."

Two of the men near the stairwell turned and came back. Others continued down the stairs, urged on by their female companions.

"Jimmy, you can let go. Carl, I'll get a bandage or something from the supply room to stop the bleeding and patch you up."

Carl dabbed the towel against his forehead a couple times. He held it in front of him, squinting to see if the bleeding had stopped. "I think it's okay now."

"Great," Isador said. "Hey, I've got an extra shirt in the storage room. Why don't you go back and change and get rid of all that blood. You might not scare as many guests away."

Carl pulled his shirt loose from where it had stuck to his chest. "Yeah," he said, "looks pretty bad."

"I'll sweep up the broken glass, then I'll get to the customers." Isador surveyed the room again. The customers who'd stayed had not taken their seats. They milled about, talking in small groups and peering every now and then at Isador and Carl.

"Ladies, gents," Isador said. "Have a seat. Everything's fine."

Isador knelt and retrieved the inverted cash drawer. He returned it to its shelf, glaring at the empty bins. Crestfallen, he plucked a handful of coins from where they'd come to rest on the floor and dropped them in the drawer, mixing nickels with dimes and pennies. When he'd whisked aside the bulk of the shards of glass to leave a clean walkway behind the bar, Isador noticed what appeared to be a dollar bill behind the ice bucket. To his surprise, the bill was not a dollar. It was the fifty dollar bill he'd removed from the cash drawer earlier in the evening and placed underneath the box for safekeeping.

Isador folded the note and stuffed it in his trouser pocket.

"Someone must have recognized them," Earl said. "Couldn't have been the cops, they'd have smashed or taken the booze and arrested you and Carl. Probably anyone else they wanted." Earl paused. "Nope, not the cops. It had to be someone we know. Some son of a bitch we know."

The two were seated at the L&M Luncheonette a few doors from the speakeasy. On Sunday, Isador had asked around and located Earl to tell him about the robbery. Earl had been "busy." They agreed to meet for lunch on Monday. In the meantime, Earl had asked Isador to estimate the amount of the loss.

"Carl didn't recognize either of them?" Earl asked.

"That's what he said."

"And you?"

"Like I told you, I'd gone to the crapper when they came in. Didn't hear a thing till I got a few feet from the back door."

"You need to have a piece under the counter. I'll get you one. If they think they got away that easy, they'll be back"

"You think?"

"I think."

"Damn."

"Didn't see anything funny earlier? Anyone you didn't know come in and leave?"

"Well, there could have been. It was a busy night."

"And a fucking fifty cents is all that's left?"

"Yeah, a fucking lousy fifty cents," Isador said, mimicking Earl.

"What did they look like? What were they wearing? Did they have a piece?" Earl fired several questions at Isador in quick succession.

"I told you before, I didn't see anything. It was over by the time I got back in there." Isador took a bite of his sandwich and chewed it for longer than he needed, buying time, trying not to hurry. "They had a piece, though, that's for sure. That's what Marty said they used to clobber Carl. Marty's a regular. Martin's his name, but he goes by—"

"Yeah," Earl said, "I know who Marty is." Earl wiped his mouth with his napkin, set it on the table, and then picked at his teeth with the edge of his fingernail.

"If you want, I can check with a few more tonight," Isador volunteered. "I haven't talked to Aken. He was there but he was so drunk, he couldn't remember a thing. Carl already talked to five or six others, including Estelle."

"Who's left?" Earl scanned the list Isador had made—from memory—of the people in the bar at the time of the robbery. They'd discussed most of the names already. "Guy Fishman and Ed Radler. And the last one, Sylvia Shaffer. That Estelle's sister? The actress?"

"Yeah. She didn't see anything. She'd gone to the back. The powder room, I think. That leaves Guy and Ed. I didn't want to scare too many away by grilling them on the spot.

Some of the ladies were in a hurry to get out of there. Didn't want to empty it out after we'd lost everything."

"Sure. I understand."

Isador breathed a sigh of relief. He'd not roused Earl's suspicions, not about his being in the back during the fracas and not about the loss of everything but fifty cents. The fifty dollar bill was safe at home, tucked between two issues of National Geographic with the rest of his savings. He took a last bite of his sandwich.

Across the table, Earl's lunch sat on his plate, untouched.

Jacob

JACOB TOOK THE STAIRS TWO AT A TIME, A SACK OF GROCERIES under each of his arms.

"Careful, Jacob. I've got eggs in one of those bags," Rose called from a few flights below.

"Yes, ma'am." When he reached the third floor, Jacob placed the bags outside Rose's door and then peered over the bannister rail at Rose rounding the stairs on the second floor. "Your eggs are safe, Mrs. Margolin. Do you want me to take them inside?"

"Just a minute. I've got the key here."

Key? Rose never used to lock her door. No one in the neighborhood locks their door. He shrugged his shoulders and waited for Rose to catch up. On the landing, she paused and fumbled in her purse.

"Here you go," she said, handing Jacob the key.

He unlocked the door, returned the key, and grabbed the two sacks.

"Put them on the counter in the kitchen. I'll be there in a minute."

Jacob set the groceries next to the bear-shaped cookie jar. He smiled, remembering how Mrs. Margolin rewarded him with a ginger snap or macaroon when he was younger. He didn't expect a cookie any more. He helped because he liked Mrs. Margolin. She was simply the most beautiful person he knew. Prettier than his teacher, Miss Alice, whom his friend Walter adored. And Miss Rose was the nicest, always smiling and sparing time for him. She and Isador were two of the youngest adults on the block, ten or fifteen years younger than his father and aunt and decades younger than his Grandma Goldstein—she'd moved in with them last week, further crowding their tiny apartment. Jacob liked Mr. Margolin, too. He could ask Mr. Margolin, Isador that is, things he would never ask his father. Isador showed him things, too, grown up things like how to tie a tie, how to comb and pomade your hair, and how to shave, though Jacob would have to wait a few years to shave. And—though he pretended not to see—Jacob liked how Isador would walk behind Miss Rose, put his arms around her, and kiss her on the neck or shoulder, even while Jacob was in the room.

"Is there anything else you need help with?" Jacob asked. She'd let him carry her trash to the bins in the alley a few weeks ago and once he'd tightened the hinge on a cabinet door, things Jacob imagined Isador might handle. Jacob preferred these tasks over the things his aunt assigned him, like washing the kitchen floor or bringing in and folding the laundry. Sometimes he bribed Leila to do the laundry for him, offering her his slice of pie on the rare occasion his aunt baked a pie. If she balked, he paid her a penny of his precious savings hidden in the back of his drawer. It was that or risk Art or Larry, who lived two doors down, catching him with his aunt's laundry basket as they'd done before. His cheeks still burned at their taunting and the embellishments Sid/Lefty had seen fit to add in front of everyone at school.

"He had on his auntie's apron, too," Sidney had said, snickering behind his cupped hand.

To which Art added, "Tied in a nice bow in the back, I'll bet."

Aunt Gladys had never made him wear an apron, but if Jacob corrected Art or denied it or showed he cared, he'd only prolong the teasing.

"Do you think you could stay for a while, Jacob?" Rose asked. "I was going to make an apple sponge cake. It won't take long, and you could take a piece home to Ralph and Leila. One for your aunt, too."

"And Grandma Goldstein?"

"Yes, of course."

Jacob's mouth watered. He'd had nothing to eat but cabbage and potatoes all week.

"Yes, ma'am, I can stay."

"Wonderful. Why don't you have a seat here at the table?"

"That's okay. Isn't there something I can do for you? Maybe a light out?"

"Hmm. Well, let me see," Rose said, tapping her palm with the bowl of the mixing spoon she'd taken from the drawer. "Would you like to polish Isador's shoes? I was going to do that for him after dinner."

"Isn't he coming home for dinner?"

"No," Rose said, her back to Jacob. She pulled a bowl from the cabinet. "With his new job, he doesn't even go to work till mid-afternoon and then he has to work late most nights." Rose put the spoon on the counter and turned to Jacob. "Come to think of it, would you like to join me for dinner?"

"Oh, yes, ma'am," he said without a second thought.

"Okay, then. You'd best get those shoes done while I finish up here."

Jacob scurried to the bedroom. Rose called out, "The black pair." He found the brogues against the wall beside the dresser and grabbed the shoeshine box from the hall closet. Isador had shown Jacob how to polish shoes and had let him do it once or twice on his own. Jacob lugged the wooden box into the kitchen and spread a piece of newspaper on the floor to catch any crumbs of polish. While Rose hummed under her breath at the sink, he squatted on the floor and picked a can of black polish from the bottom of the box along with a wooden-handled brush, stiff and thick with residue from the last use. Jacob skimmed the brush over the polish and then held it under his nose, inhaling the sharp scents of pitch and dye and oil, adult scents, masculine scents. After he'd smoothed the polish over the surfaces of both shoes, he raised a shoe and spit lightly on the toe, as Isador had done. He pulled one of the large soft-bristle brushes out, checking twice to make sure he had the black brush, not the dark brown one, and buffed the leather until he could see his reflection in the toes.

"Done?" Rose asked when he'd snapped the shoeshine box closed.

Jacob nodded and returned the shoes to the bedroom, placing them as Isador had shown him, heels against the wall.

When he returned to the kitchen, Rose had set two plates across from each other on the table. Two napkins folded in triangles beside each plate held a fork and knife. In the center of the table, though it was broad daylight, were two tall cream colored candles. "Could you light the candles for me?" Rose asked, offering a matchbox in the palm of her hand.

Jacob scratched a match against the box. The match snapped in half. "Oops."

"That's okay. Some of them are pretty old."

Jacob picked another match and tried again. This time, a bright yellow flame hissed to life. Trying to steady his trembling hand, he guided the match to the candle's wick.

"Perfect. Here, take this chair," Rose said, her hands resting on the chair against the wall. "This is where Isador usually sits."

A week after his dinner with Rose Margolin, Jacob was back in school for the fall school term. It hardly felt like fall, though, as daytime temperatures still hovered at summertime levels. If Jacob finished his chores early, he'd steal away with his friends to spend the last few hours of the afternoon at the beach, either near the rocky shore at one end or by the pier at the other. On this afternoon, except for a handful of adults strolling near the boardwalk, the boys had the beach to themselves—that is, until Isador Margolin appeared.

At first, Jacob thought he'd been mistaken.

Bored with skipping stones, taunting sand crabs, and searching for driftwood, Jacob, Walter, Michael, and Sidney—Sid/Lefty—had settled on the sandy shore to debate what to do next. A large splash near the end of the pier caught Jacob's attention. A man's head surfaced. A second splash followed. Then a third man jumped, tucked himself into a ball with his arms circling his shins, and dropped to the water. Jacob counted three heads bobbing in the waves.

Whoops of excitement erupted from the rocks above the group of boys. Three women had spread a blanket and sat side by side in their swimwear. They stared out at the ocean where the men bobbed. Two of the women waved their arms over their heads, calling the men ashore. One clapped her hands and then folded them together under her chin. All wore smiles, ear to ear, and stockings rolled down to bare their knees. Jacob elbowed Walter Abrams beside him.

"What?" Walter turned to Jacob.

"Up there," Jacob said, cocking his head towards the trio of women.

Walter whistled in the air. "Look at them. How long have they been there?"

"I don't know," Jacob said. "I didn't notice them until now."

"Me either. Hey Sidney, Michael!"

The four boys rolled on to their bellies and stared up the beach.

"Take a look at those gams," Walt said.

"Shush," Jacob said. "They'll hear you."

"So what if they do?"

"Maybe we should see if they need company," Michael said. He licked his lips.

"I don't think so," Jacob said.

"Why not?"

"Well, take a look out there," Jacob said, freeing an arm and pointing toward the water.

The three men were ankle deep in the shallows and making their way from the water to the women. The tallest of the group, dark hair, long limbs, looked a lot like Isador Margolin. By the time they stepped onto the dry sand, Jacob was certain it was his neighbor. He put his back to the men, not wanting Isador to see him, not that Isador had eyes for anything but the women.

Jacob remembered what Rose had said about Isador leaving for work in the afternoon, yet here he was, looking as if he had nowhere to go at all.

The boys stared at the women, then looked away, then stared again.

When they reached the rocks, the men stood over the women and tossed their heads back and forth, flinging drops of water like tiny sparks onto the women's heads and bare shoulders. Shrieks of mock horror erupted and the women ducked beneath towels to fend off the cold sea water. One by one, each of the men dropped to the rocks and fell into the outstretched arms of one of the women.

Jacob tried to look away, to find something interesting along the water line, but his eyes were drawn back to the young couples as if by a magnet.

Isador pulled himself to his knees and moved behind the brunette. He kneaded her shoulders. The woman's head was cocked backward, gazing at Isador. A hand with fingers tipped in scarlet pulled his head down until their lips met.

Jacob poked at a broken piece of shell in the sand by his foot. He took it between his thumb and forefinger and brought it toward his mouth, blowing against it to clean away the sand.

"Hey, sissy," Michael said. "Don't you want to watch? You might learn something."

"I already know about that. I don't need to watch."

"Oh yeah, where'd you learn anything about women? With that cousin of yours?"

Walter and Sidney snickered.

"Shut up," Jacob said, though he needn't have bothered as all three of his friends went back to ogling the women and the interaction on the rocks.

Jacob glanced at the group of adults one more time. His eyes met Isador's long enough, Jacob guessed, for Isador to recognize him. Jacob went back to examining the shell in his fingers, or at least he focused his eyes on the shell, hoping to calm his queasy stomach.

"Look out," Sidney said, "one of them's coming this way.

Turn around, quick." All three boys turned over, sat on their haunches, and stared out to sea.

A man's voice floated over their heads. "Hello there, boys. Jacob, is that you?"

Three heads turned to look at Jacob. Jacob answered without looking at Isador. "Yes, sir."

"Out of school, I guess."

"Yes, sir."

"Well, hey, can I talk to you a minute?"

Jacob rose to his feet, his head bowed, seeing only Isador's feet with their coating of sand. He supposed Isador's polished brogues were stashed somewhere up on the rocks.

"Come over here for a minute."

Jacob followed the voice and the feet. Once they were out of hearing distance of his friends and the three women, Isador placed a hand on Jacob's shoulder and squatted beside him. Eye to eye, Jacob could no longer look away.

"Now, you and I are friends, right Jacob?"

"Yes, sir."

"You don't have to call me sir. Just Isador. Like my friends. Like my friends over there. You're one of the guys. Right?"

Jacob nodded.

"Good. You have to understand, though this might seem a bit crazy to you. You have to understand, sometimes men have to have some time out with their friends. Men friends and women friends. It doesn't mean anything. It's, well, it's what adults do. Do you think you understand that?"

Jacob's head made a barely perceptible up and down motion.

"Good, I thought so. Heck, you're almost a man anyway.

But, hey, you have to understand, it's not something we talk about with the women who really, really mean something to us. They wouldn't understand. Not like you and me. We understand. Don't we?"

Jacob forced himself to make another up and down motion with his head, though his thoughts screamed otherwise. The only thing he understood was that Mr. Margolin was doing something wrong. Something Jacob could never tell Mrs. Margolin. Isador did not have to ask him to keep it a secret, but Jacob knew Isador would. Isador would make perfectly clear what he wanted.

"So, no need to mention this to Mrs. Margolin, to Rose. Got it?"

"Yes, sir."

"That's my boy," Isador said. He pulled Jacob against his hip and hugged him around the shoulders. "Hey, just a minute." Though he'd started back to his friends, Jacob turned around. Isador held two quarters in the air. "Why don't you take this and buy your friends there an ice cream before you go home. I bet they'd like that. What do you say?"

"Sure, Mr. Margolin."

Jacob took the money and returned to sit with his friends who'd abandoned watching the women to stare at Jacob and Isador.

"What was that all about?" Sidney asked.

"Nothing."

"Here," Jacob said, pressing the coins into Sidney's hand. "He said we could have this for ice cream." Jacob splayed his empty hands on the sand and rubbed his palms together, scouring his skin with the coarse grains.

Rose

EVERY SURFACE IN THE LIVING ROOM GLEAMED, POLISHED TO A high shine with wax and a considerable amount of hand rubbing. The floors were swept and mopped. Pillows and seat cushions on the sofa were plumped, erasing the curves and dips where Rose and Isador sat—when Isador was home. In the bedroom, the same. Perfume bottles stood in clusters on either side of the dresser and the wedding gift from Esther, a silver handled hairbrush and matching comb, lay on a mirrored tray scrubbed of fingerprints. A newly-framed photo of Rose and Isador in their wedding finery gleamed. The highboy had been polished too, the top as well as the sides. Rose had rubbed the brass pulls until they shone like new.

She toured the apartment, twice, failing to find something she'd overlooked—something left to fill the empty evening ahead. It was Friday, and like every weekday, Isador had left at four, missing Rose by an hour and a half.

She plopped on the bed, resting her head on her hands at the bed's foot. She gazed absently at the wedding photo and then at the floor. As usual, Isador's brogues and moccasins sat there, heels against the wall. What caught her attention, though, was a clump of dirt on one of the heels, something she'd missed. Rose retrieved a dustpan and whisk broom from the kitchen and squatted by the wall. At her touch, the clump fell apart. She'd been mistaken, the clump wasn't dirt after all. It was a crust of sand.

She couldn't remember the last time she and Isador had been to the beach. She shrugged her shoulders and swiped at the grains with her whisk broom.

As she turned to leave the room, Rose took a long look at her reflection in the mirror above her vanity table. She stepped closer, not liking the vacant eyes and unmade face of the woman who stared back. She glanced at the dustpan in her hand, back at her reflection, and then at the dustpan again. *Murphy's*, she thought. *Why not?*

Shoving her everyday dresses, skirts, and blouses and her Tillinghast uniforms to one side, Rose groped inside her small closet for something she hadn't worn in weeks. She removed the teal blue drop-waist sheath. She swiveled toward the vanity and held the dress under her chin with one hand while she gathered her hair behind her with the other. *Better, much better.* Suitable for a visit to Murphy's and the fashionable, late-night crowd Isador never tired of describing.

In a half hour, Rose looked in the mirror. A light dusting of pink on her cheeks, a smudge of deeper color on her lips, her hair tied and knotted behind her head. She liked what she saw.

Murphy's—or rather the speakeasy over Murphy's—was fifteen minutes away by foot and although Isador had been working there for over a month, she'd not been inside the place once. The café on the ground floor was not one she frequented, being well out of her neighborhood. She preferred the Revere Café near where she'd grown up; it was full of memories of celebrating one or the other of the six Forman girls' birthdays at the tiny café tables. A Forman family friend ran the café. Rose had taken Isador there after they'd first married and when he'd been working at her father's tailor shop. She hadn't realized that anything reminding Isador of the Forman family ruined his appetite and gave him a sour disposition. Once, he'd complained that the food was cold and the meat over-salted, pushing away his half-eaten plate of roast beef and potatoes. When the owner offered to bring a substitute or a slice of fresh baked apple pie "on the house" and to forego the check, Isador refused. Ever since, Rose visited the café alone or on rare occasions with Esther.

At the corner of Broadway and Cummings, Rose spotted the faded green sign with **MURPHY'S CAFÉ** in letters that had once been crisp and white. A couple of men huddled near the door. Although they had their backs to her, Rose recognized one of them, the one with the misshapen ear. Her heart pounded in her chest. She crossed the street and ducked inside a grocer. Rose walked up one aisle, stopped at a display of fresh fruit, and raised a melon to her nose. She strolled another aisle, her fingers trailing over the bananas, apples, onions, potatoes, and carrots.

Every so often, she went to the window and looked across the street, checking the access to Murphy's. On her third trip, Rose sensed she was being watched. To her right, behind the counter, the proprietor was staring at her. Rose considered buying a few apples to prove she was there for a purpose and not to pinch his produce, but thought better of the idea, picturing Isador's face as she entered the speakeasy with a sack of apples in her hand. She smiled and laughed aloud as she strode past the proprietor and out the door.

The men who'd been outside Murphy's earlier had disappeared. A couple dressed for an evening out on the town stood at the entrance. The gentleman held the door for his companion and then for Rose. As a group, they crossed to the back of the café where the couple disappeared behind a door, while Rose hung back and took stock of her surroundings.

When she opened the door, all she saw was a short dark hallway with a stairwell at the far end, but the unmistakable sounds of a speakeasy filled the void.

At the top of the stairs, she stopped and put a hand to her mouth to stifle a cough. She fanned the air, thick with smoke, and squinted into the haze. Isador had not exaggerated. Murphy's was a popular place, not a vacant table in sight. People crowded together in groups of two or three at the tables. Others sat along the bar, lips to ears, foreheads close to hear over the din. All were immersed in their own worlds, oblivious to the woman in teal blue at the head of the stairs.

Rose recognized a few faces, George and Bill, friends of Isador, whose last names she'd forgotten, if she'd ever known them. She vaguely remembered they'd been in Isador's company in the navy. And Guy Fishman with his wife, Irma, seated at a table against the wall. They lived a block north of Nahant Avenue.

She could pretend she had come to meet them, but their heads were bowed close to another couple across the table. The woman gestured wildly into the air. All four laughed and shook their heads. Guy pounded the table and laughed again.

Murphy's was not the quiet, desperate place she'd imagined. A place where men, huddled over the bar, raised glasses to their mouths and spent their precious, hard earned money on booze while their wives and children ate crackers and soup at home. Instead, the blind pig teemed with life. Two or three dozen conversations buzzed like a startled hornet's nest, glasses clinked, and chairs scraped the floor as people came and went. To Rose's surprise, the number of women nearly matched the number of men. And the women, all surprisingly young, were fashionably dressed, as if the pages of *Vogue* had come to life in front of her face. Blue sequins on a midnight background. Strands of fringe draped over bare knees. Brightly colored beads hung over breasts sheathed in silk.

Then, as if waking from a dream, or perhaps a nightmare, Rose realized how plain she must look in comparison. She turned to go but froze when she heard someone call her name.

"Rose," a voice called a second time, almost overpowered by the racket around her.

Above the heads of the crowd near the bar, a hand waved. Isador. He made his way to her through the smoke and haze.

"Rose! What are you doing here?"

"Isa. I thought I would come see the speakeasy. I was..." The word "lonely" came to mind, but instead she finished, "curious to see where you worked. That's all right isn't it?"

"Of course, it's all right. I'm just surprised, that's all. Come. Come have a seat at the bar where I can keep an eye on you."

"Oh no. Now that I'm here, I don't think I'm dressed appropriately."

"You look fine. Lovely, as always. Besides, no one cares what you wear here. Everyone's out to have a good time. Come, sit down."

Isador turned and dove headfirst into the throng, carving a path for her. She followed close on his heels, not wanting to be separated.

"Here, have a seat right here at the end. Let me bring you something to drink." Isador patted an empty stool next to another woman engaged in conversation with a couple of men, one of whom had his arm wrapped around her waist, his hand busily groping the woman's backside.

Rose was thankful for the dim lighting. Her cheeks were hot.

Isador set a glass of whiskey in front of Rose. "Here you go, sweetheart."

Sweetheart? He'd never called her that before. She started to say something, but he had gone, prancing to the far end of the bar in answer to a customer's call for another round of drinks. He topped off the glasses of two men, nodded at them, and collected their money. Before he had a chance to deposit the proceeds, another customer raised his empty glass high in the air. Isador pocketed the bills and poured another drink. This time, he lingered, chatting with the customer. He served a few more drinks and then wiped the bar in front of a woman who had stood to go. "Come back soon," he said, "sweetheart."

A hand clawed Rose's shoulder. She turned and came eye-to-eye with a complete stranger. "Well, hello there, doll. I s-s-see you've got a drink," he said. Had she not known he was drunk, Rose might have thought he had a stutter. "May I buy you another when you're done?" He grinned, his eyes hooded, drawing closed like a blind.

"No thank you. I'm just having the one." She took another sip, a long one to buy time. She emptied the glass. "That's it," she said and showed the stranger her empty glass. Instead of releasing his grip, though, he kept his hand on her shoulder.

"You sure do look beautiful, ah...what did you s-s-say your name was?"

"She didn't." It was Isador. "Vince, I think you've had enough tonight." Isador rounded the end of the bar and stepped behind Rose. He towered over Vince and lifted the stranger's hand from her shoulder. "You'd best be going home, your wife will be wondering where you are."

"Nah. Sh-she's glad to have me out of the house."

"In that case, you best have a cup of coffee before you walk in the door smelling of booze."

"Maybe I will," Vince said. "Maybe I will." He listed to the right, took a few steps, and staggered off.

"Thank you, Isador. I wasn't sure how I was going to get rid of him."

"I'm so sorry. Most people are well behaved, but now and—"

"Barkeep. Over here!" someone called from one of the tables along the far wall.

"I'll be back in a minute."

"That's okay, Isador. I'm ready to go. Try to make it a reasonable hour if you can."

"I will, dear. I promise."

Rose retrieved her purse from the bar and stepped from the stool. Near the exit, she took another glance across the room and at Isador hovering over a table of patrons. He threw his head back and with his mouth open wide, he laughed a long belly laugh. He slapped the man nearest him on the back and guffawed a second time.

Back on the street, Rose breathed a sigh of relief. She took a deep breath of fresh night air to clear her lungs but breathed in the scent of smoke and stale beer woven into the fibers of her dress. Reeling, she hurried toward home, thinking of nothing more than a long hot bath.

When Isador's weight collapsed the far side of the mattress,

Rose bolted upright. He had come to bed fully clothed, and a tang of beer and booze floated across to her side.

"What time is it?" she asked.

"I don't know. Late. Go back to sleep."

"I will, but only after you take those clothes off. They are rank!"

"I know, I know. Someone spilled a drink." Isador tried to raise himself from the bed but fell back at once. "I'm exhausted."

"I guess you would be." Rose chose not to mention the promise he'd made; she doubted he remembered making one. She watched as he tugged at his waist, his fingers dulled with alcohol, unable to handle his belt buckle. "Do you want me to help?" she asked.

"No. I've got it."

After another moment of fumbling, Isador succeeded in freeing his belt and flung it on the floor. He started on the button of his trousers.

"That place is going to wear you out, Isador. Have you thought even one minute about finding something else? Something more..."

"More what? This is our ticket, Rose. Our ticket out of here. Besides, I like it at Murphy's. You get used to it." He tore at the flap of his waistband.

"Are you sure you don't need help."

"I said I can do it myself. Go back to sleep."

The next morning, Rose dressed making as little noise as possible, though based on the rumble of heavy breathing emanating from under his pillow, an entire parade of pushcarts would not have disturbed Isador. Although he'd managed to shed his shirt, belt, and trousers, he'd gone to sleep in his underwear and socks.

Rose gathered the discarded clothes from beside the bed and carried them at arm's length to the hamper. When she dropped them inside, a gash of red on Isador's shirt collar caught her eye. Thinking the stain was blood, Rose took the shirt to the sink and held it under the faucet. She rubbed her finger across the stain, succeeding only in smearing the red blotch across the width of the collar. Rose held the shirt to the light. The stain was not blood as she'd first thought. It was lipstick, scarlet red lipstick.

Earl

EARL WAITED FOR ISADOR TO EMPTY THE LAST OF THE TRASH IN the alley, burying the liquor bottles beneath more innocent debris, unlabeled cardboard boxes, empty bottles of floor wax, and a mop with a broken handle, half its cord unraveled. Not that Earl thought anyone sifted through Murphy's trash. Still, he was pleased that Isador took the extra precautions.

"This isn't like the toy we gave you before," Earl said.

Isador accepted the revolver from Earl, taking the grip between his thumb and middle finger. *Like a lady,* Earl thought. *For Christ's sake.* Isador turned the revolver from one side to the other, his head swiveling in the opposite direction.

Earl ducked. "Goddamn, don't point that thing at me!"

"Sorry, just checking. It's not loaded is it?"

"Not loaded. Fuck. What good would an unloaded gun be?"

Isador pointed the nose at the ground and squinted at the back of the cylinder. Under the scant light of a street lamp mounted on the far corner of the building, the rounds shone with a dull glint. He hefted the gun in his hand.

"I thought you were in the army. Didn't they teach you how to shoot?"

"Navy," Isador said. "Course they did. But there wasn't much opportunity to shoot a gun aboard a ship."

"You sure you can handle this?"

"I'm sure. You think I was born yesterday?"

That's exactly what I think, Earl said to himself. To Isador, he said, "Fine. Next time you run into trouble you make sure the bastards know you have a piece." Then he added, "Try not to blow your foot off." Earl walked away, leaving Isador in the alley. He had other business to attend to before morning.

Isador's inquiries into the robbery had turned up nothing, which didn't surprise Earl. Isador didn't know the neighborhood. He didn't know the back alleys, the doors that were left unlocked, the windows that could be pried, or the fire escapes that could be lowered without waking the entire block. He didn't have the sources Earl had cultivated in the lifetime he'd spent in Revere. Nor had Isador developed the persuasive powers Earl had honed through years of observing Mr. Mosko and his lieutenants, of making notes in his head and rehearsing his lines when he lay awake at night or sat huddled over a shot of whiskey.

Mosko had once told Earl that he was destined for this life. Earl was an insider who worked on the outside. That is, he knew everyone but had no relatives and few if any friends. Earl liked it that way. *Don't trust anyone and you won't be disappointed. Don't make friends with people who might not be friends later.*

Earl figured that was what Mosko saw in him the day they met a decade ago. Earl had been at his usual spot, outside Fred's, a pool hall and local gathering spot on Shirley Avenue close to the beach. He was one of a group of boys, simulating boredom and manhood, slouched against the wall or the stoop next door, smoking cigarettes and flicking and grinding the butts on the sidewalk, doing nothing and looking for nothing to do. Four of the boys stood shoulder to shoulder and bantered back and forth. To one side, Earl stood sometimes eyeing them, sometimes checking the street in all four directions—for what, he couldn't have said. He spotted Saul Mosko first. Maybe it had been the way Mosko dressed or the way he walked or, more likely, the way the sidewalk cleared for him when he crossed the street a block or more away. Though slightly built, he stood out from the crowd, even back then.

Earl made inquiries, quietly and to the right people, not wanting to call attention to himself in the process. He'd learned Mr. Mosko's name—Mister Saul Mosko, emphasis on *Mister*. Everyone was a little tight-lipped when it came to discussing the young man they assumed would take control of the largely Jewish gang from his father.

After that, Earl kept an eye out for him. He memorized what Mosko wore, how he conducted himself, how much time he spent in the neighborhood, who he interacted with, and how he greeted everyone by name. Earl made notes of the places he frequented, many of them restaurants. The man liked to eat, yet he never put on any weight. Earl learned to spot the one or two large men who accompanied Mosko, sometimes walking side by side, more often trailing a few steps behind. They were not as nicely dressed.

Earl improved his appearance, shining his shoes and pressing his clothes. He'd done it gradually. His cohorts hardly noticed. But Mr. Mosko had, or at least Earl thought he had. Whatever the reason for singling him out, when Mr. Mosko swung by the corner and looked at Earl and when Earl did not look away as the others had, Mr. Mosko had said, "Walk with me." Earl had flicked his cigarette to the ground, stamped it out, and followed.

Earl had vouched to Mosko for Isador Margolin. He had to see this bit of trouble through. He'd done some investigating of his own on the hit and produced two names. Vic K.—"K" for Kakligian, though no one used his full name or knew the correct spelling. And Dom, no last name. Vic's cousin.

Turning the corner onto Conant, Earl proceeded to the first clapboard-sided dwelling and checked the number above the doorway. Ten. Without making a sound, he climbed the three steps to the small porch and tried the door. It opened. No need for the picklock tucked inside his breast pocket. Same for the apartment door down the hall, right rear.

Earl entered noiselessly. He found Vic sound asleep, sprawled on his back on a cot. Earl placed a hand over Vic's mouth. Vic jolted awake, thrashing his arms in the air. He stilled when his eyes focused on the revolver an inch above the crease between his eyebrows. Earl removed his hand from Vic's mouth and a put an index finger to his lips. Keeping his on eye on Vic and the revolver pointed at his head, Earl stepped to the second bed where Dom slept, dead to the world. When Earl touched his shoulder, Dom sat upright and froze where he sat.

"Get dressed," Earl said still holding the gun on Vic.

Both men eased from their beds and grabbed their trousers, one pair slung over a chair, the other tossed at the foot of the bed. Dom looked for his coat.

"Think about it," Earl said. He'd anticipated one or both would go for their pieces and had already patted down and removed the snub nose from Dom's jacket slumped beside his trousers. Vic's eyes flashed to the dresser. Earl followed his glance and saw the Colt on top of the dresser. He took a step sideways and pocketed the Colt.

When both men were dressed, Earl waved his gun toward the door. "Let's go for a walk, what do you say." It wasn't a question and neither man responded, though they exchanged glances. Earl walked behind the two men out to the street, leaving the door to the apartment and the front door of 10 Conant ajar.

"Left," Earl said, stuffing the gun in his pocket, his finger on the trigger.

"Look," Vic said, "we were just—"

"Save your breath."

After a short, brisk walk, the trio arrived at the offices of Carmine Eidenberg, Esq. At least those were the words above the mail slot on the front door of the unassuming brick building on Central. The door opened as Earl raised his arm to knock. A man Earl knew only as "Les" motioned Earl and his two charges inside.

Les shut the door and then, without a word, he headed down a long hallway toward the back of the building. Vic and Dom shuffled behind, the heels of their shoes scraping the floor as if to delay what lay ahead. Dom stole a glance at Vic who shrugged his shoulders. They passed two office doors with no markings, nothing to indicate where—if anywhere— Mr. Carmine Eidenberg, Esq. maintained his practice.

The similarly unmarked third and last door on the right stood open, a wedge of light angled into the hallway and across the floor. Les stepped aside to allow Vic and Dom to enter. Earl came behind, crossed the room, and melted into the shadows, his shoulder against the wall to take the weight off his feet.

A four-armed lamp with a single working bulb hung in the

middle of the ceiling, as if placed to illuminate a dining room table or a desk. But instead of a table or desk, two chairs sat back to back, below the bulb.

"Have a seat," Les said, pointing at the chairs.

Vic and Dom exchanged glances again.

Seconds passed, then minutes. Les, his back to the two in the middle of the room, fidgeted over a table. He moved some objects around, heavy metallic objects by the sound they made. His delay was deliberate, designed to increase the level of anxiety. Earl had witnessed countless "interviews," Les's term, most beginning with the interviewee's show of outright surprise and feigned ignorance. Vic and Dom maintained their silence, showing their understanding of the situation.

"Let me get right down to it, boys," Les said without turning around. "Seems like we're missing a little something over at Murphy's."

Vic coughed once and then choked back another, stifling the sound without raising his hand to his mouth, not wanting to attract Les's attention. Les would have heard the muffled cough and would have known it came from behind him on the right, where Vic sat. He turned, took one step, and slammed his fist into the side of Vic's head. Vic tumbled to the concrete floor. Dom flinched but did not turn to look at Vic. Instead, the muscles in Dom's jaw tightened and his eyes closed, expecting the next blow to come for him.

Les grabbed Vic by the back of his shirt and hoisted him back into the chair. "Were you about to say something, Vic?" Les asked. "I couldn't hear you."

Blood poured from a cut on the side of Vic's head. It must have ached like hell, but Vic kept his silence as he moved his head back and forth and tested his jaw. Les threw another punch, this time from the opposite side, knocking Vic to the floor again. Les rounded the chair and delivered a series of blows with his feet, the toe of his mahogany brogues ramming Vic's thighs, hips, and buttocks. With each blow, a dull groan escaped from the back of Vic's throat, and then he lay quiet.

Les circled the body and stopped in front of Dom. From his trouser pocket, he pulled a white handkerchief and wiped the blood from the brass knuckles on his left hand. Though Vic was badly beaten, Les had not delivered the hardest blow he could. With a man of Les's strength, the brass could easily have broken Vic's skull in two.

Les examined his left hand and appeared satisfied the brass was clean. He dropped the handkerchief, slashed with red, onto the table. "So, as I was saying, there's a bit of cash missing from Murphy's."

In a voice etched with fear, Dom said, "I can get it back to you." Les rubbed his fingers over his armored knuckles and then flexed his fist. "Today," Dom said. "I can get it back to you today."

"You get it back here at nine o'clock." Les looked at his watch. "That's six hours from now."

Dom nodded. "I can." His head bobbed again. "I can."

"And then," Les said, pausing for effect, "then, Monday, you go back to Murphy's and you pay the barkeep there the same amount."

Dom's jaw dropped. He choked on his saliva.

"Now, take your friend and get the hell out of here."

After Vic and Dom left the premises, Les poked his head out the back door into the alley and spoke to someone. Earl did not hear the conversation. A minute later, a man entered the room, a bucket in one hand and a mop in the other.

Les and Earl waited for the man to finish and disappear back into the alley. Although Earl knew the man was one of Mr. Mosko's men, he saw no advantage in discussing business in the open, business that didn't concern him.

"I'll be here in the morning. Can you cover Murphy's?" Les asked.

"Sure thing."

"I don't think we're going to hear from them again."

"We'll see. Nicolini's not going to like this."

"Well, if Nicolini would keep his guys from interfering in our business, this wouldn't be necessary. He'd do the same to one of ours if the tables were turned."

"I suppose."

At three o'clock the next afternoon, an hour before Murphy's opened, Earl was on duty at the corner of B Street and Cummings with a clear line of sight to the speakeasy. He would keep watch over Murphy's over the weekend and through Monday. He'd make sure Nicolini's gang didn't try anything.

He sat in the driver's seat of the Ford sedan, one of Mosko's fleet of identical inconspicuous black vehicles. Nothing like the boss's own wine red Buick touring car, but its engine and four wheels brought Earl here without wearing out his feet, and in the interim he had a place to sit. Dom might not show for hours. Vic would not show at all. His head would feel like mush.

Earl flicked his cigarette out the window, spat, and then slouched in the seat. The sun was low, and it warmed the car's interior, making Earl drowsy. He tilted his head back and lowered his hat over his eyes. Earl was not worried about falling asleep. Despite his bad ear, or maybe because of it, the hearing in his good ear was sharp and tuned to the sounds of trouble. He relied on it to rouse him when needed. For now, only laughter bubbling from passersby on the sidewalk. The laughter tickled his ear but did not wake him and soon melted into a harmless background chorus. Earl slept and dreamed.

Before Nahant, if asked, Earl would have said he didn't dream. But ever since, he dreamed a single dream every night, usually in the wee hours of the morning. At first, the dream hovered in the back of his mind, more a thought than a dream. A woman in white from head to toe, always white, and always a fabric so sheer he could not tell where a sleeve ended and the moon-dappled flesh of her arm began. Her back was to him, and when she turned, she held her arm to her forehead to shade her face. Then, she beckoned him, making circles in the night air with her free hand, over and over again, until his feet moved toward her on ground that wasn't ground; it flowed like water. He crossed the strange surface, but no matter how many steps he took or how fast his feet moved, she eluded him, never coming closer than when she first appeared. She faded in and out of sight until she disappeared through a door. He'd run to the door and throw it open only to be blinded by blazing orange-yellow sun. Then a scream as loud as a freight train rolled through his head. He'd wake, gasping for air, his own hand over his eyes.

Though he never glimpsed the woman's face, Earl knew who the woman was. In the dream, it was Rose Margolin who motioned to him. It was Rose Margolin whom he followed.

A fly landed on Earl's cheek and crawled toward his ear. He swatted at the annoyance and opened his eyes. The sun had brushed the roofline in front of him, scattering its light to the street and across the car's windshield. Earl squinted in the glare, licked his lips, swallowed, and stretched. Three-forty-five on his watch. He rubbed his eyes and lit another cigarette.

Isador appeared up ahead. He towered over everyone else and, under his chin, his customary bow tie was a dead give-away. Isador grinned and said a few words to someone by his side, someone concealed by the throng of pedestrians. Only the rounded top of a gray cloche was visible. Outside Murphy's, Isador stopped and bowed his head. Earl caught a glimpse of Rose's face under the cloche. She looked at Isador, a smile on her lips and a face bright in the late sun until Isador's shadow spread across her cheek. He kissed her on the lips, backed away, and scurried through the door.

Rose turned and walked back the way she'd come with Isador. About mid-block, she stopped and looked back, raised her hand as if to wave until, Earl guessed, she saw he'd gone.

On the sidewalk beside his car, people went about their chores. An old woman swept the sidewalk in front of her stoop, jabbing the handle at two teenage boys who'd planted on her doorstep. They stood, laughed, and settled again as soon as she retreated inside. Two women in dark clothing chatted at another doorway. Old world scarves knotted under their chins. Ample bosoms and hips. A mix of scents spilled from the open doors, cabbage, potatoes, and perhaps deep blood red borscht boiling in a soup pot on someone's stove.

If there were to be trouble, Earl decided, it would be later. He drummed his fingers on the steering wheel, thinking, planning. The hour hand on his watch pointed at four. More drumming.

Earl nudged his shoulder against the door. He stepped out and adjusted the hat on his head, the right brim tilted skyward over his ear, something he no longer noticed. He took one more glance in all directions before he darted down Cummings after Rose. Urging his feet on and craning his neck over the crowd, he spied her a long block ahead. She'd stopped to speak to a woman who held a young girl's hand. Earl narrowed the distance between them to a half block and halted, feigning interest at a fruit stand. He fingered an apple in a fruit stand but kept his eyes on his target. Rose's back was to him. She'd knelt, coming eye-to-eye with the young girl who smiled, lowered her eyes, and then snuggled into the folds of her mother's skirt. A peal of laughter traveled back to where he waited and he saw Rose with a smile on her lips. He imagined tiny creases formed at the edge of her eyes. He imagined her smiling that way at him.

Rose patted the child's head and caressed her dark hair. She cupped her fingers under the child's chin, making Earl's chin tingle as he imagined Rose's touch, light as a feather, smooth as glass. A quick flutter of her fingers signaled her departure. Rose walked away, Earl in tow at a safe distance.

When the crowd between them thinned, Earl dropped back a few steps. He walked near the edge of the sidewalk in the warmth of her steps. He filled his lungs with the air in her wake, but the smell of her had dissipated, leaving him only the scent of the afternoon.

Rose neared Broadway. Her pace slowed. She turned. Earl had anticipated the motion and ducked under an awning. He pressed his face to the glass, his nose resting on the second Z in Pizzano on the bakery's window. Inside, a clerk slid loaves of fresh baked bread onto the display shelves. The clerk shooed him away, but Earl watched until the fog of his breath on the glass evaporated. When he dared, he stepped back and caught a last glimpse of Rose across Broadway making a turn on Mountain toward Nahant. Toward home.

Rose

THE SLIGHT MOVEMENT OF ESTHER'S LIPS DID NOT ESCAPE Rose's notice. Nor did Esther's scanning of the array of foods on her plate during her silent *bracha*. All the while, Isador prattled on and shoveled more vegetables onto his plate. Rose kept her hands in her lap and waited for Esther to finish.

"...and did you know, Babe Ruth hit two homers yesterday?"

"I have to admit, I don't follow baseball very closely," Esther said, a polite smile on her lips. Her fingers fidgeted over the fork and knife in front of her.

"It's hard to keep up, that's true," Rose ventured, supporting her sister who'd agreed to an early dinner during the week, early enough to have Isador join them before leaving for work. Rabbi Daniel, Esther's husband, had made his excuses. "Isa does manage, though, somehow. He follows the Yankees and the Red Sox, of course, and he can tell you all the latest scores and statistics. Isn't that right, dear? And everything there is to know about local politics."

"Yes, I do. I think it's important to know what's going on. Did you see the headlines today? Get this. After an exhaustive investigation, our esteemed government concluded the country is awash in liquor."

"I didn't," Esther said, pushing her fork around her plate.

"I hope you like the fish," Rose said. "I bought it this morning from the fishmonger on Walnut. I don't suppose you shop there?"

"No, a bit too far for me to go." Esther took a bite and Rose exhaled, relieved. "What with the children. I have my hands full."

"I can only imagine. I don't think I could manage even one, much less three."

"Oh you could, Rose, you could," Esther said. "And I meant to tell you earlier, Judith says her baby is due in March."

"How many does that make?"

"It'll be five. Three boys and a girl so far."

"Lots of mouths to feed, I say. Right, Rose?" Isador said.

"It is indeed. And clothes to wash and mend," Rose agreed. Esther stabbed another forkful of fish.

"Judith can have another for us," Isador said. "I don't want to share my Rose with anyone." He smiled and leaned toward Rose to peck her on the cheek. Rose brushed him off with a wave of her hand. Isador continued, "Besides, when we travel, we can't be tied down with a passel of little ones."

"Oh, where are you going?" Esther asked.

"Nothing firm yet."

"Isador has been studying foreign cultures," Rose said, "Egypt, Turkey, even Japan."

Esther's eyebrows arched upward. "That would be an adventure."

"True," Isador said, "but our first priority is to move to a better side of town, away from these dingy streets. Once we've settled somewhere more comfortable, like Brookline maybe, we can start thinking about traveling."

"Brookline." Again the arched eyebrows.

"It's our dream," Rose said.

"No dream, you'll see." With that, Isador took his napkin and dotted the corners of his mouth. He pushed his chair back. "Sorry, ladies, I've got to go. Business."

Isador passed behind Rose's chair and pressed his lips on the top of Rose's head. He grabbed his hat and coat and was out the door.

"Brookline?"

"Well, we'd like to. Who wouldn't? This is not what either of us expected. It's so cramped. And you can never draw a good breath here unless you go down to the beach. But Isador insisted we have our own place, even if we had to scrape by the first year or so. Then when he lost his job..." Rose said, selecting her words carefully. "Anyway, that's in the past. He's doing quite well. Even brought home a bonus the other day. Fifty dollars. Almost what he made in a week at Logrin's."

"Goodness. That's very generous. Where did you say he was working?"

"Murphy's. It's a small café off Broadway. He's managing part of the business."

"That's wonderful."

They ate in silence for a few minutes, Rose anticipating Esther would maneuver the conversation to her favorite topic.

"And no matter what you said about traveling, what about a family? You're not getting any younger, you know."

"I know. Isador really wants to wait. And, anyway, maybe that's a good thing. It just hasn't happened. Besides, now..."

"Now, what?" Esther asked.

Rose proceeded cautiously. Later, Sarah or Leo or Lillian would wear Esther out with questions until she satisfied them with an interesting tidbit or two, particularly some failing of Isador's.

"There's so little time. Isador works nearly every day and rarely gets home before midnight. But at least he brings more money home than he used to, our savings are building."

"Money's not everything."

"No. I suppose not."

"There's something else eating at you, Rose. I can tell."

"Well, sometimes, too, I think it's all those glamorous people and then he comes home and it's just me."

"Glamorous people? At a café?"

"Well, it's more than a café. It's a café and a speakeasy, a very popular one."

"Oh."

Oh. That one word conveyed so much. A remark her father had made during Isador's courtship rang in her head, "His people"—the words her father had used—"are not our people." She maneuvered the rest of the conversation away from family matters and anything connected with Isador.

Rose never suspected that Isador had a "wandering eye" as Addie referred to men who strayed. He had all the usual male foibles. His head swiveled like a recording on his phonograph turntable when he noticed a pair of shapely calves in silk stockings pass them by during an afternoon stroll. She'd been more amused than jealous. "Watch out," she'd chided, "or you'll break your neck."

And whatever experiences with the opposite sex he'd had while in the navy she'd decided were best left unspoken. That was before he and she had met. She'd asked him once about the war and his past. He'd flinched and offered only that his parents had died while he was away and that he had no brothers or sisters, no family, just Rose and her family. After that, she asked no more questions.

Following her visit to Murphy's, though, Rose's suspicions grew. She was far more aware of the temptations he faced every day and feared sooner or later someone would take advantage of Isador's weakness for a nice set of gams. She began accompanying Isador to work, seeing him off at four in the afternoon on days she did not go to work. She dressed in his favorite outfits and sprayed a mist of perfume behind each ear. Regardless of the hour, she'd wait up for him at the end of his day, greet him with a pour of his whiskey, sit him down, and rub his tired feet. Some nights it worked and they made love—but not the way they'd enjoyed each other in the early days of their marriage. His lovemaking had changed. It was more animated. He explored places on her body where he'd never ventured before and asked her to do things he'd never asked before. Swallowing her fear and discomfort, Rose complied, preferring this form of communication and closeness to the nights when he walked past her and collapsed on the bed, too tired to undress or share a few words.

It was Jacob who confirmed Rose's suspicions. Rose had been pacing the apartment early one evening and become claustrophobic. She glanced out the window and spied a group of neighbors sitting outside, Jacob and his two young cousins, Genie Traynor, and Genie's daughter, Myra. Rose was fond of Genie, the only woman on the block close to Rose's age.

By the time Rose stepped into the street, Jacob's aunt and his grandmother had joined the group. Rose smiled and waved. Maybe Gladys would be in a good mood.

Genie had her nose in a magazine and had not seen Rose,

but Miriam Goldstein waved back. Rose took that as an invitation to join the group.

"Hello, Genie. Gladys. Mrs. Goldstein. And a good evening to all of you, too," she said, nodding at the group of children. An out-of-synch chorus returned the greeting. "Have you all had dinner?" Rose asked.

Nods up and down from the children.

"Yes, we're just enjoying the last of the day. You want to join us?" Genie asked, making room on the stoop.

"Well, I was thinking of going to the corner to get an ice cream. Anyone want to come along?" Rose added, "It's my treat."

"Oh please, may we?" Leila asked, clasping her hands under her chin, a pleading look aimed toward her mother.

"Gladys or Mrs. Goldstein? I'd be happy to bring you back a cup."

"I'll walk with you," Mrs. Goldstein said. "Want to come, Gladys?"

"No. I'm too tired to take a step. You go ahead."

"Not me, thanks," Genie said. "I'm going to finish my magazine."

"You're going to wear that thing out," Gladys said.

Genie shrugged her shoulders and brought the magazine closer to her face. *Picture Play* blazed across the front in large print. "Who's on the cover?" Rose asked.

"Betty Compson."

With a harrumph, Mrs. Goldstein started down the block. The children needed no other encouragement and sauntered ahead. Rose linked arms with Jacob's grandmother, lending support to the elderly but still spry woman.

They were gone only a few minutes, but it was long enough

for all to finish their treats on the walk back. Rose helped Mrs. Goldstein to her place on the topmost step before taking her own seat beside Genie, who still had her nose buried in the magazine. Leila squeezed between the two and whooped when Genie turned the page to reveal a woman's face, dark eyes defined with charcoal gray and a hat trimmed with white feathers.

"She's beautiful," Leila said. "Who is she?"

"Some new vaudeville actress," Genie said. "Maybe she'll make it in the cinema with those eyes."

Myra, drawn by Leila's interest, climbed behind Genie to see for herself. "Gosh, she's the most beautiful woman I've ever seen."

"No, she's not," Jacob said.

"How would you know?" Leila taunted.

"Rose is the most beautiful," he said.

Leila and Myra convulsed with laughter. Even shy Ralph joined in. Color stained Jacob's cheeks.

"Why, that's so nice of you, Jacob," Rose said, silencing the others. "In fact, that's the nicest thing anyone has said to me in a long time."

Mrs. Goldstein looked up from her perch above Genie's shoulder. Rose ignored her inquisitive stare designed to provoke Rose to continue her train of thought. The old woman rarely roamed further than the stoop on which they now sat, yet she had a way of finding things out, and given the chance, she would spread the smallest morsel of gossip across the neighborhood before dawn.

Genie flipped to another page.

A cool breeze off the ocean blew across Nahant. Mrs. Goldstein shivered and drew her shawl around her shoulders. "I'm going in."

"Me, too," Gladys said. "Come along children, you've got your chores to do."

"Yes, it's time," Genie said and swatted her daughter playfully with her rolled up magazine.

"Good night, Miss Rose," Mrs. Goldstein said.

"Good night. I'd best be getting on as well," Rose said, though she made no move to go, noting that Jacob hadn't budged from where he sat either. Gladys, Miriam, Ralph, and Leila disappeared inside, Genie and Myra to their home next door. Rose wrapped her arms around her knees and craned her head back. The stars were coming out. "Look, there's the big dipper," she said, an arm raised to the sky. Jacob did not look up. His eyes were on the ground where he scuffled a foot back and forth, turning a small pebble end over end.

"I meant that," Rose ventured. "It's a very nice compliment to say a woman is beautiful."

"I meant it, too," Jacob said, his voice little more than a whisper. "You're much prettier than that woman in the magazine, and that goes for Mr. Margolin's other women friends, too."

Rose looked away.

"I...I wasn't supposed to say anything. Mr. Margolin will—"

"You have nothing to worry about, Jacob," Rose said, turning back to face the boy. She released her grip on her knees and took his arm, circling her fingers around it gently. "It's quite all right. Mr. Margolin meets lots of fancy women. The place where he works is full of them. It's quite all right." Rose was conscious of how hollow her words sounded and that she'd repeated herself, but no other words came to mind.

Isador

EVERY MOMENT SINCE HE'D WOKEN, ISADOR HAD WORRIED whether Vic and Dom would show. And whether they'd bring the money as they had agreed, or rather been coerced, to pay. Once, he'd come close to wringing his hands in front of Earl.

"They'll be here," Earl said, swigging the last of his pint. "That wop boss of theirs doesn't want a fight on his hands." Earl sat at the far end of the bar on a stool with a clear line of sight to the alcove. Isador made a mental note to arrive early, scout out the place, and find a point of advantage. He had a lot to learn from Earl.

"Can you douse the light on this end?" Earl asked, speaking softly and forcing Isador to stretch across the bar to hear.

"Sure thing," Isador said, wishing he'd suggested the same. Earl would see Dom or Vic or both the cousins and whomever else they brought with them before they could get their bearings, especially in the darkened room. For now, except for a few early-birds huddled around a table midway across the floor and another two, backs propped against the far wall, the joint was empty, not unusual for this time of day, especially on a Monday.

After a quick check of the time, Isador sauntered back to Earl.

"So, what's up with Vic and Dom working for Nicolini anyway? Lousy bunch of goddamn Armenians."

"Been with him a long time. Guess there's a story there, but I never heard it."

Isador checked his watch and compared it with the clock above the bar.

"You worry too much," Earl said.

"I just want to patch up things with Mr. M for the earlier trouble." To take his mind off the situation, Isador tried to concentrate on what he needed to do behind the bar. He wiped a glass, held it to the light to check for spots, and then he stacked it on a shelf underneath the bar. He was polishing another when Earl rapped his knuckles twice on the bar.

"Showtime," Earl said without making a move. Vic had walked through the alcove.

Based on what Earl told him about the interrogation, Isador expected Dom instead of Vic. But he supposed Vic had a point to make. A little roughing up wouldn't keep him down. He approached the bar, treading lightly, placing one foot carefully in front of the other, as if he were inspecting the floor for a weak spot.

Face to face with Isador, the effects of the few day old beating showed. Over his right temple, Vic wore a large bandage that protruded from beneath his fedora. The puffy, black pockets of skin beneath his eyes gave him the appearance of a raccoon. Vic glanced from Isador to Earl and back again. He withdrew an envelope from his jacket and held it in front of him. Isador reached for the envelope. "This isn't for you," Vic said. "It's for that fucker at the other end of the bar."

"That's okay," Isador said, drawing himself up to where he towered over the top of Vic's head. "We're sharing."

When Vic failed to hand over the envelope, Isador glanced at Earl. Earl feigned interest in something on the bar in front of him. Vic let the envelope drop to the counter then made a show of wiping his hands. He had done what he'd been told. He was finished.

Isador opened the envelope and extracted the stack of bills.

"Jesus Christ," Vic said. "You're not going to count it are you? Not here, goddamn it."

Flustered, thinking he had violated an unwritten protocol, Isador slipped the bills back inside the envelope. "Nah, I'm sure we can find you if it's short."

"It's not short."

"Good."

Vic turned and began his tortoise crawl back to the alcove.

"And next time," Isador called after him, "take your goddamn hat off when you come in my place."

Vic came to a stop and then slowly twisted his body in Isador's direction. He slapped his right palm in the crook of his left elbow and pumped his left fist into the air. Then he disappeared into the shadows and down the staircase.

Work proceeded without incident. Most days, Isador slept late, had lunch, left home at three-thirty, and worked until one in the morning.

He'd stashed the gun Earl had given him under the counter in a clip he'd installed next to the cash drawer. Sometimes, before Carl arrived for work, Isador practiced grabbing the gun and pointing it an imaginary offender, maybe Vic or Dom returning for revenge, maybe another wop or some Irishman.

He'd shown the gun to Carl, who, despite having been on the receiving end of the coldcock from Vic, didn't like having it on the premises.

"Don't worry. I'm not asking you to use it. I'll be the one to decide if we need it, but I wanted you to know it's here."

After that, Carl avoided the area behind the counter near the cash drawer. Instead of depositing a customer's money in the drawer, or making change, he'd hand the money to Isador and escape to the far end of the bar.

By late October, the memory of the robbery had faded. Mosko withdrew the two henchmen he'd stationed in the alley. And for his part, Isador relaxed and returned to planning how to expand the business and prove his worth. He had gained an appreciation for the depth and breadth of Mosko's influence and was determined not to let anything else damage his reputation or his future in the gang.

He tested some of his ideas with Rose. "What do you think about bringing in some entertainment?" he asked during a Sunday dinner at home.

"What kind of entertainment?"

"Maybe music? Or dancing? Maybe a preview of one of the new vaudeville acts at the theater?" He'd mulled over the idea for days and rehearsed how he might propose it to Sylvia and to Rose. Then, not to arouse Rose's suspicions, he added, "Or a magician?"

Rose set her fork on the kitchen table and stared over his shoulder. She sat that way so long that Isador glanced back to see what might have drawn her attention. Isador wondered if his pretense at nonchalance been too transparent and if she suspected something. He'd never given her a reason to doubt, but as Aken said, "Women have their ways." He chased a stray English pea around his plate and waited.

"Vaudeville," she said. "You mean as in women cavorting

around the saloon in little more than a scarf and stockings? Dancing? Singing?"

"No, no, no. Nothing like that. It would be something... innocent, still entertaining of course. Maybe an acrobat or a comedy routine. I don't know. I was just thinking. Thought you might have an idea about what would work."

"Why do you need anything more than what Mr. Mosko has already set up?"

"More than what *I* have, you mean." He'd reminded Rose more than once that *he*, not Mr. Mosko, was there every night. He was the one managing the place, serving the customers, chatting with them, getting to know them. He was the one trying to make sure they stopped at Murphy's and not some other place on their way home.

"Yes, more than *you* have, sorry."

"Because I don't want Murphy's to be just like all the other blind pigs. I want it to be something special, something so popular we'll have to open another location."

"Another location? I thought this was going to be a stepping stone—"

"It is a stepping stone. A stepping stone to bigger and better. I can see expanding until we have all of Revere in our pockets. Murphy's might be as big as the Beachview and the Oceanview combined. Maybe even bigger."

"I meant a stepping stone *out* of this business, *out* of this neighborhood. What happened to that dream?"

"For Christ's sake, Rose. Can't you see? We've got plenty of time ahead of us. But right now, I have to prove myself to Mr. M. And as I see it, that means pulling in more money." Isador pushed his chair back from the table and carried his plate to the kitchen. He returned with a glass in his hand, a half-inch of amber liquid in the bottom. "I've got to think," he said. He crossed behind Rose and headed for the living room.

As it hit the ground, the lid of the metal trash can clattered noisily, drowning the scuffle of approaching steps. Isador bent to retrieve the lid, catching a full whiff of the sickeningly sweet odor of rot from the open can. Before he could replace the lid, something slammed him between his shoulder blades and threw him against the wall. A gloved hand pinned his face against the brick wall.

"So, this is Mister Tough Jew Boy, huh?" The words were spoken so close to the side of his head that a puff of air, damp with speech and spit, tickled the tiny hairs on his ear. "Well, well, well. So what are you going to do now?" Though he heard only one voice and believed only one person held him against the wall, Isador sensed there were maybe two or three more surrounding him in the alley.

The assailant removed his hand from Isador's head but dug something cold and hard, about the size of a nickel, into the back of his neck. "Maybe I should let my cousin here show you how this works?" he asked. There was the unmistakable sound of a gun cocking.

Someone patted his chest and checked his shirt pocket. Then their hands moved lower, feeling inside the pockets of his trousers. The key ring jangled, not unlike the little set of bells over Logrin's door when Isador had slammed it shut. Isador cursed under his breath, furious that he was thinking of Logrin's when he needed to get his wits about him.

Someone behind him and to his right emitted a couple of low grunts, sounding satisfied, and then stepped away, his shoes crunching on the gravel in the alley. Footsteps echoed as someone climbed the stairs.

Three men, he thought. One holding the gun at his neck. One breathing hard a few steps away. One upstairs retrieving the night's proceeds. Moments ago, Isador had counted the take, arranged the bills face up in descending order of denomination, clipped them together with a paper-clip, and slid them inside an envelope. The envelope sat on the counter next to his hat and coat. It sat there in plain sight.

Dear God. Isador couldn't imagine what he would say to Earl or what Earl would say to Mr. M. He couldn't think that far ahead. He had to concentrate on what was going on around him right now right here. The footsteps returned, ringing down the stairwell.

The two behind him shifted position. Straining to hear above the shuffling and grunting, Isador caught the sound of what he thought was one thug passing the envelope to another, someone tapping the paper against his hand, folding it, and then tucking it away.

"*Buono.* Now, Mister Tough Jew Boy, we're even. You tell your boss we're done. You're whole. We're whole. No need to talk again."

The pressure on his back lifted. Then, before Isador took his next breath, before he peeled his shirt from the brick, a blinding light flashed at the back of his eyes and a searing pain filled his head. Isador dropped to the ground.

He made it as far as the sofa in the front room and collapsed, his head feeling as large as a watermelon. Rose's scream woke him. Startled, he raised an arm in front of his face to ward off another blow, thinking for an instant he was still in the alley behind Murphy's. When he opened his eyes, Rose stood overhead, hands to her face, eyes wide in horror. He groped the pocket of his trousers with one hand, hoping it had all been a dream, a nightmare. His pocket was empty. The keys were gone.

He groaned and said, "Not so loud, Rose. My head."

Though dressed for work, she knelt beside him and pulled his hand away from the back of his head.

"Oh my God. What happened?"

"Someone coldcocked me in the alley. Stole the keys. Knocked me out."

"We should call the police."

"Forget about the police." Isador said. He glanced at his clothes. Dark stains marred his white shirt and the front of his pants. The familiar smell of garbage. He must have spent hours lying in the filth. "Phew, I stink. I'm going to take a bath."

"Let me help you. What can I do?"

"Nothing right now. Go on to work," he said. He touched the back of his head. "Ow!"

"Maybe I should go for Doctor Siegel."

"I'll be fine. No doctors. No police. Now go. You'll be late."

In the bathroom, daring a glance in the mirror above the sink, he caught sight of the right side of his face, and the large blue-black bruise where he'd scraped the wall. He flicked the raw area with a finger, brushing away grit embedded in his skin. Then he braced himself on the tub and ran a bath. Hot water. Full strength.

Rose appeared in the doorway, her usually soft-edged features pinched. "Shoo. I said I'll be fine." Though it hurt to do something as simple as purse his lips, Isador stood and pecked her on the head to allay her fears.

After soaking for an hour, Isador dressed and left the apartment, carrying his hat in his hand. He'd failed to find a position on his head in which the hat band didn't bite into the egg shaped lump over his ear. If anything, the lump was larger than before. He wasn't exactly sure where he was going. He'd never met Earl this early and was at a loss as to where to find him. He'd start with Earl's apartment. From there, he could go to the deli on Franklin. After that, he didn't know, but was confident he'd think of something.

Isador climbed the stairs to the second floor of the house on Highland Street where Earl lived. The egg on the side of his head throbbed, forcing him to take the stairs one at a time. Outside Earl's door, he stopped to catch his breath and let the pounding subside. He put his ear to the door. Conversation. Earl was home. Isador rapped his knuckles on the door. Earl's voice, the words muffled.

Dressed only in his drawers, Earl poked his head out the door. He retreated and turned sideways, the bad ear to Isador. "Get dressed," he said to someone inside. A moment later, he opened the door to allow Isador inside. "You look like shit. What happened to you?"

They faced each other in the center of the room. No one else was there.

Near the window, two upholstered chairs that had seen better days framed a low table and a rug worn thin in spots with a border of snarled fringe. Apart from these few items, the room was bare. There were two doors on the far wall, one open to reveal a small, closet-like kitchen, the other closed and presumably leading to the bedroom.

The door opened and a woman emerged. She tossed her head, sending her mane of orange-red curls flying sideways.

She'd dressed in a hurry, missing at least two buttons at her breast. In the gap, the flash of a lace trimmed brassiere.

"Honey? You want me to come back later?" The woman spoke to Earl but did not take her eyes off Isador. She took her time to raise her hand and button her blouse.

"I've got business to tend to."

"Well, okey-dokey then." The woman crossed the floor, hesitating beside Isador for an almost imperceptible moment, no longer than the time it took him to blink. Isador pivoted instinctively, his gaze fixed to her backside as she walked to the door. There, she turned and blew Earl a kiss from lips as fiery as her hair.

"Some tomato," Isador said when the sound of her footsteps had faded.

Earl shrugged. He retrieved a pair of trousers from the arm of one of the chairs in the living room. "So, talk to me," Earl said, eyeing the bruise on Isador's face. He stood on one foot and put his other into a pants leg.

"I didn't see them. I was in the alley emptying the trash when they came up behind me. Banged me into the wall. Four, maybe five of them." Isador paused to let the scene form in Earl's head as well as his own. *Four or five,* he repeated to himself. *Remember that.* "One of them had a gun. Frisked me and found the keys. One went to the drawer and took it all." Isador's pulse quickened. He should have gone by Murphy's before coming to Earl. He hoped Earl didn't ask too many questions. "Then they coldcocked me and left me there."

"Did you get a look at them?"

"Never got a chance to see their faces, but I'd bet money it was Vic and Dom and a few others from their gang. One of them called the other 'cousin.' Another one was a wop for sure. Had an accent. Said we were even."

"Fuck. Anything more?"

"The usual, I guess. Something like, 'go back where you belong.'"

"Fuck."

Earl had said he'd find Mr. Mosko and let him know what happened, sparing Isador the embarrassment. And he'd given Isador time to make it to the speakeasy to check things out before Earl came by at four. Luck was on his side, but it extended only so far. The speakeasy was a mess, chairs scattered across the floor, several broken beyond repair. Shards of glass lay strewn among the chair limbs. The placed reeked of whiskey. A glance behind the bar told him they'd hauled off most of what they hadn't smashed or spilled.

The cash drawer yawned open; the slots for ones and fives and tens and twenties empty. The envelope gone, as he'd expected. Above the cash drawer, Isador found the grip of the revolver, secure in the clip he'd installed. He wrapped the gun in his jacket and set the bundle on the counter.

By four, Isador had returned the room to some semblance of order. Murphy's would have to make do with three fewer chairs and countless fewer glasses, but he'd have to close the joint until he could get another supply of liquor.

Footsteps at the top of the alcove caught his attention. He had a whisk broom and dustpan in his hands and was kneeling to scoop up the last bit of debris when he noticed the shoes—black, polished to a mirror finish. Above the shoes, pressed pants with knife-edge creases, pointing like an arrow to the owner, Saul Mosko.

There were two men with the mob boss. They stepped inside and made a cursory scan of the speakeasy. They nodded to Mr. Mosko. Behind him at the top of the stairs was Earl. Isador breathed a sigh of relief. Earl would know what to say.

"Mr. Mosko. Please come in," Isador said.

The mob boss walked the length of the room, turned on his heels, and came back, pausing near the end of the bar, his nostrils flaring. Though Isador had mopped the floors with a strong mix of vinegar and water, the odor of spilled liquor lingered in certain spots, including the spot where Mosko stood.

"Please, have a seat, sir," Isador said, holding a chair near the entry and away from the bar. He'd broken the silence and immediately wished he'd waited.

Mr. Mosko ignored the chair. "Get a truck from the garage," he said, not addressing anyone in particular, not specifying what kind of truck or which garage. Then he approached Isador. The top of Mosko's head barely met the points of his collar, but Isador took a step back. A muscle to the side of Mosko's nose twitched—the only movement in the room for at least a full minute, a minute that to Isador lasted a lifetime. "Have your partner open tonight." Then he swiveled his head toward Earl and said, "Rizzo's. Shut them down."

Without another word from the boss, or a signal Isador could detect, one of the associates spun around and headed for the alcove. Mosko walked behind and the second associate followed, flanking the boss. Earl remained.

As soon as Mosko and his bodyguards were out of sight, Isador asked, "How did that go? I couldn't tell. Do you think he was mad? Do you think I'll lose my job?" He hated confessing his concerns, but he didn't know Mosko like Earl did.

He didn't know the unwritten, unspoken rules well enough to know what to do next.

"Mad? Plenty mad. More like fucking furious, I'd say."

Isador tried to swallow, but the saliva in his mouth had dried. He scooted behind the bar and poured a full glass of water, downing it in one long gulp. Earl straddled the wooden seat, of the chair Isador had offered to Mosko, draping one enormous thigh on each side. He made two fists and pressed them against the seat between his splayed legs, eased them, pressed them again, and eased them again. Isador waited.

"When Carl gets here, tell him he'll have to manage without you tonight. Now, I've got some things to do. I'll be back at nine. Meet me in the alley."

"What are we going to do?"

"Later."

"He said to shut down Rizzo's. What—"

"Never mind about that. Just meet me at nine. You got your piece? Or did they take that too?"

"No, I have it." Isador glanced at the bundle on the bar.

"Bring it."

At four, after telling Carl he'd have to handle Murphy's by himself for the night, but offering no explanation, Isador left. When he stepped outside, the low angle of the sun caught him square in the face, blinding him and forcing his hand to his forehead; he was still unable to seat his fedora comfortably.

He had close to five hours before his appointment with Earl. He couldn't go home where Rose would pepper him with questions, and he couldn't hang around on the corner like the latest generation of punks who loitered across the street. Isador ambled toward Broadway without a conscious direction or goal. A half hour later, he found himself crossing Ocean Avenue, a brisk breeze from the beach coating his face with a film of salt. To his right, the Jack Rabbit Coaster rattled as a car full of thrill-seekers climbed the humped back of the first hill. Isador found a bench nearby where he could sit and watch. He put his hat in his lap and leaned back, the bulge of his pistol wedged against the back of the bench.

He'd ridden his first roller coaster, the Derby Racer, when he was twelve. His father had paid a dime for the two of them to ride once around. When their car came to a stop, Isador had pleaded with him to go again. They rode the Racer five times in a row, and though Isador wanted to go again, his mother put her foot down. She had refused to ride but hovered nearby, watching, probably fearing her son would suffer some lasting ill effects from the ride's sharp curves and precipitous drops. Or maybe she'd read too many newspaper reports of the handful of deaths of riders each summer.

Later, when he was old enough to go on his own, he spent every spare nickel of his savings riding the coasters along the beach, alone or with friends, often paying their way as well.

An empty car came into position on the length of flat track used for boarding. Once a fresh set of passengers had taken their seats, the car lurched forward and began its climb up the first steep slope. It rose at a deliberately slow pace, designed to heighten the anticipation. The first peals of laughter and screams of delight would not come until the car crested the hump and pointed its nose at the ground. When the high pitch of women's voices filled the air, Isador laughed, amused by how the young ladies clutched their hats or buried their heads in their arms or their gentlemen friends' shoulders.

Soon, though, he tired of the coaster. Isador rose from the bench and joined a throng of pedestrians headed inland. Five-thirty. Four more hours to go. If he hurried, he might catch Sylvia before a performance.

Sylvia lived alone, or at least she'd been the only one home when he'd visited her apartment before. He knocked at her door and waited with his hat in his hands, more like a schoolboy shuffling his feet than a man whose head hurt so badly he couldn't concentrate. No one answered. He knocked again and called her name softly into the seam of the door frame.

Without asking who was there, Sylvia swung the door wide. She wore only a dressing gown, her hair hung loose about her shoulders, one strand of curls cuddled in the valley between her breasts, her feet bare, toes painted a deep violet, nearly black. Isador barged through, causing her to take a step back. In one motion, he threw the door closed and pressed her against the wall.

Isador seized a thick strand of her hair and pulled it behind her back, bringing her mouth up to meet his. With his other hand, he plucked the loose curls from her breasts then slipped a finger under the collar of her gown and slid it from her shoulders. She made no attempt to stop him. The gown sank to the floor in a puddle over her feet.

He grabbed her by the buttocks and together they wrestled to the floor. He'd barely managed to remove the pistol at the back of his pants and loosen his trousers before he found her. Sylvia wrapped her arms and legs around him, moving with him in a frenzied dance of limbs until a tiny scream of delight rose from deep in her throat.

Isador rolled away from her and sighed, enjoying his own release. He lay next to her on his back on the floor, staring at the ceiling, saying nothing.

"Good God, Isador," Sylvia said after another moment or two.

"I had to see you."

"I mean, it's probably six."

"So? Since when did you care what time it was?"

"Since I had to be getting ready, silly. By the way," she said, propping herself on her elbows, "shouldn't you be at Murphy's?"

"I have some other work to do for Mosko today," Isador said. "Carl's minding the place." Sylvia sat upright and gathered her robe in her arms. "Not yet. I want more." He skimmed his hand over her bare back then drew a circle around her breasts with the tip of his finger.

"Not now, mister," she said, pushing his hand away. "I'll be late."

"Please."

"No."

"Okay. But I'll wait and walk you out."

Sylvia did not answer. She pulled her gown around her hips and scurried from the room.

When she emerged from her bedroom a half hour later, he'd dressed and made himself comfortable on her sofa, his gun beside him in the crown of his upturned hat. Her eyes flashed to the weapon and then away, without a flicker of her brow or a bat of her eye. She pivoted at the front door, "Let's go, big man."

Isador jumped to his feet and went to her side, his hand reaching for the back of her head. She caught his hand in hers. "You'll mess my hair."

"All right, all right. Can I walk you to the theater?"

"No, but you can walk me downstairs."

At the door to her building, Isador stopped. He stretched an arm across the door, barring her way. "When can I see you again?"

"I don't know for sure."

"Will you be at Murphy's this week? Saturday?"

"Um, I don't think so."

Isador felt heavy on his feet, as if his heart and lungs and stomach, everything inside his skin, had fallen to the floor. "Why not?"

"Aken says it's getting too hot."

"Hot?" His heart pounded in his ears from wherever it had landed. "Why would he say that?"

"He said you were robbed. There were guns."

"It was nothing. No harm done to anyone."

"He said we should leave it alone, at least for a bit. He doesn't like the publicity."

"Fine," Isador said. After a moment he added, "I could meet you here, Saturday, after closing."

"I'll think about it."

"Think about it?"

"Isador, I have to go. I'll be late."

"Saturday then."

"Let's give it a rest, huh?"

Isador dropped his arm and held the door while Sylvia passed. She turned, placed a violet-tipped forefinger against his lips, and walked away without looking back. Then she disappeared around the corner.

Fuck.

Earl

BY NINE, THE AIR WAS MARKEDLY COOLER; THE WIND HAD SHIFT-
ed and came rushing off the ocean. Earl wore his long coat,
which he would have done even if temperatures had not
obliged. The coat extended to mid-calf. Only the last inch or
so of the barrel of the street sweeper peeked below the hem
when he walked. Few passersby gave him more than a quick
glance anyway. If they happened to make eye contact, his size
and demeanor, the firm set of his mouth, and his unwavering
gaze said he was not someone they wanted to know, nor was
he someone they wanted to be known by.

He'd waited until nightfall to leave his apartment and find
Elmer and Eugene, "The E's" as they were known, though
everyone called Eugene "Gene." They waited for him in an
alley off Blake Street in Mr. Mosko's Ford, or rather *one* of Mr.
Mosko's Fords. Without so much as a grunt or a nod of recog-
nition, Earl opened the rear door and placed the Thompson
inside, the barrel resting on the floor. He took a seat beside
the gun. As soon as he drew the door shut, the car surged
forward.

"Tell me this guy's not a goddamn virgin," Elmer said from
the right front seat.

"He'll do what I say," Earl said.

"That's not what I meant. He gives me the heebie jeebies."

"He'll be fine."

"You better goddamn hope so," Gene said.

After a short drive, they pulled into the alley behind Murphy's. Gene dimmed the lights and slowed to avoid colliding with any stray trash bins behind the five or six buildings on the block. Up ahead, a figure emerged from the shadows. Earl recognized Isador. Still hatless. As they rolled to a stop, Isador squinted and cocked his head to see inside the vehicle. Earl cracked the back door and said, "Get in."

As soon as he'd taken his seat, Isador extended a hand to Elmer in the front seat. "The name's Isador," he said. Elmer kept his eyes glued to the street in front of them, ignoring Isador's overture.

"They know who you are," Earl said.

"Oh, sorry."

Goddamn cherry, Earl thought. *Was I ever that naive?*

Gene exited the alley and made a hard right turn. The gun slid against Isador's thigh. Earl put a hand on it and swung it back beside him. They drove north, slowly, but not so slow as to catch anyone's attention. When they turned past Sal's Café—**SALS**, no apostrophe—they left what Earl considered his neighborhood and wended their way through less familiar streets.

Gene slowed the car and pulled it to the side behind a Pontiac. Up ahead was Rizzo's, an orange glow emanating from the shades drawn over its second floor windows. Gene cut the engine, sat back, and folded his arms over his chest to wait. Elmer lit a cigarette.

"Butt me," Earl said and Elmer tossed a pack of cigarettes over his shoulder to Earl.

The four men said nothing for close to an hour. Each of them sucked on their cigarettes or drummed their fingers to a tune in their head, whatever it took to pass the time. All kept their eyes on the door leading to Rizzo's, distracted only when another car pulled to the curb at the far end of the street. A man nearly as wide as he was tall exited from the driver's side and waddled across the street toward Rizzo's. He disappeared inside the ground floor entry and reemerged a short time later with a second man. The two loitered on the sidewalk until large drops of rain began to fall. The two dashed across the street and jumped into their car. They closed the doors but did not pull away.

"Torpedoes?" Earl asked, referring to the possibility of Italian strong-arms.

"Maybe. I'm sure there'll be more upstairs," Elmer said.

The rain came harder. Earl raised the window on his side of the car, leaving a crack for air. The rest of his cohorts did the same. Soon, the rain drilled against the windshield and roof of the car. Their breaths and the warmth of their bodies clouded the windshield. Visibility ahead was reduced to mere feet.

"Rain's good," Earl said, more to himself than to anyone else in the car, except for perhaps Isador. He continued, "Less chance of uninvited guests."

The downpour ended as quickly as it had started. Only a light mist persisted while fog wafted from the pavement, the heat of the afternoon dissipating.

"Crowd's thinning," Elmer said. He had the clearest view ahead.

Several people had come through the door from Rizzo's and scuttled down the block, threading their way beneath the cover of awnings. Earl rolled his window half way down. Words in Italian floated in the heavy air and then faded. Silence.

"Let's give it a few more minutes," Earl said. His watch showed ten-thirty.

Earl tapped Isador on the leg. He held out the Tommy gun, keeping the barrel pointed at the floor next to his foot. Instead of taking the weapon, Isador waggled a finger in the air and then pulled his pea shooter from his coat pocket.

"Put that away. You're going to need this tonight." He nudged the Thompson toward Isador. "You remember how I showed—"

"Yeah," Isador said, interrupting. "Yeah, I remember."

"Okay. You carry this when we go in. You keep it pointed at the ground. You keep behind me and you don't say a god-damn word. If and when I raise mine, you raise yours. When I let it fly, you do the same. Over the sons of bitches' heads. Like I—"

"Like you told me. I got it."

"And, when it's over, you toss it. Get rid of it."

"Let's go," Gene said. He popped a stick of chewing gum into his mouth and tossed the wrapper in the gutter.

The four assembled on the sidewalk. Earl took a second machine gun from Gene and stuck it inside his coat. With his free hand, he tugged at his collar, flipping it up at the back of his head to ward off the damp and the drips from the awnings and the arms of street lamps.

Midway down the block, Elmer broke from the other three and scooted out of sight between two buildings where he could circle around to the back. Gene, Earl, and Isador continued forward, their shoes slapping the shallow puddles of water accumulated on the pavement.

The stairwell was dimly lit and narrow. It forced the men

to climb in single file. Earl followed Gene and listened for the sound of Isador's footsteps behind him.

Once inside the speakeasy, they formed a row against the wall—Gene to the far right, then Earl, then Isador, closest to the door. Heads turned. A few men scooted back their chairs and rose, slack jaws giving way to glares. Several women cried out or pressed their hands to their faces, startled by the sight of the armed men, though they had not hoisted their weapons. One woman scrambled for her coat and hat, followed by another. The two made their way to the back of the saloon and the only apparent escape route. A number of men rushed to join them, urging them out the back, avoiding so much as a glance over their shoulders.

Then one woman who'd dropped something in her rush to leave ran back to her table, amid panicked calls and shouts from her friends. She snatched a parcel from a chair and hustled back to the exit.

"We have no beef with you guys," Gene said as the crowd thinned. "Just Auditore, here," he continued, using Nicolini's first name as a sign of disrespect. Auditore Nicolini, the Italian who headed the Malden Street gang, sat a few yards in front of the row of Mosko's men. He'd spun around in his chair when he noticed heads turning to glare at something over his shoulder. Recognizing trouble, he raised one hand and pointed his index finger toward the bar, his other he placed in his pocket.

"Now Auditore," Gene said. "You don't want to do anything stupid do you?" Only a fraction of a second after Nicolini had raised his arm, or perhaps it was a fraction of a second before, Earl could not tell, Gene had lifted his gun and aimed the barrel at Nicolini's head. Isador shifted his feet.

Earl thought Isador was about to draw his gun as well, despite Earl's instructions.

Gene stepped aside to let a few innocent bystanders leave through the front door. Earl counted seven men who hadn't moved when the patrons had: the barkeep, two who stood against the wall opposite, two toward the back of the saloon in deep shadow, and the remaining two who sat across from Nicolini at his table. By now, their hands underneath the table held pistols aimed toward Mosko's men. Nicolini's eyes darted from Gene to the man behind the bar and back to Gene.

"Tell your men to put their pieces on the table where we can see them. We don't want anyone to get hurt. We just want what's owed us. For our expenses. What do you say?"

"So? You. Why don't you go to Jew hell," Nicolini said, his accent heavy, his eyes passing over the faces of Gene and Earl and Isador, burning them into his memory. He spat on the floor.

Later, when he tried to recall the events of the evening, Earl remembered how the splatter of mucus glistened atop the hardwood floor. Then, he thought Nicolini was going to spin back around in his chair, putting his back to the intruders, in his own show of disrespect. He'd only made a slight motion with his knee and forearm when chaos erupted. Earl likened the scene to a vaudeville stage finale when the curtain rose and the cast swarmed forward. Heavy steps in the stairwell, shouts from the rear of the room, sirens and whistles in the street. A single gunshot cracked above the fracas. Then, after a split second of total silence, a chorus of shots erupted, snapping and popping like fireworks on the Fourth of July. Earl had no idea who had fired first, whether it was the first of several police who flooded through the half-doors on his left or one of Nicolini's men or Gene or Isador. They'd all joined the chorus after the first shot.

Before the stray bullet hit his thigh, Earl saw Elmer's face above the crowd at the back of the room. And then, as in the theater, the lights went out. Shots ceased, though the shouting continued. Someone stepped on his wrist in the confusion, perhaps trying to make their way to the street. He was on the floor in the dark. A hand slipped under his arm. Someone groaned and pulled him up, or at least to the point where Earl's feet found the floor. A whiff of spearmint in his face. *Gene. Thank God.* Despite his smaller size, Gene hooked one hand under Earl's arm and another as far as he could around Earl's waist. They struggled to the entrance and pushed through the half doors, Earl stumbling as he dragged his injured leg beside him and held onto Gene's shoulders. They were forced back into a single file down the stairwell. Below him, a shot rang out. Gene kept moving though, kicking at something or someone crumpled on the stairs.

At the bottom, they halted and listened. More shots upstairs. Gene grabbed Earl and pushed him into the void beneath the steps. The opening was small, but they squeezed together, and with their chins tucked and resting on their chests, they waited. Several pairs of feet in hard soled shoes clambered up the stairs. When the shouting and the pounding subsided, Gene and Earl emerged from their hiding place and fled into the street.

Ahead, two men stood beside their car. Gene swiveled and guided Earl in the opposite direction, hugging the sides of the storefronts and brick walls as they went. Two blocks. Three blocks. The pain in Earl's thigh worsened. His wet trousers clung to his leg, but he kept moving, limping along behind Gene in silence. Neither mentioned Elmer or Isador. The two would have to make it on their own.

"Goddamn," Earl said, grabbing the flesh and muscle of his upper thigh with his left hand. He squeezed his leg to dull the pain but only intensified the sensation of a dagger slicing through muscle.

"I said, get your hand out of the way," Salans, the not-quite-doctor said. Salans was who they turned to when they needed medical attention without the attending questions. Salans had had medical training, but Earl was not sure where or how much.

Earl sat slumped in a straight-backed chair in the doctor's kitchen, his injured leg propped up on a second chair under a lamp with its shade removed.

"Are you sure you can see?"

Salans glared at Earl. Then he bowed his head again over the wound. "You're lucky," he said after endless probing and twisting that shot waves of pain through Earl's leg.

"How's that? I don't feel so lucky."

"It's gone clean through." For effect, and to prove his point, Salans rubbed the back of Earl's thigh and brought up a set of bloody fingers. "Thought I might have to dig it out." Salans half smiled. Earl found no humor in the idea. "I'll clean it as best I can and sew it up, back and front. You'll need to keep it elevated and stay off your feet for a few days."

"Yeah, right."

"Suit yourself." Salans grabbed a sponge from a bowl filled with clean water. He squeezed the sponge and then held a dark brown bottle to it, inverting the bottle and soaking the sponge. He repeated the action a few times. "Count to ten. This is going to hurt."

"One, two—Goddamn!"

After a string of protests, insisting he could make it home, Earl relented and stayed the night at Salans's place on the couch in his living room, the injured leg resting on a chair brought from the kitchen. Regardless of which way he turned or twisted, he couldn't find a position comfortable enough to sleep. Just before daylight, Earl lowered his left leg to the floor, and with most of his weight on his right foot, he raised himself from the couch. He hobbled across the room, one hand on the back of a chair, then a table, then the wall.

There would be people out at this hour, maybe long-shoremen or other laborers, mostly bleary-eyed men who, if they noticed anything unusual, would look away. Besides, his long coat would conceal most of the blood-soaked trousers. As he stuffed an arm in the sleeve of his coat, Earl thought of the gun he'd concealed inside earlier. The police would have taken it in as evidence, but they wouldn't be able to tie it to him.

It took Earl half an hour to make it home, twice what it would have taken without his injury. Once inside his apartment, he undressed and collapsed on the bed, ignoring the small circle of blood that seeped through the layers of bandage wound around his thigh.

The dream played on the back of his eyelids. This time they were in a forest. The pale woman in front of him on the ground, her arms over her head to shield her from drops of a recent rain that pelted her each time the wind blew. Earl made a tent of his coat and held it above his head to shield her, to keep her warm, to keep her safe.

She lowered her arms. He would see her face. At last. The forest erupted with a bang. Earl scanned the canopy expecting to see a dead limb hurtling end over end toward them. The trees swayed in a fierce wind, branches scraped against each other but held fast. Then the banging resumed, behind him, in front of him, above him, like thunder but with a regular beat.

Earl opened his eyes. He lifted his head from his pillow. *The door. The goddamn door.* Earl rolled over onto his left side, the stab of pain reminding him of where he had been the night before and what had happened.

"Coming!" he shouted.

He struggled to the side of the bed and realized from the angle of the sun streaming through the windows that the day was already well along. Keeping one eye closed against the bright light, he squinted around his bedroom, looking for his shirt.

The pounding started again. Earl staggered to his feet, hobbled a few steps and then hopped on his right foot the remaining distance. "Coming!"

He cracked the door. Gene. Earl flung the door wide and retreated into the room, crumpling on a chair. With a hand on each side of his thigh, he lifted his left leg and brought it to rest on the table.

"How's the leg?"

"Seen better days. Salans said I was lucky. Bullet went in one side and out the other. Still, it hurts like hell."

Gene nodded.

"So what do you know?"

"Some good. Some not so good."

"Give me the good. I need some good news."

"Good news is the cops are investigating the scene. Apparently, we walked in ahead of a planned raid. Word is they'd staked out Rizzo's and intended to shut them down for 'illegal sale of alcohol.'"

Earl snickered. "Guess we busted up their sting."

"Guess so."

"Anyway, they haven't made any arrests, except—"

"Except, what?"

"Except for your boy."

"Who?"

"Your guy. Margolin."

"What? Don't mess with me, Gene. I'm not up to it today."

"I'm not messing with you. He must not have gotten out. He was closer to the stairs than we were. Hell. He might have been hit. I don't know. Anyway, he's downtown in the lockup."

"Fuck."

"Yeah, you can say that again."

"Fuck."

Earl massaged his thigh above the bandages. "That was the good news?" he asked.

"Yeah. Elmer didn't make it."

"Shit. You've got to be kidding me."

"My guy at the *Globe* told me. They've got some photographs. Can't imagine what kind of son of a bitch makes a living taking photos of dead people. There's no telling, at least not yet, who shot him."

Earl nodded. "There was a lot of metal flying. I don't know who started it. One of Nicolini's bastards would be my guess."

"Probably."

"I don't think it was Margolin. I think he was toeing the line."

"Maybe."

"Shit," Earl said, shaking his head from side to side.

"Do you think he'll talk?"

"He kept it together before. I think he knows what he's supposed to do."

"Mosko will want more than a 'think' so."

"Yeah," Earl said, "I know."

In the hallway, Earl explained to his downstairs neighbor, Paul Poshansky, that he'd injured his leg in an automobile accident. The old man walked with a cane Earl hoped he could borrow for the afternoon.

Mr. Poshansky made a circling motion with his wrist, as if he were swatting at a gnat. "Come in, come in," he said at last. "Only use it when I go out and I'm not planning on going anywhere today."

"Who's there, Paul?" a woman's voice called from the kitchen. The couple lived on the main floor of the house in an apartment easily twice the size of Earl's. Two overstuffed chairs, worn where he imagined the Mister and Missus spent their evenings, a footstool in front of hers, knitting needles piercing a ball of yarn on the cushion, a radio between the two chairs.

"The man from upstairs. 201," Poshansky answered. "I don't think I even know your name, come to think of it."

Earl was certain the Poshansky's knew who he was. He guessed the old man was just not sure what to call him. He did not answer and was soon spared the need.

"Maybe you would like some tomato soup," Mrs. Poshansky said, emerging from the kitchen, a ladle in one hand. "I just took some off the stove."

"Thank you, ma'am, but I've only come to borrow Mr. Poshansky's cane."

"What? Did you hurt your leg?"

"It's nothing. I've got to walk over to Nahant, so I thought—"

"You come on in and sit down. Now, if there's something you need from the pharmacy, I could go for you. I go there all the time, what with Paul's arthritis. I need some—"

"Oh, no ma'am, I have to go see some—"

"I'm sure they won't mind if you're a few minutes late. Come on in and have some soup. When was the last time you ate? You know, my son is..."

At the mention of food, Earl's empty stomach flipped and groaned. He hadn't eaten since the day before and that had been a quick bite. As he caught a whiff of the steaming broth laced with onion and garlic, even his good leg turned to mush.

"So what do you say?" she asked.

Mrs. Poshansky had droned on until Earl lost what little thread held the conversation together. He grunted a response, hoping it would do.

"That's it then. Have a seat there, next to Paul. I'll be back in a minute. Paul, would you let Mr.—" She stopped in mid-sentence, realizing as her husband had earlier that she did not know what to call their guest.

"Earl. You can call me Earl."

"Good. Paul, let Mr. Earl read the newspaper. If he hasn't had breakfast or lunch, I'll bet he hasn't read the news either."

Earl eased himself into the vacant chair, afraid it might

collapse under his weight, having only known the bird-like occupancy of Mrs. Poshansky.

Paul handed Earl the newspaper and, thankfully, swiveled in his own chair to turn on the radio. At least he'd be spared the need to make conversation. Above the crackle of the speaker as Paul dialed in a station, Mrs. Poshansky broadcast her own one-way conversation from the kitchen, neither asking for nor expecting a response.

By the time Earl unwound himself from the Poshansky's tentacles, it was close to five o'clock. He was not sure whether Rose Margolin would be home or whether she had given up on Isador returning from the night before and gone to work or if she'd somehow learned about the prior night's events.

Earl hobbled as fast as he could, using the cane as Mr. Poshansky had instructed. There was a definite trick to walking with a cane, an awkward feel until he found his own rhythm.

Standing outside 51 Nahant, Earl winced at the thought of the climb ahead. He took a deep breath, but before he could place his injured leg and the cane on the first step, a young boy darted ahead of him. Earl caught a glimpse of freckles across the bridge of his nose and forehead. The boy scampered up the three steps to the main door. There he turned. Cheeks flushed, he said as sternly as his young voice allowed, "Stay away." To emphasize his point, he raised a small pale hand, fingers outstretched, his palm facing Earl, like a policeman signaling a vehicle to halt.

Earl ignored the boy's admonition and raised his good leg to the step.

"I said, stay away from here." And then, with a hesitant tone to his voice, he added, "Leave Mrs. Margolin alone."

"I don't mean any harm," Earl said, questioning his need to explain to the boy. "I just need to speak with Mrs. Margolin for a minute."

Behind the boy, the door opened. Rose appeared in the doorway. When she saw Earl, she raised a hand to her mouth but made no move to retreat or exit. She had not screamed, though Earl thought she had every right to do so.

The boy rushed to her side. "I told him to go. I told him not to bother you."

Rose turned her head toward the boy but kept her gaze on Earl. Her eyes were glassy, uncomprehending.

"Mrs. Margolin," the boy said. He grabbed her wrist, jostling it while he called her name. "Mrs. Margolin?"

"Jacob," she said as if he'd suddenly materialized. "Jacob, it's all right."

"I told him to go away."

"Mrs. Margolin? Jacob is it?" Earl interjected, again feeling pressured to explain his presence to both of them. "I need to talk to you a moment. It's about Isador."

"You go on home now, Jacob. It'll be all right."

Clouds formed on the boy's forehead, darkening his freckles. He glared at Earl as if daring him to do Rose harm. "Yes, ma'am", he said, hanging his head. He gave Earl another glance before crossing the street to a building with an identical entryway.

"Please don't be frightened. I've only come to tell you what's happened."

Rose looked over his shoulder, checking after the boy, he thought. Then she breathed in, as if she were about to take a breath and dive into the ocean. "Come. Come inside. Out of the street."

Rose

ROSE LED EARL INTO THE ALCOVE ON THE FIRST FLOOR LANDING
of 51 Nahant. He pulled the door closed behind him. At the
sound of the door latch clicking into place, a passing neighbor
glanced up. At least if something untoward occurred, Rose
thought, they'd be seen. She planted her feet to indicate this
was as far as she would go. Despite this display of confidence
and bravery, the hairs on her arms stood erect, like small an-
tennae of insects listening for the sound of danger.

Though she faced Earl, she avoided looking him in the eye.
Instead, she busied herself with the buttons on her coat, as if
to emphasize that he was merely an interruption, a brief one
at that, and then she would be on her way.

"First, let me assure you, Isador is safe."

Despite her angst at standing close to this so-called friend
of Isador's, this thug, better yet, this animal—unfit to be
thought of as a human being—she sighed. The news was a
relief. "He didn't come home last night. What have you done
to him?" she asked, searching his face for answers. She could
not match his gaze, though, and she shifted her eyes to stare
at the floor and the space that separated them.

"We've done nothing to him, Mrs. Margolin," he said.
"He's safe. Let me explain. He did a job last night, a favor for
Mr. Mosko."

The muscles in Rose's arms flexed. She clenched her hands,
squeezing the loop of the purse she carried.

Earl continued, "We, uh, he, well, that is, you see, we got caught in a raid. A police raid. We didn't know the cops had been staking out Rizzo's. You know Rizzo's?" When she shook her head, he explained, "It's a bar up on Malden. One run by a group of Italians."

"Why would Isador be at a bar on Malden?" Rose asked, wondering whether she really wanted to know the answer.

"It was a favor, like I said."

Rose clenched her teeth and glared at the world on the other side of the glass door. "Go on."

"There were shots fired."

Her eyes snapped back to Earl's face, looking for a sign that, despite what he'd just said, Isador was indeed all right.

"He wasn't hit. Not Isador. Someone else."

"Are you sure?"

"Yes. Yes, ma'am."

Had the circumstances been different, had Earl not been one of Mosko's men, and had he not been the man who had assaulted her, Rose might have found his choice of words comical. Here was a man, barrel-chested, his hands as big as dinner plates, his neck short, little more than a stub for his head, and yet he spoke as if he were no older or more mature than Jacob.

"Where is he?"

"I'm afraid they took him in. He's being held downtown."

Rose exhaled sharply. Blood rushed to her head. She clenched her jaw again and said, "Please let me pass. I have to go."

Earl stepped back against the wall, allowing Rose as much space as possible to pass.

Once again, Rose sat across the desk from Gerald Kilcourse, leaning close and listening for words of hope.

"Now Mrs. Margolin, we don't yet know what we're dealing with. So don't panic. I've just been informed that I myself can see him, as his attorney, of course. This afternoon. He's been downtown in police custody overnight as I am sure you know."

"No. I don't know. I don't know anything. Only that he didn't come home last night and when I went out this morning, Mr.—that is..." Rose paused. She refused to speak Earl Bloom's name and grant him an ounce of familiarity, even in his absence. "Someone told me there'd been a..." again, she halted searching for the right word, "an incident at his place of employment."

"Well, that's not quite it. What I've been told—this is confidential of course, you do understand?"

Rose nodded.

"The message I received from the police captain this morning was that Mr. Margolin had been apprehended at Rizzo's during a raid. You know Rizzo's?"

"I heard mention of it earlier today. I've never been there or for that matter anywhere near the place."

"I suppose not. It's a speakeasy. Rizzo's is owned by an enterprise known as the Malden Street gang. Italians. The police had knowledge of criminal activities taking place on the premises, alcohol sales, gambling, perhaps even...ah...even prostitution. The alcohol was the least of it—hardly a secret."

"And, what did they say my husband was doing there?"

"As far as I know, and my details here are still very sketchy at this point, he was there with a few cohorts, friends of Mr. Mosko, um, er, to discuss a mishap that occurred a few weeks ago at one of Mr. Mosko's establishments. Murphy's. There was some back and forth, threats and the like, and guns were drawn. Shots were fired. At least one of the officers was injured—shot in the knee and arm. One of Mr. Mosko's men was killed. Shot dead, I'm afraid. Elmer Levine. Do you know Mr. Levine?"

Rose had stopped listening after the words "shot dead." She was well aware of the reports of robberies, beatings, and other small crimes to be sure, even shootings in the rougher parts of town. But incidents such as these happened to other people, a criminal class. They never happened to people she knew. Rose was incapable of imagining Isador involved in a shooting.

"No, I don't suppose you do. Anyway—"

"But my husband, Isador, he...Even if he were there, he can't have had anything to do with a shooting. It must have been one of the other men."

"That is, of course, a possibility. One I'll explore. Nevertheless, by the time the dust had settled, almost everyone in the place had fled. And, except for Mr. Margolin and the unfortunate Mr. Levine, the rest of Mr. Mosko's men escaped."

Rose bristled at the reference to Isador as one of "Mr. Mosko's men." However, given Mr. Kilcourse's accounting of the events, she had little to offer to contradict his characterization. "When can I see him?"

"I'm headed there myself. I can't promise you'll be allowed to see him, but I'll see what I can do."

"I would."

Access to the county jail with Mr. Kilcourse at her side was easier than Rose remembered it had been on her own. Mr. Kilcourse's years of experience had taught him how to navigate the winding hallways with left and right turns every few feet, hallways that echoed with the sound of their heels tapping against the bare floor. Each guard they encountered nodded or tipped his cap, greeting Gerald Kilcourse by name and—though they tried to hide it—staring at the woman at his side.

Kilcourse halted outside a thick wooden door, one of the few without a pane of glass or barred opening for the guards. A wooden chair sat in the hallway beside the door.

"Mrs. Margolin, please wait here. I think it's best that I meet with Mr. Margolin for a few minutes first. Alone. I'll come back to get you in a bit."

Rose glanced at the chair and down the hallway lined with identical doors and identical straight backed chairs, every ten feet or so.

"You'll be perfectly safe. Don't worry. I'll just be a few minutes."

Gerald Kilcourse squeezed his bulk through the door. She had no chance to catch a glimpse of her husband. The "few minutes" Mr. Kilcourse promised stretched into many minutes and then half an hour. She shifted positions over and over on the uncomfortable seat. She stood. She paced back and forth and pressed her ear against the door to hear the conversation taking place inside. The thick door muffled the words so that she could not be certain what anyone said or who was speaking.

Footsteps. Rose backed away. "You may go in now, Mrs. Margolin," Gerald Kilcourse said. He held the door for her, but before she passed inside, he touched her arm and said in a low tone so only she could hear, "Not too many questions, mind you. It's best to stick to saying hello and asking after him, nothing more. Nothing about the incident."

Inside, Isador sat on the far side of a long wooden table, a lone chair on her side. His face bore an unfamiliar pallor, the same sickening gray-green color as the walls. A day's growth of stubble dotted his chin and by the look of his clothes, he'd slept in them. He did not rise.

A guard entered through a door opposite the one Rose had entered. He took a position against the wall to Rose's left.

"Isa!" Rose strode to the right intending to circle the table and throw her arms around her husband, but the guard stepped forward. Rose stopped in her tracks.

"Have a seat, Rose," Isador said.

Bewildered, Rose turned and took a seat in the empty chair on the near side.

"Isador, what on earth—"

"It'll be all right, Rose. Just like last time. Mr. Kilcourse is going to take care of everything."

Her eyes flitted from the stubble on his chin to his hands on top of the table and to the glint of metal circling his wrists.

"Take my hand, Rose. I think you can do that." Isador glanced sideways at the guard.

The guard nodded.

Rose's hand crept across the table and circled his fingers, the tips of her fingers stopping short of the handcuffs and resting in the warmth of his palm.

"They said you were at Rizzo's. They said—"

"Not now, Rose. We'll talk about that later. Mr. Kilcourse has all the details. You need to take care of yourself and not worry about me. It might be a while before I can come home. I want you to promise me to take care of yourself."

"How long, Isa? How long?"

"I don't know yet. The police have to complete their investigation. That might take a few days. Mr. Kilcourse will have some more news for you then."

"When can I come back?"

Isador ran his thumb slowly over the top of her hand.

"Isa?"

"A court date hasn't been set. I'm sure they'll allow you to come then."

"Court date?"

The guard coughed, drawing their attention. He shuffled his feet and his eyes darted toward the clock on the wall.

"I think our time is up."

"But I've just arrived. I have so many questions."

"I know you do, darling."

"This is utterly insane. They cannot keep him in there," Rose said to Mr. Kilcourse as they navigated the jail's corridors in reverse.

"I am afraid they can, Mrs. Margolin. The evidence is pretty damning."

"But you'll be able to free him, right?"

Head bowed, his breath coming heavily, the attorney allowed some seconds to pass before answering. "This is not going to be as easy as it was before. After all, I don't think we can claim it was your gun a second time."

Rose pressed her lips together and walked in silence to the end of the block. Then, she asked, "What can I do? There must be something I can do or say that will help."

"Nothing right now. Once the police complete their inquiries, they'll file charges and set a court date. I'll do what I can, but I want to be honest with you. I would not hold out hope of him being released any time soon." He paused and then he added, "If at all. I fear they will be prosecuting him for murder."

Rose gasped, stumbled forward, and would have fallen had not Mr. Kilcourse caught her arm. When she'd regained her balance and her breathing calmed, she drew back from him. "That can't be. I will not allow that to happen."

"Now, Mrs. Margolin, I'll be handling your husband's case. Let me do my job. I have to do some investigating and then start preparing his defense. There's not much more you can do in the meantime."

At Shirley Avenue, where Gerald Kilcourse needed to turn to go to his office, he tipped his hat to Rose, told her again not to worry, and walked on toward Orr Square. Rose kept walking, not thinking about the direction she took or where she was headed. Her thoughts raced, spinning around as if she were astride a flying horse on one of the beach carousels.

Rose arrived at Murphy's at three-thirty in the afternoon. She hurtled through the café, aware the store manager had eyed her as she passed. She headed for the stairs without a glance at his display of lunch options. *Let him think I'm one of the quiffs that hang around here*, she thought. *I don't give a damn.*

Surprised at her use of profanity, even if not uttered aloud, Rose halted halfway up the staircase. She blanched, imagining the profanities she'd need to confront Mr. Mosko and his men.

Carl, whom she'd had the advantage of meeting on one or two occasions, was nowhere to be found. A stranger stood behind the bar, setting up for the night. "Where can I find Mr. Mosko?" she asked.

"Mister who?"

"Please, you can spare me the pretenses. My husband is Isador Margolin. You may have heard of him. He's the manager here. I know he worked, that is, he works, for Mr. Mosko. I need to see—"

"Well, sometimes he's here and sometimes he's not. I really can't say when he might come by."

"Then who can?"

"If you come by later, there might be someone who can take you to him."

"I'll wait." Rose took a seat near the bar where the barkeep or anyone else who wandered in could not ignore her presence.

"Suit yourself. It might be a while though."

"I have all day." Rose placed her purse on the table and clasped her hands in her lap. She scrutinized the barkeeper's every move as if he were executing a feat of extraordinary difficulty and interest rather than wiping glasses and polishing the counter. After some minutes under her watch, he'd worked his way to the far end of the bar and slipped down the hallway and out of her sight.

After another several minutes had passed and he had not returned, Rose thought she might have to check on his whereabouts. The washrooms, as she knew, were in the hallway, but she was not desperate enough to pursue him there. She'd give him some more time. Five more minutes passed. At last, she heard steps returning. It was the barkeep, and behind him was a figure she recognized.

Earl hobbled to her table while the barkeep returned to polishing and wiping.

"Are you injured?" she asked. She eyed his cane and his left leg, the one he'd favored as he crossed the room. "Were you there?" Earl said nothing. "Of course you were."

Earl removed his hat and held it in his left hand along with his cane. "Just a touch of arthritis," he said, showing no re-action to her accusation but avoiding looking directly at her.

"How is it you escaped and Isador was left behind, arrest-ed, incarcerated, and likely to stand trial for murder?"

"I can take you to Mr. Mosko."

"Good."

He turned and started toward the back of the room. Rose gathered her things and caught up with him on the stairs. He led her away from the ocean and into an unfamiliar section of town, stopping outside a café on the ground floor of a build-ing unlike any other in Revere. Two spires towered above the entrance, each tower striped with gold paint and topped with a bulb-like dome. Each dome capped with a symbol she sup-posed was meant to represent the orient.

"He's in there." Earl gestured with his cane at the equally gaudy doors beneath the words **IMPERIAL CAFÉ** embla-zoned in red.

"How will I find him?"

"He'll find you."

Rose took a deep breath, summoning the courage to go in-side. One indisputable fact propelled her forward: Isador had few, if any, options left. "Thank you," she said, thinking she owed the man at least that common decency. Earl, however, had disappeared into the crowd on the sidewalk.

Stepping inside the café, Rose was struck by a wall of un-usual and powerful aromas. Spices she could not fathom or name mingled with the odor of garlic, onions, and peppers.

Meat sizzled somewhere on a hot skillet. Rose's eyes teared; she couldn't imagine anyone eating whatever it was the café served. Judging by the tables piled high with food and patrons occupying every available chair, though, she was alone in her opinion.

A head turned at one of the tables nearby. A man eyed her and then turned back around, leaning close to his fellow diner. Both men turned to look. Rose shifted from one foot to the other and fidgeted with an earring. She could only stand there so much longer and was about to retreat when a man approached and said, "Come this way."

"I'm not here to eat," she said, assuming he was a waiter. He pivoted and headed to the back of the room. Rose had no choice but to follow in the zigzag course he charted.

Her escort stopped near a beaded curtain strung under an arch. He held the curtain aside for her to pass. Inside was a small, low-ceilinged room containing a single dining table, round, with six chairs. The man she'd met at Tillinghast's, Saul Mosko, occupied the chair furthest from her. The rest were empty. He dabbed his lips with his napkin, rose, and circled the table. He held his palm upward and gestured to the chair next to him.

"I need to speak to you—"

"Please, come in and have a seat. You must be Mrs. Margolin. My name is Saul Mosko." He took a step backward and held the chair for her.

Rose stared at the empty chair. She looked back at the curtain and then again at the chair. Saul Mosko had not moved a muscle.

"I, I am..."

"Please have a seat. Make yourself comfortable. Sit here

beside me where we can talk. I know you have many concerns and I will try to address them."

Rose took a seat, as he suggested, or commanded, she did not know which. Her thoughts of blurting out her demands vanished. She found herself unable to remember what she had intended to say.

"May I offer you something to eat or perhaps a cup of coffee?"

"Nothing, thank you. I—"

"Perhaps some *rugaleh*. Bernie, the chef here, makes the best in town."

"Coffee. I'll have a coffee."

Mr. Mosko nodded at someone behind her, perhaps the man who'd escorted her to the private room. He'd said nothing and she'd forgotten that anyone else was in the room besides Saul Mosko, Jewish gang leader, mob boss, racketeer, gambler, rum runner, hijacker, and thief—all of the words she'd heard to describe him. *And*, she thought, *Isador's boss*.

"And please bring Mrs. Margolin some *rugaleh*, with raisins." Though Rose shook her head, he said, "I insist," and then took his own seat.

In no time, a waiter appeared and placed the coffee and pastry in front of her. She turned her head and watched as he disappeared through the curtain, the tiny beads on the strands clicking as they parted and came together again. Before she turned back, she caught sight of someone else in the room, someone she had not noticed until that moment, his jacket and trousers plain against a wall striped with flecks of gold paint. She turned back to her coffee and dessert and ventured a glance across the table.

"Lenny," Mr. Mosko said, perhaps noticing her unease,

"you can leave us now." Then, without another word, he returned to his meal.

Rose finished the small helping of *rugaleh* in a few bites and moistened her dry throat with the coffee.

"Was the *rugaleh* as promised?"

"Yes. It was very good." With food in her stomach and caffeine from the coffee flooding her veins, Rose woke from the stupor of the polite conversation. She reminded herself where she was and with whom she was dining.

"Have we met before?" Mosko asked.

He was not only excessively polite, she thought, but also endowed with a remarkable memory, given how many people he must encounter in a day. *Stop! Remember why you're here.* "We have. Briefly. I work at Tillinghast's and helped you with a purchase some time ago. But the reason I am here—"

"Yes, well. I thought so. And, I apologize for not addressing your concerns earlier. Let's discuss your husband's circumstances." He set his fork down and pushed aside his plate, half of his large steak untouched. "I am sure you are very worried. If I can, I will try to calm your fears."

"I've spoken to his lawyer, Mr. Gerald Kilcourse. He says Isador might be charged with murder. I don't know the details of what happened, only that my husband is no murderer." Rose continued without stopping for several minutes. She repeated everything Mr. Kilcourse had told her and everything she had concluded about Isador's activities. She spoke passionately and quickly, as if her words were hurtling down a chute. Her voice was strong, though. It did not quake as she thought it might, and she did not break down in tears. Her confidence grew. She concluded with her demand, the one she'd rehearsed. "You simply must have him released."

For a moment after she finished, Mosko said nothing. A long, uncomfortable moment. Rose sensed he was waiting for her to continue, to offer further arguments on Isador's behalf or to retract her demand and beg for his help. But she had finished what she had to say. She would wait all night without saying another word, without ceding him the advantage, whatever it took. She set her eyes level with his and willed herself not to blink.

Saul Mosko fingered the large signet ring on his left hand. Then, he cleared his throat and drained his coffee. "Mrs. Margolin, you know very well I am not the police, or the judge, or the mayor. I do not have the power to do such a thing."

"You have all that power and more," she dared, interrupting him and contesting his false modesty.

"Not in this case," he said, ignoring her insinuation. "Not when there's been a homicide." He fingered the ring again and stared at her over his hands. "I will look into the situation and see what I can do. I promise you that."

"When?" she asked.

Rose thought she saw the hint of a smile forming at the corners of his mouth. If it had been a smile, it disappeared as quickly as it had come. He answered, "I'm afraid nothing can be done until after the investigation. That will take several days. We have some time."

"I don't have that time. Isador doesn't have that time."

"You don't need to worry. Or to want for anything." He fumbled in his pocket with his ringed hand and withdrew a stack of folded money as thick as the unfinished steak on his plate. He peeled a few bills from the outside.

"I don't want your money."

"He would want you to have this. Consider it his salary. He

still works for me." Mosko laid the bills on the table, but Rose kept her hands in her lap and her eyes on his face. He looked at something behind her and nodded. His man must have returned. "Mrs. Margolin," he said, rising from his chair, "you have my word. I will do what I can for your husband. Before the week is out, I'll bring you some news. But now, if you will excuse me, I have a funeral to attend. One of my men is not in jail. He is in a coffin. His family, too, has needs. Lenny will see you safely home." He nodded at the man behind her and extended his hand.

She stood and took his outstretched hand. He closed his other hand over hers and pressed gently. She turned to go, noticing the bills on the table had disappeared.

Lenny accompanied her to the door and exited along with her. "I'll be happy to drive you home, courtesy of Mr. Mosko."

"Thank you. I'll walk." Rose said. She sped away, needing to distance herself quickly. Her courage was failing. As soon as she turned the first corner, out of sight of the Imperial Café and Lenny and Saul Mosko, she stopped and leaned against the wall for support. She took several deep breaths and then placed her hand against her heart. It had been racing for the better part of an hour.

When she felt rested enough to walk, she continued down the unfamiliar street. Without Earl Bloom as an escort, she wasn't certain which way to turn. She headed east, to the ocean. She'd find her way from there.

It was only later, after she'd collapsed onto her couch at home and searched for a handkerchief in her purse, that she found the bills nestled at the bottom.

Isador

At first, Isador balked. "I didn't shoot anyone. Hell, I didn't even fire the gun. I had it in my hand and when the shit started I, I...the gun wouldn't fire. It jammed. They might be able to examine it and see I'm telling the truth," Isador said, wondering how convincing he sounded. He'd told no one that when the first shots rang out, he'd panicked and cowered behind an upended table. Instead, he invented his own version of what had happened. He continued, exactly as he'd rehearsed. "Bullets were flying everywhere. Anyone could have fired the shot that killed Elmer. Even Earl or Gene. Who knows?"

Kilcourse nodded and pursed his lips. He said nothing.

"Did you ever try talking to the cops?" Isador pressed on. "Maybe they were the ones that shot him. The whole thing was one big piece of bad luck. Fuck. No one was supposed to get hurt."

Kilcourse rocked back and forth, his hands clasped over his stomach.

"Say something for God's sake."

"I've told you, Isador. He doesn't want any more of his men exposed. Gene and Earl made it away without being seen. Earl was hit, you know. He's still walking around with a limp. And they've both done time before. It would go down harder for them. They might never see the light of day. As far as the police go, you can be sure their weapons have been cleared or if your speculations are right, they've 'disappeared.' They're probably somewhere at the bottom of the ocean right now."

"So I get to take the rap? That's it? It's a goddamn done deal?"

"I'm afraid so. However, like during your last brief incarceration, you'll be taken care of. If—"

"Yeah, if I keep my trap shut. If I don't implicate anyone else."

"Mrs. Margolin will be looked after, too."

At Kilcourse's reference to Rose, the anger evident in the lines on Isador's forehead mellowed. He was grateful for Mr. Mosko's help and what he thought awaited him on his release, the single bright spot in his future. "How many months do you think?" he asked.

Kilcourse withdrew a neatly folded white square from his pocket and wiped his forehead. He took his time returning it to his pocket. "We could be looking at more than a few months."

"Huh? You mean years? Christ! Jesus fucking Christ."

"We will throw ourselves on the mercy of the court. We will claim it was an accident."

"Ourselves?" Isador slammed his fist and stood, towering over Kilcourse. "In case you hadn't noticed, there's no one but me on this side of the goddamn table."

The trial was over before it started, at least it seemed that way to Isador. Kilcourse had predicted as much, preparing Isador for what would happen once he entered a guilty plea. Isador sat before the judge, saying nothing, staring at the pattern made by the grain of wood in the table, imagining a cloud formation, a river draining into the ocean, a face. He could not testify in his defense, could not say he had never fired his weapon, could not mention the names of others present at the time, could not proclaim his innocence. The only words Kilcourse allowed him were printed in the attorney's hand on a piece of paper. When at last the judge asked if the "accused" had anything to say, Isador stood and read, "Your honor, I am deeply sorry for the result of my actions. I humbly ask for mercy from the court."

He received a sentence of ten years. *Some mercy*, he thought sarcastically.

After the judge delivered the verdict, Isador turned to Rose, who'd sat behind him during the proceeding, sniffling into her handkerchief every few minutes. She came to her feet at once, the alarm on her face evident. He wanted to put his arms around her to comfort her, but as before, two officers slapped handcuffs around his wrists and swept him from the courtroom.

Kilcourse tried to reassure him by saying no one actually served the whole term. He'd be out in four or maybe five. *Five fucking years.*

Hell Gate

With its darkened interior, Hell Gate simulated a descent into hell. Riders of this Wonderland amusement boarded small boats that meandered through narrow tunnels and "fell" into the abyss near the end of the ride before emerging once again into the bright sunlight of a summer's day near Revere Beach.

Rose

MONDAY MORNING. ROSE TURNED OVER IN BED. SHE'D SLEPT, AS always, in one place on her side of the bed, the side facing the window. No one thrashed about on the other side, nudging her to the edge and rolling away, the covers going with them like a receding wave. Invariably, when she rose, she found the sheets and blanket on the far side turned down and folded as neatly as the moment she'd crawled into bed the night before.

She delayed rising as long as she could, anticipating the chill of the bare floor against her feet as she never remembered to place her slippers where she could find them. She hopped from the bed, wrapped her arms around herself, and scurried to the closet for her robe and slippers. Then she smoothed her side of the bed until it was a mirror image of the other half.

Rose put a pot of coffee on the stove. It had taken her weeks to adjust to making one serving. Standing at the kitchen sink, she drank her coffee in deafening silence, not bothering to savor it as she'd done in the past, seated across the table from Isador, his running commentary on the news or his plans filling the kitchen with the sounds of a life with a future. Rose rinsed her cup and checked the pot. She'd wasted nothing.

Sometimes when she left for work, she found Jacob leaving for school at the same time. It happened so often that she suspected he watched the front of her building and waited for her to step into the street before making his way to his own front door. His cousins had gone ahead or were late, he'd say. Either way, they walked together along Shirley Avenue heading inland. Then, he'd turn to the right and she to the left. Often, before she'd gone another block, she'd sense his presence and turn to see him observing her from where they'd separated. Only after she waved and made a shooing motion with her hand did he turn and scamper on to school.

Denial, sorrow, and anger had been her companions in the weeks after Isador's sentencing. Acceptance finally came when she stood in front of the mirror and forced herself to say the words aloud: "Isador is not coming home anytime soon." He might be gone for a decade, though she refused to let her thoughts spring that far ahead.

She filled the hours of solitude with borrowed magazines, Addie's fashion magazines and occasionally one of Genie's issues of *Picture Play*, full of gossip about vaudeville and the cinema. Isador would have disapproved and chided her endlessly for wasting her time on such insignificant fare. But the light subjects took her mind off her situation, and for the first time, she had something to add to Addie's otherwise one-way dialogue about celebrities and the latest styles.

"Oh, don't you just adore this little number?" Addie would ask during lunch, the latest shade of polish on her fingertip pointing at a scandalously short skirt featured in one of her periodicals. "I wonder if I would have the courage to wear something like that. Hugh would probably box my ears and toss me into the street."

"I can't say I'd have the gumption either. It's the latest thing, though. Times are changing."

"Aren't they ever? Oh, I have the last issue for you. I finished it yesterday." Addie fumbled in her bag and withdrew the November issue of *Ladies Home Journal*. On the cover was a blonde in a peignoir. She was pictured alone, but Rose imagined that she was gazing at an admirer just outside the frame. Addie handed the magazine to Rose. "Keep it for yourself. I've thumbed through it so many times, I think I've worn the print off."

Rose was the sole breadwinner in the Margolin household, her earnings no longer a supplement to Isador's wages. She'd signed on full time with Tillinghast's. The work took her mind off her situation. And every hour she worked at Tillinghast's was one less she spent alone before bed.

On one of her visits to the state penitentiary, Rose had told Isador about working full time. She expected a pat on the back, but he'd scowled. "You don't need to work full time," he'd said. "Only lower class women or widows work full time. They have to."

Rose lacked the heart to explain that without his income she had in fact joined the ranks of the lower class and had more in common with the widows he mentioned than he realized. But Isador had always lived blissfully ignorant of the status of their household finances, not the least bit curious as to how much came in the door, and worse, how much leaked out each crack and crevice. Rose, on the other hand, kept scrupulous records. She knew how close to the brink that had appeared when Isador walked away from Forman & Forman Tailors and later from Logrin's.

After listening to him fume and leaving him to return to his cell in a foul humor, her own mood little better, Rose vowed not to mention the subject again. On the next visit, if he asked, she'd find a way to change the subject or claim to have heeded his advice. A small lie, if necessary, but one that would keep the peace. Isador appeared to have enough issues of his own anyway. The last time she'd seen him, he'd not shaved and on one side of his head his hair lay flat while it stood practically erect on the other.

She also chose not to mention that Esther made a point of bringing food to Rose whenever she stopped by for lunch or dinner. Esther would claim she and Daniel had far too much roast for the family to finish or she'd baked a double batch of something "by mistake" and didn't want it to spoil, and surely Rose would avail herself of some for dinner, and besides, wasn't she looking frail, and had she lost weight and on and on. Esther would lecture without taking a breath until Rose agreed to a bite of whatever she'd brought.

Rose had not been too proud to accept her sister's offering. Although she had the means to stock her pantry if she shopped carefully, she had difficulty summoning the energy and desire to cook.

1922. A new year. Rose's life had returned to normal, albeit a new normal, days during the week at Tillinghast's, days on the weekends cleaning, mending, or reading, nights survived.

"Cesareo. Guilty. Cesareo. Guilty of Murder. Verdict just in. Cesareo." The newspaper boy on the corner barked the headlines about a verdict rendered after a recent gang shooting. A man tossed the boy a coin and walked away with the latest news tucked under his arm.

The nightmare of Mosko's world blanketed Revere like snow. She supposed it had always been there and that she had just been oblivious, denying its existence or looking the other way as so many others did. Rose hurried past, heading home from work, refusing to look at the boy and his papers, much less purchase a copy and take the gang-related news into her home. Wind off the ocean, though blocks away, roared through the channel of brick-lined streets. She tugged the edges of her coat close around her and clutched the ends of the collar together with one hand. At the end of each block, she switched hands, plunging the first, cold and stiff, into her pocket. She'd spent every day of her twenty-three years in this town, but had never become accustomed to its winters.

Rose forced her thoughts to spring, when the leaves first appeared, crinkled like a newborn baby, unfolding, spreading and stretching as they welcomed the season. Even summer was better than winter, though most of her neighbors abhorred the hot days with heat rising from the pavement until they swore the walls outside their windows would melt into the ground. They'd flee to the streets, sit on the stoops or rooftops, and hold the collars of their blouses open to any passing puff of fresh air.

But with months of bone-chilling cold ahead, there was no point dreaming about spring or summer. Rose huddled against a store window to put her back to the wind, if only for a few minutes. Visible in the window's reflection, a car came to a stop behind her. For the last several blocks, she'd been barely conscious of it inching its way down the street and too cold to bother to look around. She squinted into the window at the reflection while examining the store window's contents. Rose cupped her hands in front of her mouth and blew on them, though her breath had the opposite effect of what she'd intended. Her fingers shone with a glint of moisture that the cold would turn to ice in short order.

She rammed one hand into her coat pocket and turned. A

few steps later, a rapping sound caught her attention. The car had rolled forward. Someone tapped the glass.

"Mrs. Margolin," a man's voice called through the inch of space above the lowered window. Rose squinted. Her reflection on the glass stared back. She could not make out who'd called her name, only the rough outline of a man's head and shoulders. "Mrs. Margolin, please forgive me, I didn't mean to startle you." The voice was familiar. The odd melding of one word and another. The overly polite phraseology. It was Saul Mosko. Rose tightened her grip on the edges of her collar, her knuckles white from more than the cold. "Ah! Yes. It is you," he said. "I thought so." Rose stood stock still. He lowered the window another couple of inches, revealing his face, perhaps thinking she had not recognized him. "Please. Please allow me to drive you wherever you are headed. It's much too cold to walk in this weather, even a few blocks."

All of the reasons why she should not accept Mr. Mosko's offer ticked off in her head and in the balance the one reason to accept, the cold. A fresh blast of ocean wind screamed through the street, forcing Rose's hand to her head to secure her hat. Five or six long blocks lay ahead. She shivered. The door to the car opened. Rose stepped forward and took a seat inside, the enveloping warmth worth any risk she could imagine at the moment. The door closed with a solid click and the driver, Lenny, the man who'd offered her a ride home from the Imperial Café, resumed his seat at the wheel.

"I am so glad you allowed me this service," Mosko continued. "What address would you like?"

Rose rubbed her hands back and forth. She croaked, "51-3B Nahant," her throat parched from the cold, dry air. Lenny, who'd turned an ear to the back of the car, nodded, turned back, and then steered the car from the curb. Rose sat perched on the edge of the seat, not daring to allow herself to relax into the comfort of the cushion, not daring to sit any closer than she must to the gang leader, her husband's boss.

She'd grown used to thinking of Mr. Mosko in those terms, as her husband's boss, even with Isador behind bars. Last November, the first month after his incarceration at the state penitentiary in Charlestown, she'd gone to her landlord's home to pay her rent. Mr. Gopen looked at the cash in her hand with a befuddled expression. He dragged a ledger from his desk drawer and read aloud from it, "Nahant, 61, 57, 55. Yes, here it is, 51. And, 3B." He stabbed the page at the check mark in ink under the column "Paid." He looked at her, his eyebrows arched into perfect peaks.

"Oh. I must have forgotten. Silly me. I'm sorry to have troubled you," had been all she could say. At first, she thought the trauma of Isador's sentencing had eclipsed her memory. Then, in December, when she returned to Mr. Gopen's, she found again the rent had been paid. This time, Rose was prepared. Rather than leave her landlord with the impression she was distraught or worse, a tad deranged, before she handed Mr. Gopen the money, she inquired if had it been paid. Again, he took the ledger from the drawer of his desk and showed her his entries and checkmarks.

"Paid in full," he said. "I trust you are well, Mrs. Margolin."

Rose nodded. She groped for something to say. "Yes. I'm quite well." She paused and then added, "Thank you."

"You know you may call on me anytime should you need

something. Someone to lend a hand, a loan, or to fix something around the house."

"I'm quite well," she repeated. "That won't be necessary." That he knew someone was paying her rent was one thing. Having him meddle any further in her affairs was quite another.

Mosko's car pulled alongside the entry to 51 Nahant. Outside, snow was falling, swirling with each gust of wind. Rose shivered in anticipation of stepping back into the frosty air and climbing the stairs to her cold and empty apartment.

Lenny opened the car door and stepped aside. Rose exited, muttered a quick thank you over her shoulder, and hurried inside without another word or glance.

"Psst. Psst." A voice beckoned from behind the millinery counter. "There's a package for you, Miss Margolin." Only one side of Wilfred's face was visible through the crack in the door behind her counter. Wilfred worked in the mail room. He was a shy boy and rarely, if ever, showed himself on the sales floor.

"Well, bring it to me, Wilfred," she said.

"Oh no, Miss Margolin. I'll leave it for you in the millinery mail slot."

"Really, Wilfred. It's okay for you to bring it to me, but I'll come find you on my break, if you prefer." Mail? A package? At work? Before the visible half of Wilfred's face receded from the opening, she said, "What's the postmark?"

"There's no postmark," Wilfred said. "It came by delivery."

"Okay, wait just a minute."

Her curiosity had overcome her sense of decorum. Rose

craned her neck to see the opposite side of the sales floor where Mabel, a fellow sales clerk, wiped fingerprints from the glass over her counter. Rose sprinted across the floor. "Mabel, could you watch my station? I'll be back in a jiffy." The word "jiffy" was the ladies' code for needing to visit the washroom outside of breaks.

"Sure thing," Mabel said, without looking up from her position, eye-level with the counter, scanning the glass for any remaining smudges.

Rose hurried back to her station and through the half open door where Wilfred waited. He proceeded down the hall with Rose in tow, as excited as a child about to receive a gift.

Outside the cubbyhole where Wilfred sorted the mail and stored brooms and mops—he also doubled as the store's janitor—he excused himself a moment, ducked inside, and returned with a small, flat package wrapped in the store's distinctive gift paper, a pattern of Tillinghast crests stamped in silver on a smoky gray background.

"Here you are," Wilfred said, handing her the package.

Rose turned the box over. "Was there a card?"

"No, ma'am. Just the package and instructions to deliver it to you."

Too excited to wait until later to unwrap the package, Rose slid her finger under the flap of familiar paper and tore it from the box. A small cry escaped her lips. Inside, beneath tissue secured with a red ribbon, lay a pair of leather gloves with lambs-wool lining.

"Those sure are nice gloves, Mrs. Margolin."

Earl

"Is there some place we can talk?" Rose asked.

Rose Margolin had located his apartment and then waited outside on the chance she'd find him coming or going. Earl wondered what the Poshansky's thought seeing a refined woman like Mrs. Margolin in the street opposite his building.

"There's a coffee shop on the corner. A couple of blocks that way," Earl said, cocking his head to the left. In the window above the street where Earl and Rose stood, someone had drawn back the curtains. Earl caught a glimpse of a hand, tendons and bones prominent and puckered with arthritis, more like a bird's claw than a human hand. Mrs. Poshansky. Ever since he'd borrowed her husband's cane and joined them for dinner, the couple had taken an interest in him and his daily activities. On his way down the stairs, if he happened to step on the outside of the second stair from the top, it would creak and bring one or the other of the two to the door. "How's the leg today," Mr. Poshansky might ask. "Need the cane? Looks like we're in for a cold one today. Don't forget your gloves." Or any one of a number of innocuous greetings meant to entice him to linger.

Mrs. Poshansky was at the window with her face pressed against the glass. She smiled, glanced at the woman with Earl, and waved. Rose had turned away. Earl nodded at Mrs. Poshansky, no doubt she approved of what she imagined to be his new woman friend.

Rose did not speak the entire way, so Earl made himself content to breathe the faint aroma of lilies in the air around her and listen to the click of her heels on the sidewalk. Twice, hoping she didn't notice, he angled his head to the side to watch the way her skirt flounced beneath the hem of her coat after each step.

At the corner, he reached for the door, but Rose ignored his attempt to be a gentleman and strode through. Her affront was a small wound to his psyche, one tiny prick of a needle. Two elderly women rose from a table beside the door. He waited for them and held the door to show Rose he had manners. The women nodded as they passed.

Earl motioned Rose to an empty table in bright light and away from the window, assuming she wanted to meet in plain sight but not at a table on display to every passerby. Rose removed her hat and gloves. When he offered to take her coat, she shook her head. He wondered if she were cold or just avoiding contact.

A waitress came, took their order, and left, returning in no time with two coffees. Rose, who had been scanning the room, lowered her eyes and added a teaspoon of sugar to her cup. While she stirred her coffee, for what to Earl was an extraordinarily long time, he waited, matching her silence. Around them, though, conversation buzzed. Glasses, cups, and saucers clattered together. Forks and knives rubbed against the china.

Earl broke the silence. While Rose had been bold enough to seek him out, once she found herself face to face with him, he figured she'd lost her nerve. "How can I help you, Mrs. Margolin?"

Rose took a sip from her cup. She set it back on the table and stared into the steaming brew as if the answer were there.

"I don't know what to do. I don't know what I am supposed to do."

"On what account?"

"On Isador's account, of course. On getting him released."

"Of course."

"I've tried everything I know to do. I was wondering if there's something you could suggest? Something I've over-looked. You surely have more experience in these matters. Isador told me you had once..."

When she hesitated, Earl filled in the rest of her sentence, "Been in the..." then, he hesitated too, taking in the polite company surrounding their table, "been at Charlestown."

"Yes, exactly. Is there something you would advise me to do?"

"Have you been to see Mr. Kilcourse?"

"Yes. And, of course, he claims he's working on an appeal and says I should be patient. But he seems to be taking such a long time."

"Who else?"

"Well, as you know, I spoke to Mr. Mosko. He also told me to be patient."

"Yes. Patience is in order."

"I was thinking, perhaps you could do something. You were there that night. You must know what happened. What if you went to the police?"

Earl tried to arrange his face as he'd seen Mosko do when pressed, his brow smooth, nostrils and lips relaxed, as bland a countenance as if a curtain had been drawn over his face. But Earl guessed he'd flinched or blinked too rapidly because Rose rushed to add, "Not to turn yourself in, of course. Just to tell the authorities that Isador did not shoot that man. They won't listen to me. I tried to see them, but they just shoo me away."

Earl held back, letting Rose continue.

"I don't think Isador can make it much longer. Much less survive five years there."

Rose paused.

"Five years?" Earl said.

"That's how long Mr. Kilcourse thinks it might be before he'll be considered for parole. I'm afraid for his health and for his state of mind."

Earl sensed her desperation. Her eyes darted back and forth from one of his eyes to the other as if each belonged to a different person—if one eye did not hold the answer, perhaps the other did. Her hands were in her lap, hidden from him. He imagined she clasped and unclasped her fingers, made fists and clenched and unclenched them, over and over.

"I see you've given this a lot of thought."

"Every waking moment. And then, at night, I lie awake thinking there's something I've overlooked, someone I haven't spoken to."

"You did the right thing by coming to me. Not that I have the answers, but I can try to help. If you'll let me." Earl stirred his coffee though he'd not added cream or sugar. He took a deep breath, kept his eyes on his cup, and said, "I have so much to make up for."

"I'll do whatever you say," she answered, latching on to the slightest ray of optimism in his response and ignoring, if she heard it, his attempt at an apology and hope for reconciliation.

"I don't have any suggestions at the moment. And I'm not sure that I can do anything, anything at all. My guess is that he'll have to serve a good portion of his sentence." Rose exhaled and her shoulders slumped. Immediately, Earl regretted not being more optimistic. He was unaccustomed to speaking to ladies over cups of coffee, or for that matter, speaking to ladies at all. He didn't count Caroline and Emily as ladies. Nor any of the other women he paid for sex. "I'm only trying to level with you, Mrs. Margolin," adding her name to approach her on a more personal level, though he dared not go so far as to use her given name. "Let me do some checking before I say anything more."

With that tiny glimmer of hope, her eyes brightened. "Oh. Please. Take whatever time you need, if you think you can help."

"Your other comment, um...Oh. Yes. You mentioned Isador's 'state of mind.' His health. Is he in a bad way, that is, is he sick?"

"Well, he coughs a lot. It's been a hard winter and I am sure the conditions inside are deplorable. I wonder every night if he has a blanket. I wonder if he's able to see a doctor."

"Has he complained of being sick?"

"No, but when I ask, he turns his head or changes the subject."

"What do you think is wrong?" Despite his sincere desire to help Rose, Earl's highest priority was to discover if Isador's resolve was weakening, if he posed a threat to the gang. He needed to know if Isador might be desperate enough to talk, to tell what he knew or name names.

"I can't put my finger on it, exactly. He's just, well, 'morose' I suppose is the right word."

"Morose."

"Yes, morose. It's like—"

"Yes, I know what it means—"

"Oh, I meant no offense, Mr. Bloom. I don't know how to describe it any better."

When Rose spoke his name, the chasm between them narrowed, at least it seemed so to Earl. He shifted in his seat, pulling his shoulders back and his chin up. "No offense taken, Mrs. Margolin," Earl said, scrambling to cover his abruptness. "Charlestown can be very lonely and depressing, I know, but I can tell you what got me through."

"What's that?" Rose leaned closer.

"I made a few friends. And if you can't be home with your family, at least you can have some chums close by to share your time."

"I hardly think Isador will find friends there."

"Don't be too sure. I might be able to do something about that. We need to make sure he knows people are looking out for him."

"I'd be forever in your debt."

"No, ma'am, not at all, it's my debt to you."

Rose's eyelids flickered, a momentary hesitation, but one Earl caught. What he'd done could never be undone and would never be forgiven, even if the memory of it collapsed and faded with the years. The memory lived somewhere deep inside them both and made their eyes twitch.

"Was there anything else?" he asked.

"Only, ah...Mr. Mosko." She paused. Her cup was empty and bought her no more time.

"Mr. Mosko?"

"Yes. He's been very kind. He pays Isador's wages to me, but—" she stopped abruptly and bit her lip. "Well, no. I'm sorry. Nothing else."

Clearly, Rose had more to say, but Earl did not press her. He'd made a huge leap forward. Best to end on a positive note. "Well, you've nothing to worry about. You'll see. Mr. Mosko is a man of honor. He will make sure Isador is safe."

A flicker of a smile crossed her lips, but her eyes showed doubt.

Isador

"HEY, BOOK, YOU'VE GOT A VISITOR," LEROY, THE SECOND floor guard at Charlestown, called out as he passed Isador's cell.

Isador bolted upright. "What? What's the date?" He knew it was Sunday, since he'd returned to his cell after breakfast rather than reporting for duty as he would every other day of the week. But he couldn't recall which Sunday it was. Visiting day was the third Sunday. He snapped shut the book he'd been reading, a travelogue of a visit to Italy, and set it beside him on the cot. On the wall to his right, a calendar displayed the page for January with its thirty-one small squares, barely enough room to mark an appointment or anniversary or any other important event. In November and December, Isador had waited until the "lights out" call at nine o'clock in the evening and then drawn an X through each day filling the squares. He'd soon tired of the effort. The squares for January were blank, empty, unmarked.

Leroy called over his shoulder, "Five minutes." Isador scrambled to his feet, pulled a comb from the cup on his sink. He felt for the natural crease along the top of his head with the fingers of his left hand and combed his hair without benefit of a mirror, as he'd become accustomed to doing. Then he brushed his teeth with the tooth powder he'd purchased from the penitentiary's store and ran his hand over his chin. The stubble was noticeable but it would have to do.

The metallic clink of a jumble of keys announced Leroy's return. Isador liked Leroy. Everyone did, but in his case, Isador thought the feeling was mutual. Leroy lingered at Isador's cell a bit longer than he did with the others, always making idle conversation or asking about whatever Isador was reading or sharing a smoke when Isador ran low.

When Leroy unlocked Isador's cell, Isador slid through the narrow opening and formed a line with two other waiting prisoners. Leroy took point and led the group away, a second guard falling in behind. As he followed in Leroy's footsteps, Isador had a clear view of the bald spot on the back of the man's head. Leroy barely reached Isador's chest. The old man walked slumped over, his chest a backward C, compacted with phlegm. He wheezed constantly, and at night, the sound carried as far as two corridors away. Beneath the cavernous sleeves of his uniform, his arms were no bigger around than the spindles on a kitchen chair. Anyone who wanted to could overtake the man with a single punch to the jaw.

The visitors' room teemed with people as it did every month on visiting day, but Isador easily spotted Rose amid the throng. Dressed in shell pink from head to toe, she sat in an area of relative calm, her hands on her lap, her eyes on the door, somehow ignoring the chaos around her. Flocks of children scampered between the tables and chairs, gay and without understanding, men and women chatted, some even laughed. Isador, a wide smile on his face, waved to Rose. He strode across the room through a pattern of light and dark stripes cast by the requisite bars on the floor to ceiling windows.

His mood brightened when he came beside her. Unlike the Suffolk County Jail, the penitentiary allowed physical contact.

Isador wrapped his wife in his arms and planted a kiss on the top of her head and another on her lips when she lifted her face. "You are more beautiful than ever," he said. "Let me look at you." He straightened his elbows and held her at arm's length.

"Don't make such a fuss, Isa."

"Book."

"Book?"

"Yes. That's what everybody calls me here."

"What for? Or should I ask?"

"Sit. Sit," he waved a hand at their end of a shared table. At the opposite end, a couple sat with their heads close, deep in a conversation of hushed and hurried words of all that had passed in the world outside since their last visit.

"Isa—"

"Shush, shush." For his part, Isador preferred to say less and feast on the sight of his wife. He tilted his head from side to side until she shifted uncomfortably in her chair. "You look splendid," he said, "if not a bit thin. Are you eating enough?"

"I'm fine. Don't worry about me. And I'm happy to see you looking better than the last time I visited."

"I am better. I got a job here. One of the better ones."

"A job? Doing what?"

"I work in the library."

"I had no idea there was such a thing in..."

"In prison. Yes. We're the beneficiary of one of those *shiksa* do-gooder societies."

"Isa," Rose interrupted, casting furtive glances left and right, "you shouldn't speak like that."

"What are they going to do? Tack on a month?"

"Don't even joke about that."

"Anyway, I'm in charge of working with the Ladies of St. Michael's and their Incarceration and Reform Benefit Society. They raise money for the 'humane' treatment of the prisoners and some of it goes to books. I guess I'm one of the few smart enough to sort through what we get, organize it, and sometimes suggest what we'd like to have. But best of all, I get to read everything new that comes in. That's what prompted the nickname. Someone said all I ever do is sit on my bunk with my nose stuck in a book."

"I'm sure having a job helps pass the time."

"You bet it does. Guess what?"

"I have no idea. What?"

"I've been reading about Italy. And I'm making a list of all the places we're going to go and things we're going to see. Rome, Florence, Venice. Did you know Rome's Colosseum is the largest amphitheater in the world? And all along I thought our own Fenway held the record. You know, in Venice, they have all these canals. I've read you can rent a gondola to tour the city by boat. You might like to see the glass blowing demonstrations and then, then..." When the words had run out, he studied Rose to gauge her enthusiasm, but her head was turned away and her eyes rested on a young girl sitting on her father's lap. "So, what do you think?"

"I'm sorry, Isa. Think about what?"

"About Italy, Rose. Italy. Did you hear any of what I just said?"

"Yes, Rome, Venice. I'm sure Italy is a wonderful place."

"We'll have to decide, though."

"Decide what?"

"Whether we want to see Italy first or whether we want to go to London and then to the continent."

"It's a long way off, Isa. Right now—"

"Long way? Well, Hell, I guess it is. I know exactly how long it is," Isador said, his voice rising and his brows diving into the furrow between them. He exhaled sharply and then tried to draw a good breath. His eyes shifted to the bright light outside the windows, unable to fathom what a breath of truly fresh air felt like.

"I just meant—"

"Do you have any idea how long it is? I bet you can't tell me how many days I've been in here, or how many days I've got to go. Can you? It probably doesn't matter to you."

"You can't mean that. Of course it matters to me. All of your plans matter to me," she said, fumbling to find a handkerchief in the purse tucked beside her on the seat. She dabbed at her eyes.

"Oh Rose, I didn't mean to make you cry. It's just that this is all I have. Thinking about our future, thinking about any place but here."

"It's all right. I can't begin to imagine how hard it is."

"It's rough," he said, leaning close. "I've been thinking, too, about other things."

"Like what?"

"Like how I can get out of here."

"I wish there were a way. I'd give anything to have you home again. Anything. I went to see Mr. Kilcourse and that man, Bloom."

"You did what? Why would you go see Earl?"

"I didn't want to leave any stones unturned. I had to ask if there were something more I could do on my own. That attorney of yours hasn't said a word."

"So, what did Earl say?"

Rose shook her head and fixed her eyes on her lap. "Not much. Only that he would try to help make sure you have what you need here."

"Have what I need?" Blood rushed to his head again. "Have what I need? How would he know what I need?"

"Well, you said he'd spent time here. And he said he knew how awful it was."

"He did, huh? What else did Mr. Bloom say?"

Rose looked toward the windows. "Nothing. Just that."

"He didn't do anything, did he?" Isador asked, knowing Earl's temperament and persuasive abilities. "Like try to take advantage of you? Nothing like that?"

"No. No, of course not," she said.

Isador noticed a flush in her cheeks, the slightest blush of peach. When he looked again, it had gone. "You stay away from him. You don't know what he's capable of."

On the third Sunday in February, Rose did not show. Isador worried all day and throughout the night. He sent word to Gerald Kilcourse asking him to check on his wife, hoping he could find out if she were all right. The cumbersome communication process took longer than he liked. Yesterday, he'd turned the page on the calendar to March and still had not heard a word. He had close to three weeks to sit in his cell and worry before the next visitors' day.

After finishing his breakfast, another bowl of the usual Sunday fare, Isador sat cross-legged on his cot, an article on Tuthmosis III in the *Journal of Egyptian Archaeology* in his lap. The scholarly journal included black and white plates of a glass chalice and other finds from recent archaeological explorations. He hadn't actually read the journal, just looked at the plates and their captions. Three times. Mrs. Titorchook from the Ladies of St. Michael's had donated the journal to the library. She showed it to Isador, holding it in front of her as if it were the chalice itself on a silver tray, her face flush with expectancy, sure he would share her excitement.

"These are some of the very latest discoveries," she said. "My late husband, God rest his soul, and I had a chance to visit Egypt and to see the pyramids. They are astonishingly beautiful even, of course, as ruins."

"I hope to see them one day myself," he'd replied.

"Oh?" A look of surprise flashed across Mrs. Titorchook's face, as if she'd noticed a wart on his nose or seen him sprout horns. She'd not likely imagined him anywhere but here in the penitentiary and one of the presumed grateful recipients of her charity. "That's a noble goal, Mr. Margolin. You should make a point of reading up on it then."

Isador closed the journal and rested his head against the wall. *I was crazy to think I'd ever see the pyramids or stand in front of the Sphinx beside the likes of Mrs. Titorchook and ladies from Boston's high society. I'll never see Egypt or any of the other places on my list.* Isador threw the journal at the wall, knocking the calendar loose. Both the calendar and the book slid down the wall, hit the edge of the sink, and vanished under his cot.

"Hey, man," Harris said. "What's up?" Harris, his cellmate, had been napping on his bunk when the thud from the book woke him. He'd bolted upright.

"I'm so tired of this goddamn place," Isador said.

"Well, you better figure something out 'cause you aren't going anywhere." Harris rubbed his knuckles over his eyes and propped himself on his elbows.

"I'm not going to rot in here for the next nine and a half years. I'll figure something out."

"Far as I see, you got three options," Harris said. He placed one foot and then another on the floor and sat on his bunk to face Isador. He counted the possibilities on the fingers of his right hand. "One. You can get sick and die and they can carry you out of here."

"What if I get sick and go to a hospital."

"Doesn't work that way, man. You get sick, you'll be lucky to see a doctor. Or maybe they'll give you a powder, but you won't see no hospital. No hospital with all them sweet ass nurses. Nope, you get a powder and back to work. You don't get better, you die."

Isador grunted.

"Two. Your lawyer finds the guy who really blipped off the dead guy and he confesses. Like you said, you're innocent. Right?"

"Right."

"Now what are the odds on that one?"

"Not good."

"That's what I thought."

The prison block horn bleated eight o'clock, time for their hour of exercise in the prison yard. Isador and Harris rose to their feet and approached the bars, waiting for the sound of Leroy's rubber-soled shoes on the concrete. "What's three?"

"Three? Well, that's where you start yapping. Talking to the guards, then the warden, and then the police. Telling them what they want to know."

"What would I be able to tell them?"

Keys jangled in the adjacent cell, halting their conversation. Then Leroy stood outside their cell. "Morning, gents," his daily salutation at each cell. Isador had a bet with Harris on whether Leroy would ever vary his greeting.

"Morning," they replied in unison, the edges of Isador's lips twisted upward in a smirk. He turned to the left, lining up behind the two men from the adjacent cell and Harris fell in behind him. Harris handed Isador a cigarette, passing it over his shoulder. Leroy continued on to the next cell.

With his voice lowered, Isador cocked his head over his shoulder and continued, "What would they be looking for?"

"Plenty. Names. Places. Who works for whom. Who's on the take. Whatever."

"I'm no goddamn snitch," Isador said, his voice rising with his anger. The inmate ahead turned and eyed Isador.

"Pipe down, Book," Harris said. "I didn't say you were. Relax. You asked."

"That's it? Nothing else? Just those three?"

"That's it."

Rose

FOR THE ENTIRE THIRD WEEK OF FEBRUARY, ROSE HAD THOUGHT of nothing more than the upcoming visiting day. On Saturday, she searched through her closet and selected one of Isador's favorite outfits. She hung her choice on the back of the bedroom door, set out her shoes, hat, and gloves, and then found a chain of beads to compliment the drop-waist sheath's lemon yellow sash. For what promised to be a dreary day, another overcast late winter day, she thought the bright color might cheer Isador.

Sometime in the middle of the night, however, Rose woke, shivering in the cold. She groped about for the covers, finding them in a heap on the floor and the sheet beneath her wet with sweat. She felt her head with the back of her hand, confirming her suspicion. She had a fever. After pulling the covers tight around her and tucking them under her chin, she fell back asleep. Then, at first light, she tried to get out of bed, stumbling only as far as the bathroom in time to heave the contents of her stomach into the toilet.

Rose rinsed a washcloth in the sink and held it to her head. Weak with fever, she returned to bed and slept and when she woke again, through heavy-lidded eyes, she saw the yellow dress on the hanger. The dress she'd planned to wear for visiting day. She needed to get up and dress, but her head, feeling as if it were twice its normal weight, held her to the pillow. After another short nap, she rose and wandered into the kitchen, glanced at the coffee pot and the food on the pantry shelves. Her stomach churned.

"Rose? Rose? Yoo-hoo?"

It was Pauline Seidman from downstairs. "Pauline?"

"There you are! I wanted to check—oh my. You look awful."

Rose put a hand to her head and ran her fingers through her hair, pulling it behind her neck. "I was sick last night. Or was it yesterday?"

"I thought you might not be feeling well. That's what I told mother when we didn't see you the whole weekend. I told her I'd go—"

"Whole weekend? What day is it?"

"Monday, of course. Goodness, you have been sick. Is there something—?"

"Monday."

"Yes. And you look like you need to go right back to bed."

Isador. Visiting day. She'd slept through it and could only imagine how disappointed and worried he must have been. Her stomach roiled, disappointment mixing with nausea.

"Can I get you something?"

"No. No. I think I will go back to bed. I'll have to get word to Tillinghast."

"I'll have mother call for you, Rose. You go back to bed. I'll check on you later."

By Tuesday morning, whatever Rose had contracted had subsided. Her stomach ached with hunger, not nausea—another sign the worst was past. Rose draped her robe over her shoulders and headed for the kitchen, propelled forward by just the thought of coffee. She put a slice of bread into the toaster as she waited for the coffee to brew.

Two taps on her door. *Pauline again,* she thought. She glanced at the clock. Almost noon. Two more taps.

Rose stuffed her arms in her robe and then cracked the door open. Black brogues polished to a high shine, the reflection of the hallway lamp glowing like a star opal on the toe, charcoal gray wool, a pinstripe running its length, a black felt fedora between two hands, the right bearing a signet ring. "Oh!"

"Please, Mrs. Margolin. I am so sorry. I didn't mean to startle you."

"I'm not dressed. Give me a minute." Without waiting for Mr. Mosko's reply, she closed the door and sped to her bedroom. She grabbed the yellow sheath from the back of the door and flung it over her head. Her fingers flew as she poked each of the mother-of-pearl buttons through a loop. She double checked to see that she hadn't missed one. Stockings. Shoes. A quick glance in the mirror above her dresser. Her hair lay in tangles about her shoulders. From the top drawer of the dresser she pulled a ribbon, unconcerned whether it matched, and fumbled until something resembling a bow held her hair at the nape of her neck.

She went to the door but stopped a foot short. A thousand thoughts raced through her head. *Apologize for making him wait. Then, send him away. Thank him for checking on me. Wait—how did he know I was ill? How did he know I'd be home? And what did the neighbors think, seeing him come into my building? Tell him I was just going out. Say I was having breakfast.* Only the last was true.

"Mr. Mosko. I...Please," were the only words out of her mouth.

He came into the room, his fine clothes accentuating the faded pattern of peonies on the worn sofa, the unpolished floor, the scatter of dog-eared magazines on the table, the large blank areas in the room. Rose eyed her meager surroundings, as he must have, seeing them as she'd never seen them before.

Words of apology formed in her head. She started to speak when he interrupted. "I apologize for appearing here without notice, but as we turned onto Nahant, Lenny reminded me we were passing your home."

"Oh." Rose said, struggling to find air to create words.

"I thought since it is such an unusually fine day for February you might accompany me for a short drive." It was a statement, not a question. Rose sensed he had little experience with refusals. While she stood transfixed by his appearance in her home, a line of gray smoke wended its way from the kitchen into the living room and along the ceiling, bringing with it an odor of burnt toast.

"Oh." Rose turned and ran toward the kitchen, Mosko in tow.

She pulled open and shut several cabinet drawers as she searched for tongs or a towel.

"Here," he said, lowering the oven door. He extracted the two crusty black squares with his bare hands. He held the nearly unrecognizable pieces of toast aloft, dangling them from his fingertips until she pointed to the trash bin behind the door. "Now I've caused you to ruin your breakfast. My foresight to bring a picnic lunch appears to have been on point. Shall we go?"

Rose found herself passing through the open front door, moving in the direction his hand suggested, moving as if she were sleep walking. Yet she was conscious of him extinguishing the oven behind her, collecting her coat, and retrieving his hat from the floor where he must have dropped it when he'd hurried to the kitchen. She heard the door latch behind them. She was conscious too, in some distant recess of her mind, of the implausibility of his earlier statement. He'd only happened to pass by her apartment, yet he'd also brought a picnic lunch. Beside him, Rose descended the stairs, as if it were he who willed her feet forward.

Lenny drove them toward the ocean and then turned north away from the crowds. He turned the car onto a short gravel road and inched his way to a small rise. There, he got out, spread a blanket on the ground, propped two small folding chairs against the car, and set a lunch basket on the blanket. He walked some yards away, paused to light a cigarette, and took a few more steps in the direction they'd come, whether to afford them privacy or to stand guard, she didn't know. Mosko carried on as though they were alone. He was, she guessed, so accustomed to the bodyguard-chauffeur's presence that he failed to notice the third pair of eyes and ears as they ate and talked.

Later that evening at home, Rose tried to recall details of the afternoon and their conversation. All she remembered was answering questions, or rather responding to Mosko's gentle prodding. She'd told him of her family and her father's work as a tailor. He'd laughed when she'd mentioned her five sisters and no brothers and in effect how she'd grown up under the eyes of not one but six mothers, always pampered as the baby in the family. She'd told him of her work at Tillinghast's, and they'd recounted the circumstances of their first meeting at the millinery counter.

Once, during a break in the conversation, when the silence had lingered too long, she pointed toward the end of the beach. "Look, you can still see where Wonderland used to be," Rose said.

"Wonderland," Mosko said. As always, a statement, not a question.

"I thought surely everyone knew about Wonderland. Of course, I was very young and never had a chance to go there, but—" Rose caught herself, not wanting to bring Isador's name into the conversation. "So I've been told," she continued, explaining the individual amusements in as much detail as she remembered from Isador's descriptions. "There were coasters then and a tunnel of love, like today. Love's Journey, I think it was called. Flying horses and odd things too, a room full of incubators for babies."

Mr. Mosko had gazed into Rose's eyes, hardly blinking his own.

"I'm boring you, aren't I?" she'd asked.

"Not at all. I find it very interesting."

"You're just humoring me."

Rose did remember clearly that neither had mentioned their meeting at the Imperial, Rose's demands, or Isador's name.

"I've had an invitation for dinner," Rose said, as casually as she could.

"That's wonderful," Addie said. She said nothing more for a moment, as if she wanted to avoid showing too much interest, or so Rose thought. Then, when Rose offered nothing more, Addie continued, "You haven't been out in a long time. You need a break from the house."

Rose played Addie's game and munched on a cookie she'd brought from home.

"Who's the invite from?"

"Just a friend."

"Oh."

"A male friend."

"Ah ha."

"Don't go jumping to conclusions. It's hardly worth mentioning. Actually, it's just Isador's old boss."

Addie grunted her disappointment as if she had hoped to hear something more salacious.

"I don't know if I should accept," which was a half-truth though she'd already agreed to go, Rose had her doubts. She had not had the strength to say no to Mr. Mosko. To Addie, she said, "I don't think Isador would want me to go."

"Isador is hardly in a position to say yea or nay, don't you think? Besides, like you said, it's his boss." Then after a moment, "What could be wrong with that?"

"That's what I said."

"You told Isador?"

"No, not yet. I will when I see him."

"Then what are you worried about? Sounds like he's just being considerate. Looking after you. I wouldn't make much of it. You might just say his old boss stopped by to check in on you. Skip the 'out to dinner' part. After all, you can imagine what he might be having for supper himself."

"I suppose you're right. I'll probably have forgotten by the time I see him anyway."

"There you go. Go out. Have a nice time. You deserve it."

The two finished the last bites of their lunch. Addie lit a cigarette. "Where are you going?"

"I'm not sure. He didn't say."

"Do I know him?"

Rose raised the napkin to her lips, folded it, and placed it on the table beside her cup, all with deliberately slow motions, buying time. "No, I don't think you do. I'm sure you don't." Rose crumbled the empty wax paper wrapper into a ball and pushed her chair back from the table. After a quick glance at the clock in the break room, Rose said, "We'd better hurry. We'll be late."

For the next several days, whether at home in the evening, on her way to work, or helping a customer, the idea of having dinner with Mr. Mosko haunted Rose. She'd wake in the wee hours of the morning, thoughts swirling in her head. The next morning, she'd swear to herself that she'd find Mr. Mosko even if she had to go through Mr. Bloom. Rose ran through a litany of options in her head, everything from saying simply that something had come up to explaining in detail that one of her sisters was ill, or that she was not feeling well. She'd discard each one and then go through the alternatives and excuses again until she exhausted herself and fell asleep.

Friday arrived. Rose had done nothing about canceling the appointment—the word she'd chosen for the dinner invitation after convincing herself Mosko was only interested in her well- being. After all, he'd not given her any reason to believe otherwise.

At half past six, she waited, perched on the edge of the sofa and staring straight ahead at nothing. She'd checked her watch every five minutes, combed her hair in the bedroom mirror twice, and smoothed her stockings repeatedly.

At six forty-five, there was a light tap at the door. Rose swallowed and took a deep breath before answering. To her surprise, it was Lenny. He nodded and said Mr. Mosko was waiting downstairs in the car. Flustered and wholly unprepared to offer her excuses to Lenny, Rose grabbed her hat and followed the driver to the bottom floor and out the door. In her imagination, if not in fact, every window in every apartment along Nahant held the silhouette of someone peering down with what Rose imagined was a disapproving sneer, their eyes fixed on the married woman from 51-3B dressed for an evening out and stepping into a sleek, black Pontiac, a car polished to such a high gloss that the dim streetlights twinkled in the fenders and hood. Rose did not have the courage to glance up at the windows.

"Good evening, Rose," Saul Mosko said once she was seated.

"Good evening," she said.

The car pulled away.

"I do hope you like French food. I thought we would have dinner at one of my favorite places in all of Boston, Simone's. Have you eaten there before?"

"No, I can't say that I have." Simone's had a reputation for exquisite food, as well as prices beyond anything Rose could imagine. The dinner would cost five or six times what she and Isador had ever spent for a meal, including their wedding dinner. Lost in her thoughts but suddenly aware of the silence in the car, she blushed and apologized for being distracted.

"It was nothing," he said. "Only idle conversation. I am embarrassed."

"Embarrassed? You?"

"What I meant to say is, I realize now my gift is inappropriate." Mr. Mosko handed Rose a small package, no bigger than a deck of cards. "It's a bottle of perfume. But the scent you are wearing is already very pleasing. Lilies, is it? "

Rose looked at the package and its aquamarine wrapping paper, tied with a matching satin bow. "Mr. Mosko—"

"Saul."

"Mr. Mosko, I can't accept it. It's very kind of you to ask me to dinner, but there is no need for the gift."

"Nonsense. It would give me great pleasure if you wear it on another occasion. Please. Go on," he nudged her hand. "Open it."

Rose threw her purse on the couch and stormed into the bedroom to take off her clothes, burying her dinner dress at the back of the armoire where she hoped she'd never see it again. Though it was near midnight, she ran a bath with the hottest water the pipes had to offer, refusing to let her mind dwell on the events of the evening until she was safely immersed to her neck.

"Aarh," she said aloud. Then again, "Aarh," louder. She didn't care if the neighbors heard. They were surely awake, all those silhouettes waiting by the windows to watch for her return and note the time on their clocks. Eleanor Seidman would no doubt be pacing back and forth at the building's entrance waiting for Rose at dawn the next morning.

Rose grabbed a bar of lavender-scented soap and a sponge and scrubbed every inch of her body, finishing with her face, willing the scalding water to burn the open pores of her skin and erase the feel of Mosko's arm around her shoulder, his hands on her neck and his lips on hers when he'd embraced her outside her door. When she was done scrubbing, Rose began again. Then she closed her eyes and slipped below the water line so nothing, not a toe or knee or tip of her head was exposed to the world. She held her breath, counted to twenty, and then burst through with an explosive gasp for air.

As Rose expected, when she left for work the next day, Eleanor stood outside 51 Nahant, busying herself or, more accurately, pretending to busy herself by sweeping the walk. She had nothing more to show for her labor than an anthill-sized mound of twigs and gravel. "Hello, Eleanor. I see you're up early," Rose said.

"Always. And you, too," she said.

"Not early enough. I promised to be in before eight and look," Rose made a show of pulling back the cuff of her blouse to expose her wristwatch, "it's almost eight now. I'd better hurry. See you later."

Leaving no time for Eleanor to interject one word, Rose skipped past the woman. As soon as she was out of sight, Rose grinned, satisfied that she'd avoided the litany of questions Eleanor would have rehearsed all night and most of the morning. She imagined the bewildered look on Eleanor's face.

Her next challenge was Addie. She regretted having ever mentioned the dinner to Addie. She'd have some explaining to do, and she'd had little practice with nonchalance, let alone outright lying.

No more than five minutes after Rose took up her station, before any customers had arrived, and before Rose had time to set up her display, Addie appeared across the counter. They had plenty of time to chat, but Rose dove into her morning routine, pulling pairs of gloves from the drawers and arranging them to best compliment the hats, scarves, and other accessories under her counter. She turned the items this way and that, feigning rapt attention. Anything to avoid looking Addie in the eye.

"So, I'm dying to hear. How was your dinner?"

"Oh. Thanks for asking. It was fine. Nothing special. I don't know why I even mentioned it."

"Now, what was his name again?"

"How does that look?" Rose asked, hoping to deflect Addie's curiosity. "Do you think the blue scarf goes better with the black or the gray?" Rose peered through the glass into the cabinet, turning her head from side to side.

"I like it set against the gray, seems to bring out the color more."

"I think so, too." Rose dipped below the counter again. "We went to a little café in the North End. The food was so-so. In fact, Isador's dinner might have been better than mine."

"You're probably right. You know, I'm always disappointed when I eat out. I make better meals at home than I've ever had at one of those hoity toity restaurants."

"Speaking of which," Rose seized on Addie's train of thought, "can you write down your recipe for date bars? I'm having dinner with Esther this weekend and I thought maybe I'd make a batch to take with me."

"Only if you give me your special roast chicken, like you promised."

"Deal," Rose said, a smile on her lips—she'd managed the conversation as she planned and the subject of her dinner with Mosko was a thing of the past.

Rose's smug attitude didn't last long. Addie had scribed the recipe from memory on the back of a blank receipt from her clerk's ledger and left it on Rose's counter on her way out at the end of the day. She also left Rose her last few issues of *Movie Weekly* and Sunday's *Boston Post*. Rose tucked the bundle under her arm and carried it home. She was glad to have both the recipe and the periodicals. She was indeed going to see Esther on the weekend and with Addie's recipe she could make one of her favorite desserts to take along. And the magazine and newspaper would provide her a full evening's entertainment.

After dinner, Rose put a pot of tea on the stove. While she waited for the tea to brew, she sat at the kitchen table and flipped through the newspaper. A photograph of sumptuously dressed figures caught her eye. The caption below read "Boston's Gala Affair for Fenway Court." The accompanying article described a social gathering to support the city museum's acquisition of a collection of art. Rose pulled the photograph closer to check the hairstyles and fashions of the high society patrons. She squinted at the profile of a woman in the center, admiring her bobbed hair. Unconsciously, Rose ran her fingers through her own hair. It lay loose around her shoulders. She gathered it in one hand, rolling it up and under. The blunt cut was all the rage. Addie had done hers and encouraged Rose to do the same. But Rose could only imagine Isador's look. He'd be shocked. He had no way of knowing what the latest styles were.

Rose released her hair and studied the photograph again. Dapperly dressed gentlemen stood on both sides of the central figure. One of the men looked familiar. Rose brought the page into better light. Mosko. Rose looked again to be sure. She could hardly believe it, but then again, he had the means and power to rub elbows with the city's upper crust, so why was she surprised.

Tweet. The teapot whistled behind her on the stove. When she returned to the paper, she skimmed the article for more details, pausing once or twice to blow across her cup of hot tea. "Here to welcome the first exhibit of Fenway's latest acquisition were Mr. and Mrs. Leslie Thibault, Mr. and Mrs. Harold Vozella, and Mr. and Mrs. Saul Mosko."

The tea cup fell from Rose's hand, spilling hot tea onto the paper. A puddle of brown liquid seeped across the page, smearing the photograph, and melting the figures together. The empty cup lay toppled on its side. *Mrs. Mosko? Mrs. Mosko?* Dotting the wet page with a dishcloth, she succeeded only in marring the photograph and congealing the pages into a wad of newsprint.

Rose dumped the ruined paper into the waste bin. For good measure, she gathered the stack of magazines and tossed them on top of the soggy mess. *Aarh.* Rose mopped the spilled tea, wiped the floor with the already damp towel, and then threw it into the bin as well.

For the rest of the evening, she paced back and forth across the living room, muttering to herself. She'd never stopped to consider that he was a married man. She'd accepted his charity—the rent, the gloves, the dinner, even the perfume—foolishly attributing them to nothing more than his looking after Isador and her on Isador's behalf. Finding he was a married man and worse, if it were possible, that he might have a family, she felt betrayed and ashamed. Mosko was no longer "looking after her." He was no longer indulging a lonely woman whom he'd found in dire circumstances. He was a married man with something more on his mind, and Rose refused to be part of his sordid and underhanded plan.

She dug her fingers into her arms crossed in front of her, digging deep as she paced the floor. For an hour or more after she fell asleep, four tiny pink crescents decorated the flesh above each elbow.

Isador

"I WAS SO WORRIED WHEN YOU DIDN'T SHOW," ISADOR SAID, AS he sat beside his wife in the penitentiary visitor's room. "But Kilcourse, you remember Gerald, don't you? He got word to me."

"He did?"

"Yeah, said you'd been sick. Which made me worry even more, at least until he told me you were better."

"I have to say I'm surprised at how well news travels in here. It's as if you had your own newspaper," she said.

"Hey. We look out for each other. For friends, that is. You should meet Harris. He's my cellmate. If it weren't for him and a couple others, even some of the guards, I think I'd have gone out of my mind."

"I'm glad, though, I wouldn't have thought you'd find friends in here."

"Well, let me tell you, the first few months I would have agreed with you. My first cellmate lasted about a day. He kept yelling that he didn't want to share a cell with 'no goddamn Jew,' yelling it at the top of his voice each time one of the guards showed so much as his nose on the corridor. He was no one I wanted to be friends with. That's for sure."

"How horrible."

"Yeah, well, he got himself transferred to a cell in some other block," Isador said, "not soon enough for my tastes. And then, Harris moved in. We hit it off right away. He's been here a lot longer than I have, and he told me there's a system here, like anywhere else. I just had to figure out what it was and how to make it work. And you know what?"

"What?"

"I did. I figured it out."

"You did?"

"Well, it's kind of hard to explain. I got so low I think I came close to giving up. I wasn't myself at all. I just moped around, did my job, didn't complain, didn't think about my plans and our future. Numb, I suppose. And then, well, like that," Isador snapped his fingers, "things started getting better."

"I'm so happy for you."

"I guess I had to find the bottom before things could improve. Not that things are great here, but with Harris and a few others..." Isador paused and nodded at an inmate across the aisle. "See him," Isador tipped his head toward a man on his left, "he's another one of our guys. But then, way back behind me, at the front of the room. You see that guy with a scar down the left side of his face?" Rose scanned the tables to his rear, her eyes settling on the table furthest away. She looked back at Isador and nodded. "He's a snitch. Everyone knows it."

"How did he get the scar? It looks horrible."

"I'll tell you." Isador took a drag from a cigarette he'd pulled from a pack tucked in his shirt pocket. "He's been in here five years and has another ten to do."

Rose sighed audibly, her shoulders slumping.

"Yeah. And I thought I had it rough. Well, he was looking for a quick way out. Started flapping his jaw. Telling a few of the guards he had names someone up in the tower might want to hear."

"The tower?"

"Yeah, it's on the north side of the prison. The warden's office is there. Anyway, this guy tried bargaining with the guards, said he'd give them some names in exchange for time off his sentence."

"What happened?"

"The story here is he gave them one name, a pretty low level operator in an Italian gang. Wanted to see what he'd get in return. Then, before he made it back to his cell, someone or rather several someones jumped him. No one knows, of course, who was in on it, but they sliced him up good. You should see underneath his shirt. One big long gash from here to here." Isador gestured with his finger, drawing a straight line from his collar bone to his waist. "We thought he wasn't going to make it, but he surprised everyone."

"Did he get his sentenced reduced?"

"Nope. Not one day. I figure they already had the name. And now he swears he never snitched and he couldn't have because he doesn't know anyone anyway. Who knows? Let's just say he doesn't have many friends around here anymore. No one wants to be seen with him, not the guards, not the inmates. We give him a wide berth."

"You wouldn't think of doing anything like that, would you? Naming names, I mean," Rose spoke through her hands, leaning close and keeping her voice soft.

In the distance, a forest and a soft murmur of trees rustling in the wind. The murmurs became whispers, the whispers words. The words indistinct but insistent, pinging him, rousing him.

Isador cracked one eye. No forest. No trees. Only iron bars.

"Psst." Isador lifted his head from the hard pillow and squinted in the half-light, catching the dull sheen of a badge and Leroy's stooped frame by the door to his cell.

"Whaa?"

"Keep it down," Leroy whispered, making a tamping motion with his hand.

Isador stole a look at Harris. He was fast asleep in his bunk. His snores rumbled with the regularity of a metronome. The man could sleep through an earthquake.

Leroy edged the cell door open, slowly, trying to keep it from scraping the cement as it usually did. He managed to prevent all but a tiny scratching noise, like mice skittering across the floor. Creatures all too familiar to the Charlestown inmates. Leroy held a forefinger to his lips and with his other hand motioned for Isador to follow him. Isador stuffed his arms into his shirt and pulled on his trousers. He carried his shoes with him and slipped them on once outside the cell. Two o'clock in the morning according to the clock on the wall. Normally he woke with the breakfast bell, four hours from now. Isador rubbed his eyes with his knuckles.

The two walked in silence, Isador setting his feet on the concrete floor with care, mimicking Leroy's noiseless padding ahead. The old man veered left down a corridor that Isador knew led to the guard station and bunkhouse, but Leroy passed the door to the bunkhouse and continued ten or twelve paces farther to another door where he halted. He tapped his knuckles on the door three times, waited, and then tapped twice more. If Leroy hadn't already shushed him twice, Isador would have asked what was up.

Mitch, a guard from South Block, appeared. He glanced at Leroy and then at Isador, but as Leroy had done earlier, he said nothing. Leroy motioned Isador through then shut and locked the door. Isador nodded to Mitch but was, if anything, more puzzled. The room was no bigger than his cell but held two chairs, a desk, a square table on which playing cards sat face-up in neat rows, and shelves of file boxes stacked to the ceiling. A bare bulb shone from the socket overhead. He guessed that the night shift whiled away their duty here when not sleeping in turns in the bunkhouse.

Laughter. A snort. Isador's head snapped to the right to a half open door he'd not noticed on entering. Several voices shushed each other at once. Then a few giggles and more shushing. *Giggles? Women?* Isador's eyes darted to Leroy.

Leroy smiled. "Hey, in there," he said, his voice aimed toward the door, a notch higher in volume than his earlier whispers. "Time's up."

"What—" Isador started, keeping his voice low.

But Leroy interrupted him. "Thought you might like a little break in the routine," he said, "but you've got to keep it down." Leroy leaned over the desk and removed a pint from one of the desk drawers. It was half full with an amber liquid. He splashed a bit of whiskey into a couple of makeshift shot glasses, small paper cups like those used in the infirmary, and handed one to Isador.

The shot burned the back of his throat. It been since he'd had a nip of liquor. Isador put his fist to his chest as if to knock the alcohol down his pipe. He coughed. "Fuck me," he said.

"Thought you'd say that," Leroy said.

Isador had a thousand questions but decided they could wait. He held out his cup for a refill, his tongue and throat burning with anticipation. He'd almost forgotten the commotion in the adjacent room when Bill, a cohort of Leroy's, strode through the door, buckling his belt. Behind him came Henry, an inmate everyone called "Hatchet" because he'd hacked a man to death. "Bye, ladies," Hatchet said, poking his head back through the open door and waggling his fingers at whoever remained inside. Hatchet spied the whiskey and the cups on the desk. "How about a nightcap?" he asked with a glance at Mitch and Leroy.

"Sure," Mitch said. Leroy passed the bottle to Mitch, who sloshed a bit of whiskey into Hatchet's cup. Then, Leroy plucked Isador's used cup from his hand and stuck it inside his own before placing the two on the desk. He grabbed Isador by the arm and nudged him toward the door Bill and Hatchet had exited. "Go on. Enjoy yourself."

"What the hell?" Isador blinked several times in amazement. "Fuck me," he said again.

Before the door closed behind him, he heard Mitch say, "Just keep it down."

"God almighty." The room held two cots, one on each side of the room, a small table between the two on which a metal office lamp stood, its bulb casting a well-defined spotlight onto the floor like a doll-sized stage, vacant but anticipating the appearance of its tiny actors. Isador would recall these details later, when he reconstructed the scene in his head to prove to himself he'd not imagined what had transpired. But now, his eyes were glued to the bare shoulders and arms of two women sitting side by side on the far cot. They laughed, a synchronized series of chords and then laughed again at the fact that they'd laughed together.

Isador's eyes flicked from one to the other and back. As far as he could tell, they were twins. "Come here, darling," the one on the right said. She scooted to the side to make room for Isador to sit between them. The second woman did likewise, her bobbed hair swinging like a curtain over her face and then opening again, a peek-a-boo motion that stirred every prison-dulled nerve in his body.

"I can see you're happy to see us," the one on the left said. She stared at his crotch and the erection he hadn't thought or cared to hide as he squeezed between the two women.

"What's your name?" he asked the woman on his right. The question was instinct or nerves.

She threw her head back and laughed again. "You can call me Sophie," she said.

Lips tickled his left earlobe. A tongue slid along his neck. He whipped his head around. The lips pulled away. "And you can call me Celia," the second woman said as her hand settled on his groin. She located the flap of his trousers and fumbled with the buttons while Sophie pushed herself on top of him. The three fell back onto the cot. The laughter faded, replaced with softer sounds of pleasure from three voices, rising and falling in unison. Then Isador tuned his ears to the sounds of the release in his veins, his skin, and the hairs on his scalp.

When Leroy knocked on the door and said, "Time's up," Isador wanted to plead for more time. He could think of nothing better than to spend his remaining four years, two months, and seventeen days in that small room, hidden away with Sophie and Celia. He imagined Leroy and Mitch bringing his meals to him on a tray. He imagined days filled with wine, whiskey, and sex—joyous, raucous, unending sex. *Four years. Four, if I'm lucky.* He refused to acknowledge his full sentence and relied on Gerald Kilcourse's promise he'd only serve five.

It had taken all his strength to unwind the women's arms from his neck and shoulders. How he managed to dress and force one foot in front of the other out the door, he did not remember. But he'd trudged behind Leroy, past the bunkhouse, through the series of turns, and then back along Corridor C.

Leroy turned the key in the lock and disappeared without a sound. Isador did not climb back in his bunk, instead, he propped himself against the cell door, his hands gripping the bars for added support. Harris mumbled something incoherent, rolled over, and faced the wall. Isador prayed Harris would not wake; he wanted time to relive the events in the room beside the bunkhouse. Isador clenched his fingers around the bars. Were it not for the palpable ache in his groin, he'd swear he'd dreamt everything. How anyone succeeded in smuggling two women inside the prison without being seen was beyond his comprehension. How anyone could have found two more perfect women with identical mouths, arms, hands, and thighs; he could not fathom. Still reeling from the experience, the bite of the liquor gone, replaced with the taste of perfumed skin, Isador collapsed fully clothed onto his cot.

When the wake up bell sounded, Isador rolled over and put his feet on the floor.

"You look like shit," Harris said, eyeing Isador's rumpled clothes.

"I feel great. In fact, I feel superb. Maybe even fantastic."

"Aren't you Little Miss Ray of Sunshine. I don't care what you say, you still look like shit."

Isador examined his wrinkled trousers and shirt sleeves and smiled. "What the hell. It's Monday. Clean ones coming anyway."

Then he remembered, Monday meant Leroy's day off. He'd have to wait another twenty-four hours to pull Leroy aside and ask the questions swarming his head, the foremost being when he'd see the twins again.

"You sure are in a good mood," Harris said.

Then, Bert, one of the least friendly of the guards, appeared at their cell door, keys in hand, no greeting. "Let's go," he said. Harris and Isador exited and fell in line.

As the inmates walked in single file to the cafeteria, Isador passed a cigarette over his shoulder. He heard Harris whisper, "You can't even walk straight, Book. Did you get any sleep at all last night?"

"No talking," Bert called out over their heads.

Rose

With a tin of charoset for Passover tucked under one arm, Rose climbed to the front porch of her parents' home and knocked on the door. She took several deep breaths. It had been over a year since she had seen her mother and father and, except for Esther and Sarah, her other siblings and their spouses.

Her last visit had been a brief meeting with her father. A meeting she'd kept from Isador. She'd met with him after the falling out and pleaded for Leo to give Isador a second chance, but he wouldn't listen. "I've given him a second chance. And a third. And, besides, well, there are things you don't know. He's...I told you. I've said it for the last time. He is not welcome here." Leo had refused to clarify his comments.

Rose decided that if her husband weren't welcome in her parents' home, then neither was she. She'd left, hurtling herself through the door before her father could see the tears stream down her cheeks.

It was Esther who had pressed Rose to come for Passover. For their mother's sake, if nothing else, she'd said. Lost in her thoughts, outside the door, Rose failed to hear Ruth come up the steps until her sister stood beside her. To her surprise, Ruth pressed her cheek against Rose's and put an arm around her shoulders, though she withdrew it quickly. "We don't have to knock, you know, just go on in."

Rose bit her lip. *That's fine for you to say,* Rose thought. *You come every week.* Ruth continued on to the kitchen, but Rose held back, waiting just inside the front door. Her eyes skimmed the familiar surroundings. Nothing had changed. Three doily-covered armchairs sat in the same arrangement along one wall. They faced a sofa with its own pair of doilies. Room enough for four, her mother, her father, her sister Sarah, and Sarah's husband, Alfred. The two had moved in with Leo and Lillian after Sarah and Alfred's wedding, Sarah becoming a second pair of washing hands, and cooking hands, and child bathing hands, and mending hands, and whatever else their parents, her husband, and her two children needed. Rose imagined them in the room, each in their designated place reading a newspaper or book, a child in their lap or on the floor or on an impromptu assembly of straight backed chairs belonging to the kitchen or back porch.

"Rose. You've come," her mother said, dabbing away tears with the corner of her apron as she inched closer. Rose held the tin in front of her at arm's length.

"Set it down, dear," her mother said. "Let me give you a hug. It's been so long." Rose did as her mother asked and accepted the embrace, her mother snuffling as she buried her face in Rose's shoulder.

Rose glanced about for her father. He'd not offer a hug, but she hoped he'd speak. They'd been so close before she'd married.

"Where's father?"

"He's outside with Alfred and Frank and the children. They'll be in when dinner's ready. Come sit with me here in the living room. I want to know everything that's going on with you." Lillian took hold of Rose's hand and urged her toward the sofa.

Sarah emerged from the kitchen, the hair around her forehead in tight curls, her forehead damp from the steam rising off pots of soup. "Hello, Rose."

"Sarah, can you set the table?" Lillian asked.

"I already have," Sarah answered without inflection. Rose caught a hint of annoyance and offered to help. "That's okay," Sarah said. "You visit with Mother. Esther will be here in a minute and she can help."

Lillian pulled a pack of Chesterfields from her pocket and held it out, but Rose waved her hand to decline. With a cigarette balanced between two fingers and held aloft beside her head, Lillian eyed her youngest daughter. "You've lost weight," she said. She took a puff of her cigarette, drew it into her lungs, and then blew a stream of gray smoke toward the ceiling. She coughed for a solid minute afterward, and then tamped the cigarette against the edge of an ashtray before taking another puff.

"You must not be eating right," she continued. "Does that man of yours not keep enough food in the house?"

It hadn't taken long for Rose's thoughts of a happy reunion to vanish. "Mother, don't start, please," Rose said. "If you want to know, I've gained weight."

Hyman, Sarah's youngest boy, burst into the room and ran across the living room floor, naked from the waist down, with a top-of-his-lungs half-scream half-chortle. He dashed into the dining room.

"Shush! Stop screaming this minute," Sarah called from the kitchen and ran after the boy.

Rose used the interruption to change the subject. "He's gotten so big I didn't recognize him." She bit her tongue, realizing she'd opened the door to another, more fragile topic.

"Just two of my daughters left now. Leah and you. Tell me there's something to hope for."

"Not yet, Mother."

Rose stiffened under the old woman's eyes scanning her face, examining every worry line, the wrinkles at the edge of her eyes, the dimple on her chin. Lillian took another drag on her cigarette while Rose studied the intricate design of the carpet with its dots and squares and curlicue shapes and wondered which painful topic her mother would turn to next. She cringed at the thought of the conversations full of the Oh-Poor-Poor-Rose's and I-Told-You-So's taking place behind her back.

A clatter from the kitchen broke the silence and offered Rose an escape. "Let me go help," Rose said, rising and moving to the kitchen with an invented sense of urgency.

Esther was in the kitchen, having arrived and come in through the back door. Her hands were occupied, so she cocked her head and offered her cheek to Rose.

"Hello, Esther. Sarah, what can I do to help?"

"I think we're ready," Sarah said. "Everyone's out back. Why don't you call them in?"

Through the back door's window, the glass rippled and pocked with the imperfections, Rose peered over the loose circle of family below. The clap of a hand on a shoulder, the proximity of two heads, and a child's hand grasping an aunt's finger, evidence of familiarity and contentment. Inside the protective circle, her brother-in-law, the Rabbi Daniel, tossed a ball to one of Rose's nephews, the group applauded and cheered as one whether the child caught it in his small hands or not. Rose turned the handle on the door and stepped outside. "Dinner is ready." No one turned or looked toward the sound of her voice. She wondered if she'd spoken the words aloud or if they'd heard and chosen to ignore her.

Peals of friendly laughter bubbled up. One of the little ones had taken a few steps, his fat little legs pumping against the ground like pistons but unable to match the forward lunge of his body. He tumbled to the ground.

Rose cleared her throat and said the words again. This time, her father looked up. Without a smile or wave, he turned back to the others and repeated her words. "Dinner is ready."

The circle unwound and threaded up the stairs, mothers with young ones in their arms, fathers or uncles with one hand on the rail and the other on the shoulder of a son or nephew. Rose retreated into the kitchen, turned, and greeted them as they passed.

"Rose, so good to see you."

"It's been so long."

"Peace unto you," said the Rabbi.

"Hello, Auntie Rose."

"We've missed you."

"Rose," said her father, the same as if he'd said "chair" or "wall" or "stone."

A long embrace from Leah, the only one to touch her. "Come sit beside me," she whispered.

The family filed into the small dining room, spare chairs added to the six that usually ringed the table.

They bowed their heads and Daniel said the blessing. When he finished, Rose silently gave thanks for the small children—they dominated the conversation and demanded the better part of the adults' attention, diverting the uncomfortable gazes and awkward questions about Isador, so blatantly absent that Rose felt him standing behind her, hovering over her, or seated beside her. She froze her lips into a smile while her eyes wandered over the children's faces, seeing traces of their parents and grandparents in an unruly head of hair, or a line of nose, or the cupid's bow of their lips. On her plate, she pushed a few morsels of food from side to side, separating them then herding them around a piece of meat, her throat too small and dry to venture a bite. She stole a glance at her father's face across the table to find his eyes fixed on the motion of her fork. When he raised his eyes to hers, she looked away and took a sip of wine.

Soon, the children fidgeted in their chairs and played with their cutlery. Donald yelled and pointed a tiny finger at his cousin, accusing Samuel, Judith's eldest, of jabbing him under the table.

"Boys, behave," Sarah said. She pushed her chair back and stacked a few plates. Rose jumped up. "No, no, you sit," Sarah said.

"I'm fine. I'd like to help."

"Both of you come back here before you wash up. We need to have a photograph," said Frank, Ruth's husband.

Chairs scraped the floor as the group crowded together on one side of the table, Frank opposite with his camera. He motioned one relative to move closer to another, someone to back up, someone to stoop, another to lean in. "Ruth, look here, look at the camera. Donald, you too." He snapped a shot. "One more, hold it, hold it." The camera clicked again.

Rose never saw the finished product, but she held the scene in her mind's eye. Her father stood behind her mother, hands on the back of her chair, his eyes piercing the air between him and the camera. Her mother caught glancing at Sarah beside her. Alfred behind, holding Donald's hand to keep him still.

Little Hyman in Sarah's lap. Esther and Daniel arm in arm behind Ruth. Beside them, Leah and Judith, whose husbands could not attend, and Samuel. Ruth's two girls, their heads in their hands, elbows propped on the table. Behind them, Rose stood with her hands behind her back, snapped with eyes downcast in each of Frank's several shots.

Once the dishes were washed, dried, and put away, Rose gathered her things. She said a quick goodbye to her sisters, one by one, and then pecked her mother on the cheek opposite another cigarette in her hand. She waved to her father and the rest of the men as a group as they headed back out the kitchen door.

As she crossed the living room, Rose felt something crack beneath her foot. On the floor, a tinker toy spool lay snapped in two. She bent to pick up the broken toy, but Esther interceded and tossed the pieces into a box.

"Why don't you stay awhile? You don't need to hurry off," Esther asked.

Feeling as damaged as the spool, Rose shook her head and slipped through the door without a word.

By the time she returned to Nahant, the street was crowded with children, their mothers inside cleaning up after their own *Seders* and their fathers settled into their easy chairs with a pipe or already nodded off. Rose sat on the step outside her entryway. A couple of girls nearby played hopscotch on the sidewalk, across the street another played with a doll, and farther on several boys were immersed in a ball game of one sort or another, all competing for space on the short block.

She had no idea how long she sat there, content to watch the hive of activity and listen to the cacophony of high-pitched voices, afraid to climb the stairs to her empty apartment and its tomb-like silence.

"Miss Rose?"

"Why hello, Jacob," she said, startled, wondering how long he had been there.

"Did you have a nice Pass——" he began. He stepped back with one foot and then forward again. "Are you crying, Miss Rose?"

It was almost quitting time, by the clock on the wall. Rose stared at the second hand, willing it to slow down. Unlike Addie who sped out the door each night within minutes of closing, Rose dawdled, tucking ladies hats into boxes, covering items in the drawers with tissue, cleaning her counter, and from time to time sweeping the floor.

A bustle at the front door caught her attention. A last minute customer. Mosko. This time without an entourage. He veered left toward the leather goods. She breathed a sigh of relief, and though she was curious, she turned her back, hoping he would not visit her counter. She stole a glance at her watch. With a mere five minutes left until closing, he'd have only time enough to make his purchase and leave. Rose adjusted a wide-brimmed woven hat on the display counter, though it had sat in the same position all day. She tugged the brim lower and cocked the hat at a jaunty angle, work she could do while her ears strained for sounds of activity across the floor.

Tap. Tap.

Rose turned. Her heart fell to the floor. Mosko.

"Good evening, may I help you?" she asked.

"A good evening to you as well. I'm looking for something very special."

"Something for your wife, perhaps?" she dared, her eyes locked on his face, wanting to see his expression.

"Perhaps." He'd missed or deliberately ignored her allusion. "What would you suggest? Nothing elaborate. Something subtle but with obvious quality."

"This might do," Rose said, lifting a light beige hat from the back counter. She placed it on the glass for Mosko to examine. He did not glance at the hat.

"It's perfect. I'll take it."

He said nothing more while she placed the gift in a box and wrapped it. "Here you are, sir," she said, offering him the box.

He accepted it with both hands, his finding hers and covering them. "Will you do me the favor of accompanying me to the theater tonight?" Then he added, giving her no time to think of what to say, "You can't say no. You don't have anywhere to go. There is no one at home who needs you to make dinner for them. Please. I would enjoy it so."

"I, I..."

"Excellent. My car is waiting outside. As soon as you are free to go, you'll find me there." He scooped up the box and turned, leaving her stranded without a chance to consider whether or not she'd accepted his invitation.

When Rose joined Mosko in his car, the boxed hat rested on the seat between them. She ignored it and stayed close to the window.

"I'm sure you are hungry after a long day's work. We can eat a light meal before the theater."

Rose was not at all sure she was hungry or, if food were placed in front of her, whether she'd be capable of lifting a fork. She wasn't sure she could speak, much less eat. Seeming oblivious to her discomfort, Mosko chattered on as they drove, mentioning the fine spate of weather they'd had in the last few weeks, telling her a bit about the night's program, and pointing out a few sights along the way. Rose did little more than nod politely and smile in response, until he brought up the subject of Isador.

"How was your husband the last time you visited. Last week was it?"

Her heart beat faster, not so much at the mention of Isador, but at the realization that Mosko knew she'd been to visit him the past Sunday. "He was quite well, in fact."

"Better then. How so?"

"He's found friends and a good job, such as it can be, in there."

"Imagine that. And was he eating well? Did he mention the extra food, the beef roast?"

Rose looked down half expecting to see her chest ripped open and her heart beating furiously in her lap. "He did."

Mosko turned and looked out the window, saying nothing more for the remainder of the drive. He'd made his point. Rose understood.

Four acts passed before Mosko took her hand, a musical excerpt from a play on Broadway, an act featuring a psychic, a brother and sister performing tumbling feats in clown costumes, and a cycle of songs by Marguerite Hourihan, "fresh from her international tour" the bill claimed.

Mosko caressed her hand with his thumb probing the hills and valleys of her knuckles, the tiny gaps between the fingers and the hollow area at their base. He shifted in his seat, drew closer, and slid a hand along her arm. Rose coughed, pulled her arm from his grasp to cover her mouth, adjusted her new beige cloche, and bothered a loose curl behind her ear. She returned her hand to her lap and held her breath. Mosko resumed his posture, his fingers to the sensitive skin at the crook of her elbow, groping, seeking.

"Please," she whispered without turning her head. She wanted him to stop. At the same time, she feared offending him. Mosko did not remove his hand.

The beauty of the theater with its glistening chandeliers dotting the ceiling, sconces every few feet along the walls, the finely dressed patrons, women in feathers and sequins and jewels in the orchestra section—all of it faded into the background. She read the playbill in her lap. Sabino & Company had the stage. It was the final act. The ordeal was almost over, or so she thought at the time.

When Mosko's car pulled to a stop, Rose unlatched the door and dashed out, nearly colliding with Lenny. Her move failed to deter Mosko however. He was at her side, his hand, palm up, inviting her to lead the way. As she climbed to her apartment, she heard the sound of Lenny pulling the Buick away from the curb and, behind her, Mosko's footfall echoing softly on the stairs.

The ordeal was not over. It had just begun.

Jacob

ALL MONDAY NIGHT, JACOB LISTENED TO RALPH GROAN IN HIS sleep. At first light, he woke his aunt. She came at once, trailing behind him, and placed her hand on the young boy's forehead. She pulled the covers back and found Ralph's side of the shared bed soaked. "He's hot," she said. She turned to Jacob, "You best go sleep on the couch. Here, take your pillow." He accepted the pillow, but instead of going to the couch, he backed into the shadows and watched as Aunt Gladys tucked the blanket under Ralph's chin. She sat beside her son and wiped beads of sweat from his forehead, cheeks, and neck with the hem of the shawl around her shoulders.

Then she leaned over him and whispered his name, "Ralph. Ralph, baby, how do you feel?" Ralph groaned in response, or perhaps it was only a reflex to the sound of the voice above his head or the feel of his mother's cheek against his. "Ralph," she said again, her voice softer and more soothing, but Ralph did not respond. Gladys pulled him into her lap and cradled his head in her arms. With her eyes closed, she rocked him slowly back and forth, humming the tune Jacob's mother had sung, so many years ago.

...The goat will go to the market to bring you wonderful treats
He'll bring you raisins and almonds, sleep, my little one, sleep.

For weeks after Jacob and his newly-widowed father had

come to live with Aunt Gladys, herself a widow, he'd sung the song to himself at night, mouthing the words with his face turned away from his cousin. He'd never heard Gladys sing or hum, he'd never been the beneficiary of her kinder side, even when he'd fallen and scraped his knee in the street. All she'd said was not to bleed on the rug.

Sleep, my little one, sleep.

Gladys opened her eyes and saw Jacob clutching his pillow in his arms. "Go, boy. What are you standing there for?" She turned back to the child in her arms and rocked.

Jacob padded to the front room and propped his pillow on the couch. He folded his arms over his chest and listened, straining to hear the humming over the intermittent groans and whimpers from Ralph.

Later, Jacob woke, teeth chattering, though it was almost summer. He fumbled for the covers but found only the sides of the sofa. He opened his eyes and remembered. The door to his bedroom was closed, but a short time later, Aunt Gladys emerged carrying a pail. Jacob asked, "Is Ralph going to be okay?" His only frame of reference for illness had been the flu epidemic that had ravaged the country a couple of years earlier. Everyone he knew lay feverish in their beds at the time. Doctors came but could do nothing to relieve their suffering. Some went to the hospital, sweating and feverish, unable to dress themselves or walk. He'd watched his own mother thrash in her bed, moaning and rolling about on the damp mattress. He'd watched as his father wrapped a coat around her shoulders and took her out the front door and down the walk, supporting her with an arm around her waist.

She'd gone to the hospital and never returned. He waited for his Aunt to wrap Ralph and take him away.

By mid-morning, Ralph began vomiting, hurling what remained of his last meal and, later, clear but foul smelling fluid from his stomach. Aunt Gladys cleaned the floor and disappeared into her room to dress. She returned and issued instructions to Jacob and his sister not to go into the bedroom under any circumstances. "He's sleeping. Leave him alone. I'll be back as soon as I can." Jacob and Leila nodded. They sat side by side on the couch in the living room, frightened and wordless and staring at the dark rectangle of the door to the room where Ralph lay, blinds closed against the sun.

Gladys returned and found them still sitting together. She was alone.

"Is the doctor coming?" Jacob asked. Aunt Gladys hadn't said the word "flu", at least not in front of Jacob, but he saw the way she wrung her hands and paced.

"Later. Why don't the two of you skedaddle, go outside." She hadn't noticed it was a school day. She hadn't noticed they hadn't eaten. She walked into the kitchen and returned with another pail of water in one hand and dry towels under her arm.

Jacob shoved forward in the couch and placed his feet on the floor. He grabbed Leila's hand and urged her with him to the kitchen. There, he sliced two pieces of bread from the loaf in the bread bin. After handing one to Leila, he guided her back through the living room and outside.

When the doctor arrived, he nodded at Jacob and Leila huddled together on the stoop. Leila rose and followed him into the house, but Jacob dared not go. He'd wait until the doctor had seen Ralph. He thought of going to the beach to delay hearing the words he knew would come. Jacob jabbed a small rock with a pointed end at the cracks in the steps. He lost track of time, but the sun was higher and the temperature rising. He pulled his cap off and closed his eyes, his face to the sun.

"Jacob." A voice from somewhere nearby. "Jacob." Miss Rose stood beside him, bent at the waist. "Why so glum?"

"It's Ralph, he's sick. I think he's going to die."

"Die? Jacob, don't be silly. What's wrong? Has your aunt called for the doctor?"

Jacob nodded.

"What did he say?"

He shrugged his shoulders in response. "He's upstairs."

"Let me go check and see if there's something I can do."

Midway up the three flights, Rose stopped. She took a couple of deep breaths and braced herself against the bannister.

"You're not ill, too, are you, Miss Rose?" Jacob asked. He'd trailed behind her, but caught up when she'd stopped.

"I don't think so. I'm just out of breath."

They met the doctor as he was leaving.

"Doctor Siegel," Rose asked, "how's Ralph?"

"He'll be fine. Quite a scare though for Mrs. Cohen."

"Does he have the flu?" Jacob asked.

"No, not the flu. Say, young man, you didn't see him eat or drink anything he wasn't supposed to? Anything he might have found around the house or in the basement?"

"No, sir."

"Are you sure?" the doctor asked again.

"Yes, sir," Jacob said, more forcefully this time.

"What do you think it is?" Rose asked.

"To be honest," he said, glancing at Jacob then back to

Rose, "I think he got into some bad booze. I'd like to find it before someone else takes a swig. It's happening more and more these days. Darn government poisoning the alcohol. Still, people won't stop."

"How is he now?" Rose asked.

"He's resting. But he's got to get it out of his system."

"He's not going to die!" Jacob said.

"No. But let this be a warning—to him and to you. Keep away from that stuff. It can hurt you. Don't be trying to show everyone how grown up you are."

"No, sir," Jacob said, trying to catch a glimpse of Ralph behind the doctor.

Earl

"HAVE YOU EVER HEARD OF SOMEONE DYING AFTER DRINKING alcohol?" Rose asked.

"What?" Earl had heard Mrs. Margolin plain enough, but the nature of her question surprised him.

She repeated the question, slowing her speech and enunciating her words with concerted effort, as if she thought him hard of hearing. They sat across the same table in the same coffee shop where they'd met months earlier. This time, he'd received word through Elliot Kriger that "a lady" wanted to speak to him. How Rose knew Kriger or that Kriger was a member of Mosko's gang he didn't know. Kriger had said this dame had walked straight up to him on Shirley Avenue, a real Sheba. Said she needed to talk to Mr. Bloom. "*Mister* Bloom," Kriger had repeated. Elliott had had a good laugh at that and asked Earl if he'd changed his taste in women and gone all high society.

"I heard you, ma'am. Just surprised you'd be asking something like that. There are some cheap juke joints around who sell some bad stuff. A lot of people making their own, too, not being careful and then selling it or passing it off to someone else. I heard one guy went blind. Down in South Boston. Mostly people just get pretty sick. It's rare, but I won't lie to you, there have been a few fatalities."

"Accidental?"

"Well, yeah. No one drinks the stuff if they know it'll kill them."

"Would they know if it were bad? That is, does it smell or taste bad?"

"Not always. Sometimes it's so diluted with sugar or fruit juice or something. Never know what hit them until later. You know someone?"

"A little boy across the street. He became quite ill. His mother had to call the doctor."

"He going to be all right?" Earl asked, presuming that was the polite thing to say.

"Yes, I think so." Rose drummed her fingers on the table, the shell pink nails with white crescents and tips danced up and down inches from his own fingers. Earl imagined how smooth they'd feel gliding against his skin.

She said nothing more, but Earl sensed that she had other questions. He took a sip of coffee, lit a cigarette, and took a few long pulls, allowing her time to think and summon her courage. He tried to avoid staring at her during the silence but found his eyes wandering to her face, seeing her bite the side of her cheek, her eyelids flutter, and her brows knit together.

"How's Isador?" he asked, thinking a change of subject might work.

"Oh, thank you for asking. He's fine. He seems to be enjoying life again, if that's possible to do there. So much better now than his first few weeks." Another pause. "I think Mr. Mosko is looking after him."

"Well, when someone does the right thing—does Mr. Mosko a favor, so to speak—he returns the favor. It's the way he does things."

"How long will he continue?"

"As long as necessary. Unless circumstances change, of course."

Rose drummed the table again.

"You're not drinking your coffee?" Earl asked.

"No. I've not had much appetite of late."

"Are you ill?"

"No, at least, I don't think so. I'll be fine."

"Is there something I can help you with?" he asked, not wanting to pry but thinking she might never get to the reason she'd asked to see him.

"Do you have a gun?"

His face betrayed his astonishment. "Well, yes," he said. "But why do you ask?"

She bit the corner of her lip, before answering. "What I meant to say is can you get me a gun?"

"You? What would you want a gun for?"

"Protection, I suppose, is the right way to say it. In case, well, of trouble."

"You can't be in any sort of trouble. If you are, all you have to do is say so. I'll take care of anything or anyone worrying you."

"No, no, there's nothing I need you to do. I thought, well, I'm alone in my apartment, it might be good to have one."

"I'd advise against it, but if you're sure, I'll see what I can do," he said, keeping his voice lowered, matching the level of hers.

"I'm sure."

A week later, Earl tapped on Rose's door. When she cracked it open, he stepped back onto the landing, conscious of the last time he'd stood there. But she showed no signs of concern.

"Come in," Rose said.

Her face was flushed and Earl thought he detected a slight

odor, as if she'd been ill. He noted the open door to the bath-room and for the first time, the damp cloth in her hand.

"Mrs. Margolin, I have something for you."

Her eyes fell to the brown-paper-wrapped package under his arm. "Oh. I hadn't expected you so soon," she said.

"Do you want me to leave it with you?"

Rose did not answer.

"Would you like me to show you how to use it?" he tried again.

"I suppose that would be best. I've never actually held one before."

They stood together on a small rise at the edge of the marshes north and west of Revere. Earl unwrapped the package and presented the gun to her as if it were a plate of cookies.

"Is it loaded?"

"Not yet. Go ahead, take it."

She placed her fingers around the handle and lifted it from his hand, the tips of her nails grazing his palm. "It's smaller than I thought it would be. Heavier, too."

"Small, but just as deadly. Whoa, there—It's not a toy!" Rose had bounced the gun in her hands, feeling its heft and had inadvertently pointed the barrel at Earl. "Never point a gun at someone unless you intend to fire it. And if you fire it, fire it at the head or heart."

"I thought you said it wasn't loaded." She lowered the end of the barrel toward the ground.

"It's not, but you don't want to take any chances. Always assume it's loaded, even when you know it's not."

He stepped beside her and pointed to and named the basic parts. Then, he demonstrated how to cock and aim the gun.

"Here," he said, fumbling in his pocket. He withdrew a handful of bullets and took the gun from her. "I'll load it."

"Now," Earl scanned the area for a target, "over there, see that dead log on its side?" He turned to face the log. "Square your body to the target, put your feet shoulder-width apart, and bring the gun up, shoulder level. Like this." As he raised his arm, Rose put a finger in each ear. Earl fired a single shot at the log. The bang echoed across the marsh and several birds took flight, cawing raucously as they rose into the sky.

"That's it? That's all there is to it?"

"That's it. Here, you try."

Rose squared herself to the target and raised the gun as she'd seen Earl do, though with the weight of the weapon, her arm sagged. Earl placed a hand underneath hers to steady it.

"Try using both hands."

As Rose cupped her left hand under her right, Earl withdrew his, slowly. She squeezed the trigger. Nothing happened.

"Harder."

She tried again and this time the gun fired, startling her and causing her to jump backward. She tried again. She raised her arm, closed one eye, and pulled the trigger three times. Two shots missed the log, the third one hit.

"You've got promise," he said, smiling.

She did not return his smile but handed him the firearm. "Could you reload it?"

"Now that I see you didn't mean to fire it at me, sure."

Rose did not respond to his attempt at levity. Instead, she studied his moves as he loaded the bullets one by one. When he returned the gun, she placed it in her purse and then, instead of carrying the purse by its handle, she tucked the purse under her arm as if it were a rolled up newspaper.

"Good, it's safer that way."

They had little to say on the return trip, but when they pulled to a stop alongside the entry to her apartment building, Rose turned and said, "I can't thank you enough for your help. I want you to know that...what's past is past. I've forgiven you."

Earl had trouble finding his voice. "I'm not sure I deserve that," he managed.

"You've been honest with me and helped far more than you know." Rose stepped from the car. She turned back and leaned through the open door. "Would you help me with one more thing?"

"Anything."

"Will you help me keep Isador safe?"

Earl looked at Rose, puzzled. "Of course," he said, though he did not know what she meant.

With that, she was gone, though the scent of lilies lingered. Despite the heat, Earl closed the windows and drove the car for miles, going nowhere but circling through the Revere neighborhoods, inhaling the aroma of flowers as long as it lasted.

Nautical Gardens

The Nautical Gardens attraction adjacent to Wonderland was festooned with lamps at night. It contained a ballroom that witnessed many of the popular dance marathons during the 1920s. It was also the gateway to the ocean and held changing rooms for bathers of the day.

Rose

IN FRONT OF THE MIRROR IN HER BATHROOM, WITH THE GUN still inside her handbag and the handbag on her shoulder, Rose smiled at her reflection. She turned one way, then another, and then back around, eyeing the bulge on one side of the bag but satisfied a passerby would notice nothing awry.

She adopted a new routine. Each evening when she arrived home, she placed the weapon in the middle of the counter next to her spices where she would see it as she prepared dinner. Before retiring for the night, if she had a few minutes to read, she'd sit on the sofa thumbing through the latest of Addie's magazines, the deadly instrument propped against her thigh. She wanted the gun to be as ordinary an item as one of the needlepoint pillows on her couch, as familiar as an old friend, and as comfortable as a glove or a scarf or a hat.

One weekend, she rode the streetcar for hours, going four or five blocks in one direction, before turning around and retracing her route. Each time, she took a seat next to a stranger, placed her bag on her lap or beside her on the bench and slipped her hand inside, her fingers finding and gripping the gun's handle. She practiced the move over and over until she found the handle with ease and could smile or nod at her fellow passenger without a rush of blood to her face.

She'd grown accustomed to the added weight and to finding the gun handle when she fumbled inside her purse for her comb or her compact.

But handling the gun was not the only new skill Rose practiced. She also worked on concealing her emotions, wanting to mask her face with an expressionless gaze, as if she were a geisha on a page of one of Isador's magazines, the white powder paste concealing her fears, her worries, and her lies.

A week ago, at lunch with Addie, instead of setting her purse on the floor or in a vacant seat as she usually did, she set the purse on top of the table. Addie had not given the purse a second glance, at least not until Helen Rust, the store manager's secretary, approached their table and asked to join them. Rose pretended not to notice her purse sat in Helen's way.

"What are you carrying in there?" Addie asked as she set the purse aside to make room for Helen. "A brick?"

"A gun," Rose replied, her face blank. Easier to keep to the truth than stammer over a fabrication.

"Feels like it," she said. Then she turned to Helen to inquire about Helen's latest nephew. Rose failed to follow the conversation. She'd been too intent on searching for signs of suspicion or curiosity from Addie.

On Wednesdays, the days Mosko visited, Rose broke her routine. On those nights, she followed Mosko's routine, a fixed series of actions of which she realized he was unaware. Each time he came through her door, he announced he'd brought along something special. Something very special, he claimed, not knowing how weary Rose was of his "something very specials." Every time he said the words, she knew to expect a gift—perfume, a scarf, a hat, or worse. Of late, they'd grown more and more intimate, matching his advances. At first, he'd satisfied himself with an innocent caress, then a kiss, then, about the same time as the grabbing and pawing had started, he'd given her a pair of silk stockings. The night he forced himself on her, the gift had been a silk negligee.

If she balked and held him at arm's length, as she had done at first, he'd remind her in some oblique way of her influence on Isador's tenuous state of existence. It was a threat that was never made clear, but a threat nonetheless. A threat she understood. He expected to have his way with her, whenever and wherever he wanted, with or without notice.

Rose suspected his absence from his home on a night during the week was easier explained away than one on the weekend. She wondered if his wife knew where he was and what he did on Wednesdays. She wondered if he visited other women on Mondays, Tuesdays, and Thursdays.

Early on, Rose had tried to take control of the situation. She joined Addie for dinner on a Wednesday and lingered over coffee, talking of nothing for hours. Each time the conversation flagged, Rose introduced another subject despite the yawns from Addie and Hugh and a look Rose saw flash between them once or twice. At ten o'clock, having worn out her welcome with her friends, she walked home, her steps light and her head clear. Thinking she'd succeeded in avoiding Mosko for one Wednesday, she nearly skipped the last block along Shirley Avenue. But when she turned the corner onto Nahant, the black Pontiac was there, parked under a street lamp.

"I'm a patient man, Rose," Mosko had said later, poking a cufflink through the slot on his cuff. She stole a look at the clock. Twelve-thirty. He tucked a finger under the hem of the sheet she'd pulled over her shoulders and slid the sheet to her waist. Then, he cupped one of her breasts in his hand. "But I am a busy man, too." His hold on her breast grew firm, uncomfortable. "It's late. Later than I like to keep you awake and later than I like to be kept from my obligations." He relaxed his grip and slid his hand from under her arm. "Till next Wednesday, my dear."

When she heard the door snap closed, she did as she always did on Wednesdays. She stripped the bed of its covers, changed the sheets, and then drew a bath of scalding water.

A clear blue sky. July and the height of the summer's heat. Rose donned a light cotton dress and ventured outside to search for Jacob before he had a chance to join his friends or his Aunt Gladys snared him for chores. He was not in the street.

After knocking twice, Rose heard Gladys approaching, her habitual wheezing evident through the closed door. "Coming," she said, though it sounded like "Cughmingh."

"Hello, Miss Gladys," Rose said, more cheerful than normal. Gladys never seemed in a mood for cheer. "I was wondering if I could impose on Jacob this morning. I could use some help..." She let her words trail away, expecting Gladys would tire and turn away before Rose would have to invent a chore or two.

"Jacob," Gladys called out over her shoulder without bothering to hear what Rose needed. "Jacob," she called again. Then to Rose, she said, "Better he does something useful for you than waste his time at the pool hall with those good for nothing boys from Walnut."

"I quite agree," Rose said.

Jacob appeared underneath the sagging flesh of Gladys's arm propped against the doorframe. "Yes, ma'am?"

"Have you finished cleaning up from breakfast?"

"Yes, ma'am."

"Good, then see if you can help Miss Rose out. And make sure you don't get in her way or give her anything to complain about."

"No, ma'am," he said as he pulled his hat from the hook beside the door.

Rose placed a hand on Jacob's shoulder and guided him down the stairs. When they were halfway across the street, Rose bent over and whispered in the boy's ear, "How would you like to go to the beach and ride the coaster?"

"Really, Miss Rose? I thought—"

"I wasn't sure your aunt would approve if I asked to take you to the beach, so we'll think of some chore I need you to do later. But the weather is so nice I thought we might go for a few rides. What do you say?"

"Yes, ma'am!"

The couple, looking as much like any other mother and son, walked down Shirley Avenue toward the beach. She held Jacob's hand in one of hers and in her other hand, Rose held her purse.

They rode the Jack Rabbit, walked through the funhouse, and then, though her stomach still felt queasy from the first Jack Rabbit circuit, she acquiesced to Jacob's plea to ride it again.

"You really should open your eyes," Jacob said as they climbed aboard. Jacob had fought his way through the crowd to board the first car. "When we get to the top, when I say 'let go,' you raise your arms in the air."

"I don't know about that, Jacob." Rose had no intention of opening her eyes or loosening her grip on the handrail, at least not until they had crested the top of the last incline and the train had come to a full stop where it had begun. She secured her handbag under her right leg as she had the first time around.

"That was great! Again?" Jacob said as the two exited their car.

"Maybe another day. Let's get some ice cream."

The two found a bench in the shade where they ate their ice cream before it dripped through the thin wax paper cups. When they'd finished, Rose asked, "How about one more ride?"

"Which one, Miss Rose?"

"Not the roller coaster, that's for sure. How about the Tunnel of Love?"

"Tunnel of Love? That's a Leila ride."

"I know it's not very exciting. Not like the coaster. But just once, okay? For me?"

"Sure, Miss Rose."

"I promise not to tell Sidney or Michael."

"Or Walter."

"Or Walter."

As they waited in line to board the white cars with pink and red hearts emblazoned on their sides, Rose noticed Jacob looking left and right and behind, checking the faces in the crowd every few minutes and pulling his cap low on his forehead. A car came along the track and Rose stepped inside. There was little room left for Jacob, exactly as the amusement's inventor had intended. In the cramped space, lovers were forced to sit close, rubbing shoulders, hips, and thighs as they traveled through the dark interior.

The car crawled away from the starting point and passed beneath a small opening, so low that Rose and Jacob bowed their heads toward each other to pass. The perfect place for a young lover to steal a first kiss from his sweetheart. Once inside, her eyes darted along the trail ahead. *Left once, twice, right once, right twice,* Rose said to herself, counting the turns on her fingers. She was oblivious to the hearts hung from the ceiling by thin wires and to the numerous cherubs bearing bows and arrows affixed to the sides of the walls. The car trundled on through the dark. Rose could just make out the sides of the tunnel and a path on the right no more than a foot or two wide. After the fifth turn, the car proceeded down a long straightaway. The outline of a door appeared ahead. Another right and a last left turn and then the light from the plaza ahead after a final low crescent shaped opening, a place for one last kiss before the daylight returned.

When the car stopped, the operator opened the side door and offered a hand to Rose. She kept her seat and turned to Jacob, "One more time?" He clearly did not want to go again but was too polite to say so. "Please?" she asked.

He forced a smile to his lips and nodded.

"Thank you." Rose faced the operator, handed him a dime, and pulled the car door shut.

This time, eyes closed, Rose called out the sequence of turns in her head. As the car rattled around the fifth turn, she opened her eyes and slid her hand inside her purse, clutched the gun in her fingers, counted to twelve, and then on the straightaway, took a long look at the door embedded in the wall. She squinted in the dark and located the handle and the hinges, noting the direction it would swing.

When they returned once more to the start, the operator nodded and smiled. "Again?" he asked before bothering to open the door.

"No. That's it. Thank you."

Jacob cleared the car before she did.

"By the way," she said to the operator, "there's a door inside along the track. Is it there in case of emergency? In case of a fire or if the ride broke down?"

"A door?" he paused. "Oh, you must mean the access door. I suppose it could be used in case of an emergency, but that's how we go in and out for maintenance. There's no need to worry, though, the ride's in fine shape. Never had a problem yet."

"Thank you. I didn't want my young friend here to be in any danger. Ready, Jacob?"

Rose had little need to fake feeling out of sorts. She remembered denying the truth for the first week, attributing her breathless episodes, dizziness, loss of appetite and then being sick each morning to her hopeless situation and constant worry. But she knew better. Her time of the month had never been a day off schedule. Two weeks passed. Then three. After the second miss, denial was not an option. She was pregnant.

She'd done her best to disguise her symptoms and to make plausible excuses. "I don't know if I'm coming down with a cold or what," she'd said to Helen. "Maybe I didn't sleep well last night."

"I can ask Miss Winchester to fill in for you if you need to go lie down."

"Oh no. I couldn't impose on her. I'll be fine." Madeline Winchester was a clerk in the store's accounting office, a mousy woman with few social skills, always looking at her feet and responding to attempts to engage her in conversation with one- or two-word utterances.

"She'd be happy to, Rose. You let me know if you change your mind," Helen said.

"I think I can make it to the end of the day, but thank you."

But just after lunch, Rose bolted from her counter. Inside the cramped ladies washroom, she leaned over the sink and vomited, taking care not to soil her blouse or skirt. Rose ran cold water over her hands and patted a few drops on her forehead and neck. She rinsed the basin and bent over a second time, cupping her hands under the faucet and pooling enough water to rinse the sour taste from her mouth. This time it was fear and nerves, not morning sickness.

A knock at the door. "Rose. Rose. Are you okay?" It was Addie.

"Yes. I'm fine. I'll just be a minute." Apparently, her dash from the sales floor hadn't escaped notice. In the mirror, her face was pale, whether due to feeling light headed or to the dim, dust covered bulb overhead, she couldn't tell.

On her way out, Rose nearly collided with Addie. "Everything all right?" Addie asked.

"I was feeling a bit faint. But I took a sip of water and I'm much better now." The whiff of tainted air had dissipated behind her, but it was still noticeable.

"You should go home and lie down. You look frazzled."

"I'm fine, really. Just a couple more hours to closing anyway."

Rose minded her station for the rest of the afternoon, slumping uncharacteristically against her counter every now and then. She dared not pull a chair close by, a forbidden act at Tillinghast's, lady and gentlemen attendants must remain standing behind their counters during sales hours. Four o'clock, then five after the hour. The hands on the clock refused to speed up. If anything, they slowed, inching their way around the dial. At four-thirty, with half an hour left to closing and no supervisor watching, Rose packed all but one or two of the display items and pulled her personal things from the empty drawer below the counter, placing them in easy reach. Four fifty-nine. Rose rushed through the door without so much as a nod or wave to Addie.

The air outdoors cleared her lungs and settled her stomach but did nothing to calm her nerves. Rose quickened her pace and looked straight ahead, ignoring nods and greetings from a few passersby and avoiding even a flick of her eye toward the gaily decorated cakes in the pastry shop window. Her feet advanced mechanically, as if guided by the string of a puppet master; they turned when she was supposed to turn, paused for traffic, and went forward when it was safe.

Rose ran up the flights of stairs to her apartment, the adrenaline in her veins compensating for her lack of breath. In her bedroom, she shuffled through the closet and chose a chocolate brown sheath. *Perfect,* she thought.

She slipped into the dress, feeling a slight tug as she pulled it over her hips and stomach. She inhaled and tightened the muscles across her belly. A sideways glance at the mirror convinced her that her pregnancy was not noticeable. Not yet.

Rose powdered her nose, dabbed a bit of color on her cheeks, and patted her hair in place. In the living room, she leaned over the couch and lowered the double-sash windows, trapping the already warm air inside. Then, she took a seat on the sofa to wait.

Six-thirty. The hum of a car below in the street, a distinctive velvet-smooth purr that floated beneath the chirps of a dozen or more American Swifts, darting unseen above the building's chimney, coming home to roost. The slight telltale squeak, as Lenny applied the brakes. The motor died. Rose held her breath. A car door opened and closed. Moments later, a knock at the door. Rose pushed herself from her perch on the sofa.

In one motion, he came inside, brandished a bouquet of flowers in front of her, and then wrapped it behind her back as he pulled her close and covered her mouth with his. Though she bristled at the light sweat on his upper lip, the heat of his body from climbing the stairs, and his probing tongue in her mouth, she did not push him away, she did not resist. She knew her role with all its lines and gestures.

"You look lovely, Rose," Mosko said. "But my gosh, it's warm in here."

"I'm so sorry. I rushed to change when I got home and hadn't noticed. Here, let me take your coat."

"No, go on, open the windows. Let's get some air for a bit. Perhaps we can go down to the boardwalk."

"That would be delightful. I'm sure it will be cooler by the time we get back. Let me just put these flowers in some water." Rose disappeared into the kitchen. She listened but couldn't hear the sound of Lenny driving away as he normally did, returning only much later in the night to retrieve his boss.

When she returned to the living room, she raised the two front windows and glanced outside. The car was still in the street. She slipped the strap of her purse over her arm and followed Mosko outside.

Rose gave a furtive look to the left and right and then peered through the glass at the driver's window. Lenny was nowhere to be seen.

"I gave him the night off," Mosko said. "Decided I'd drive myself."

"But—" Rose started. She fidgeted with her purse string.

"Did you forget something?" Mosko asked, his hand on the passenger door.

"No. It's nothing." She ducked into the car and smoothed her face. It was a change in the Wednesday routine she'd not anticipated. While Mosko took a seat behind the wheel, Rose removed her compact from her purse and stared at her eyes in the tiny mirror, seeing through them into her head where her thoughts raced, assessing the situation.

"You needn't fuss. You look beautiful."

Rose snapped the compact shut and smiled her geisha smile.

Mosko parked the Pontiac along Beach Boulevard. "We can walk to the pier from here," he said, offering his arm. She laced her arm through his, as he'd bid, and walked beside him along the Boulevard and to the end of the pier. There, they stood side by side, elbows on the railing, a sliver of the moon hanging in the still light sky. "You were right, it is so much better here," Rose said.

"Cooler yes, but here I have to share you with everyone else."

"You'll have me all to yourself later," Rose said, affecting a light tone.

"That I will." He paused. "When I first arrived, I thought you looked tired, but you've got color back in your cheeks and you're much more cheerful, unusually cheerful, in fact."

"I felt ill earlier today, but I feel so much better now," Rose said, finding a suitable explanation, one close to the truth. "I suppose I should have stayed home, but I've missed so many hours already this year, I was afraid Tillinghast might start looking for a replacement."

"Well, we couldn't let that happen, could we? I could speak—"

"No. I didn't mean that. I mean...I was exaggerating, I'm sure," she said, realizing how a subtle phrase, an offhand comment, or a sigh at the wrong moment could trigger a barrage of unfortunate events.

"You take me far too seriously, Rose."

"Oh. You were kidding."

Mosko tilted his head back and laughed so hard and long that several couples turned to look. Rose bowed her head and hid her face under the brim of her hat. "I'm sorry," he said, when he'd regained control, "your expression was priceless." He chuckled, "And you're blushing. I can see that even in this light." Mosko circled his arm around her waist and pressed his body against hers, the heat of his limbs palpable through his clothes.

Rose gazed out at the sea and then to the darkening sky above. The first few stars had emerged.

"It's probably cooled off now. Shall we go back?" Mosko asked, looking toward the street where the car was parked.

"Yes, of course." Rose turned and slipped her hand through the crook of his elbow, doing her best not to rest her arm on his. A few feet short of the beach, Rose turned and pointed toward the amusements, their facades glowing with strings of light and the lanes crowded with people. "What about a small detour?"

"Uh, no detours, let's go back," he nuzzled against her ear, his breath on her neck.

"Something I'd wager you've never done before."

"What's that?"

"You'll see."

"Rose..."

"It won't take long. This way. It's right over there," she said, her hand flitting in the direction of the row of amusements, intentionally vague.

On the steps below the marquee that read TUNNEL OF LOVE, Mosko stopped and took in the gaudy hearts, the silent wooden cupids with their frozen bows and arrows, and the annoying off-key tune emanating from inside the darkened interior. "Now it's you who must be joking."

"Not at all. I'll bet you've never been inside. It's fun. You'll see."

Mosko hesitated, turning his hat in his hand.

"Unless you're afraid of the dark," Rose added, sure that a challenge to the ego of someone of Mosko's stature would not go unanswered.

"Lead the way," he said.

Jacob

"TAKE YOUR COUSINS AND GET OUT OF HERE," AUNT GLADYS said.

Jacob recognized the signs his aunt was having another of her "spells." That's what she called them. The children knew from prior experience not to yell or scream or stomp around the floor or ask for anything including lunch or dinner during these periods. Sometimes the spell came on while they were away in school or outside. When they came home, they'd find a closed door and a darkened apartment. Gladys would be sitting with her head in her hands on the sofa or lying in her bed, the shades drawn, the door closed, the bed covers or a pillow over her head.

She must have felt it coming this time, as she was in the kitchen gripping the counter, staring at a pile of dirty dishes and utensils stacked in the sink. Jacob set the last pot from the stove onto the counter and looked at his aunt. She put her hands to her head, one on each temple, pushing and pulling the loose skin like the dough she kneaded each week.

"Do you want me to do the dishes?" Jacob asked in a whisper, hoping she would say no.

Her head moved from side to side, slowly, still clasped between her hands. "No," she said in a hushed tone as if she feared the sound of her own voice might aggravate her spell. "Just go and take them outside for a while."

Before she had a chance to change her mind, Jacob took

hold of Leila and Ralph and pulled them out of the kitchen. He grabbed his hat and Leila's and then, on tiptoes, the three walked out the front door, closing it behind them without making a sound. Jacob gave his two charges his best imitation of his father's expression. The look, a wide-eyed stare straight into their upturned faces. Their mouths were open and ready to complain, but the look told them to say nothing and do as he said.

Outside on the stoop, he laced Leila's shoes. She'd been ready to kick them off when Gladys had given her warning. "Where are we going?" Leila asked, her tone whiny and hesitant; she would have preferred to go back inside.

"Shush," Ralph said. "Mama needs to rest." Then he turned to Jacob. "Where are we going?"

At that moment, Jacob didn't know, but he wasn't about to allow his indecision to show. They'd sense his uncertainty and complain. This was the first time he could remember a spell coming in the evening, on a week night. At least it had chosen to scuttle under the door and into the apartment after dinner rather than before they'd eaten or Leila and Ralph would complain of being hungry. "We're going down to the beach."

"But it's night," Leila said, one hand rubbing an eye.

"It's not night. It's just after dinner. You'll like the lights. I'll bet you don't remember seeing the lights on the Jack Rabbit."

"I don't want to ride a roller coaster. I'm scared."

"Baby," Ralph said.

"I am not."

"Be quiet," Jacob said, wresting back control of the situation. "We're not going to ride the coaster, anyway. We're just going to look."

Though the complaining and questioning continued unabated for several blocks, as soon as the rocky wall of the beach came into view, the conversation shifted back to what they were going to do. "No, we're not going swimming. Like I said, we're just going to look."

"There's a place we can sit," Ralph said, pointing to a bench nearby. An elderly couple occupied the far side, but there was room to their left. Jacob took the middle and settled Leila and Ralph to his side.

"I want an ice cream," Leila said.

Jacob had overestimated her ability to sit and watch in silence. "You're not getting one. You just ate dinner."

"I want to go on a ride."

"We're not going on a ride."

Leila would not be placated.

"You're doing a fine job of minding your sister, young man," the woman next to him said. Jacob wanted to explain that Leila was not his sister but decided it was not worth the effort.

"I want to ride the flying horses."

"I said we're not going on a ride."

Ralph added, "We can't. We don't have a nickel. Now shut up."

The couple rose from the bench. But before they ambled away, the old woman called to Jacob. Expecting an admonishment for Leila's constant whining, he said, "I'm sorry ma'am, we didn't mean to disturb you."

"Oh, no, dear, you needn't worry. We were just leaving. Such a lot of responsibility for someone so young. You remind me of my grandson." She scratched along the bottom of her purse. "Here," she said, "take this and buy your sister and brother an ice cream." She dropped several coins in Jacob's hand. He closed his fingers around them, hiding the gift from Ralph and Leila.

"Are you happy, Leila?" Jacob asked. He and Ralph had gobbled their scoops of ice cream and thrown away their cups. Leila, though, ate hers slowly and ran her spoon around the edges of the cup, gathering the last remnants of the sugary concoction. She nodded.

By chance, when Jacob glanced over Leila's head, he caught a glimpse of Rose Margolin coming from the pier, a man holding her close, pressing his body against hers. He blinked, looked at his feet, and then back at the couple, sure he'd mistaken someone else for Mrs. Margolin. But it was Miss Rose, though she looked unlike herself. She had the same hair and skin and carriage, but wore an expression on her face that he didn't recognize.

Jacob placed a knee on the ground. He bent his head over and fumbled with Leila's shoe, untying and retying her laces. He took his time, keeping an eye on the chocolate brown skirt that passed only a few yards from where he and his cousins stood. When he was certain Miss Rose and the stranger had not spotted them, he started after them. "Let's walk this way," he said to his cousins, oblivious to whether or not they trotted behind him. He craned his neck this way and that, catching slices of Miss Rose through the intervening arms and legs and torsos.

"Where are we going, now?" Ralph asked.

Jacob did not answer. He knew where Miss Rose was going. She was leading the stranger to the Tunnel of Love, the ride she'd shared with him a few weeks ago, the one she'd said was her favorite. At the entrance, Jacob watched as Rose stepped up to the boarding platform. She laughed, but it was not the laugh Jacob knew, the one that sounded like bells. Isador's words flooded his head. "Men friends and women friends. It doesn't mean anything. It's what adults do." Jacob wanted to ask someone if this laugh, mouth full open and throaty, was a laugh reserved for adults. She boarded the car. The man followed, his hat in his hand. As the car set off along the track, the man put his arm around Miss Rose's shoulder.

"Come on. Quick. Come on," Jacob called, urging the two younger children along.

"Where are we going?" the question came again.

"We're going on a ride."

"But I want to go on the flying horses."

"Okay. Okay. We'll go there next."

Jacob handed the operator fifteen cents and the three piled into a car, two cars behind Miss Rose and the man.

Once the car passed under the crescent opening, Jacob willed his eyes to adjust to the dark. He slowed his breathing, clenched his fingers around the car's rail, and tuned his ears to the sounds ahead. The laughter had ceased, replaced by strains of the recorded tune piped inside the tunnel. Rose had said it was *For Me and My Gal* and had hummed a few bars. The volume of the music grew as they penetrated further inside the tunnel until it dampened the occasional squeal of riders on the nearby amusements, the jingle jangle of the barkers outside, and far off the clamor of the flying horses going through their circuit.

"It's dark in here," Leila said, squirming in her seat.

"Don't be a baby," Ralph said.

Jacob did not respond. He kept his eyes fastened on the car ahead as it angled to the right, the heads of the riders joined as one.

"I'm scared," Leila said.

"Close your eyes," Ralph said.

A few more turns and then a straightaway, the cherubs on the walls lit by tiny lamps where their hearts would be.

"I want to go," Leila said.

"Hush."

The first shot brought no response from anyone in the tunnel. Jacob suspected most of the riders had been in the arms of their fellow riders and attributed the sound, if they'd noticed it at all, to another of the beach-side amusements or a car backfiring. The second came swiftly, and this time the sound reverberated across the dark tunnel. Gasps and shouts came from passengers in front and behind Jacob and his cousins. They twisted and turned in their seats to locate the source.

Leila whimpered and plugged her ears.

"What was that?" Ralph asked.

Jacob knew where to look. A glow of light filled a rectangle on the right. A second later, it was gone. Only someone who had anticipated the side door opening and who had known where to look would have seen the silhouette against the light as a woman's figure passed through.

"You take Leila when the ride ends and you go home," Jacob said to Ralph. "You understand?"

"Where are you going?"

"Just do as I say. Take her home."

With that, Jacob squeezed under the rail in front of him and jumped from the car onto the small footpath. Keeping close to the wall, he felt his way to the door. He located the doorknob, opened the door, and shut it behind him as quickly as Rose had.

Jacob found himself alone in a small room, brightly lit compared with the pitch black in the tunnel. The room was little more than a closet, filled on one side with switches and wire and on the other with hooks holding brooms, dustpans, mops, and a few tools. On the far wall was another door that he guessed opened to the outside. Miss Rose, if it were Rose that he'd seen, had come and gone, exiting through the far door.

He'd guessed correctly. The door emptied into an alleyway running the length of the Tunnel of Love. Jacob glanced to his right, toward the entrance and then back to his left. Only one or two fun seekers ambled by. Rose was nowhere in sight. He ran toward the far end of the alley, toward the Aeroplane Whirl, the carousel, and several other amusements. If Rose wanted to disappear, she'd be more likely to head deeper into the crowds around the amusements.

At the end of the alley, he stood on the tips of his toes. There was no sign of Rose or the man with the hat in his hand. A few discarded crates sat alongside the wall behind the carousel. He turned one upright and boosted himself on top. Beyond the sea of black-banded straw hats and countless numbers of dark haired women, he spied a head of blonde hair.

Jacob tore through the crowd, weaving left and right, bumping into one person then another, not bothering to apologize. Behind him, he left a trail of astonished men and women and a chorus of "Slow down there, young man" or "How rude." The thought of what his aunt would say on seeing Ralph and Leila return alone made him hesitate. Then, behind him, where he imagined the entrance to the Tunnel of Love was, he heard a high pitched sound. A scream. Another followed.

Screams of horror, easily distinguished from the excited peals of the passengers aboard the Jack Rabbit careening around another sharp curve.

Jacob knew what the screams meant. He knew the car two cars ahead of his had emerged from the dark and had rolled to a stop at the boarding platform, its lone inhabitant slumped over the rail, perhaps an arm lying limp outside the car, the curve of the shoulders concealing the blood on the man's shirtfront. He saw in his mind's eye the operator lean forward and tap the man on the shoulder, calling out, "Sir? Sir?" He saw the young couple waiting to board, their hands going to their mouths, the woman's high pitched scream splitting the air when the stranger's body fell lifeless to the ground, half in and half out of the car.

"Rose!" he shouted, though he knew she could not hear him. He ran to where he'd seen her last and then to the far side of the Aeroplane Whirl where she might have headed back to the boardwalk. Jacob could not imagine where else she might have gone. He spotted a lone figure on the beach near the shoreline. A woman's figure, too dark to see clearly, but of Rose's height and build and dressed in chocolate brown, blending into the dark. She walked, bareheaded toward the ocean.

"Rose!" he screamed. "Miss Rose!" but the ocean drowned his words.

Earl

EARL HANDED VIRGINIA A CUP OF ICE CREAM, ACCEPTED A SEC-
ond from the vendor, and then wandered away with his lady
companion into the crowd. Virginia raised her cup and held it
to her forehead. "Ooh. Try this. It's deliciously cool."

"You're supposed to eat it," he said, "not wear it."

Ro.

"Oh shush, you. I'm so hot I could put it down my blouse."

"If you did, I'd have to take it off and lick it up right here."

Rose.

"You would not. You might want to, but you wouldn't"

"Don't try me," Earl said.

Miss Rose.

Earl took a spoon of his cup of ice cream and raised it to
his mouth. They headed away from the boardwalk, down to
the beach.

Later, when he recalled the events, Earl relived them as if
they had unfolded slowly, as if they had oozed past like warm
maple syrup, when in fact they had hurtled by.

At the instant he put the spoonful of ice cream on his
tongue, Earl was conscious of a sound out of kilter with the
other sounds of the beach on a hot summer night. He turned
toward the ocean.

Slap. Plop. Ping.

Against the placid surface, where a moment before the

ocean shimmied in and out with hardly a ripple, something or someone was tearing through the water.

Virginia pointed a red-tipped finger at the disturbance in the water. "Can you believe that? Someone's going swimming at this hour. They must be crazy or really, really hot."

The figure in the water flailed its arms, creating sprays of froth that caught the fading light and then fell back into the gray blue water below. Earl's eyes traveled back from the figure to the beach where two shoes lay discarded half-way to the water and then to a boy's cap in the surf, riding an incoming ripple of water before retreating to the ocean. The figure was not swimming as Virginia had suggested. It was erect, running back and forth in the shallows. Then a strong wave rolled in on the otherwise calm water and washed over the figure's head. Earl stared and held his breath until the wave passed.

"Where'd he go?" Virginia asked, putting words to Earl's thoughts.

A hand broke the surface of the water and thrashed, pawing at the air and at the water, but finding nothing. The hand slipped below the surface.

When Virginia opened her mouth again, a cup of ice cream and a tiny wooden spoon lay on the ground, the cream losing itself in the sand. Earl was twenty feet away, his straw boater taking flight like a gull behind his head, his legs pumping, and his arms tearing at his jacket. He stopped long enough to remove his shoes and then ran into the ocean. His legs churned through the shallow water, cutting a deep swath and creating his own spray of white. Once waist deep, he threw himself at the horizon and slapped his arms one after the other toward his goal.

Earl stopped swimming at the point where he thought the hand had disappeared. He treaded water, circled, and flung his head one way and then another, tossing strands of hair from his eyes and water from his lashes. He took a deep breath, held it, and dove below the surface, arms circling and reaching where his eyes could not see in the murky water. Nothing. He breached the surface, paddled a few feet to his right, and submerged again. This time something soft brushed his fingertips. He kicked his feet, propelling his body toward the mass, grabbing and clawing at the form. He found an arm, a shoulder, and then a head. Another kick brought Earl back to the surface, with a head cupped in his palm, the face skyward.

The body was small and thin, a boy, not a man. Earl paddled with his free arm toward the shore.

Once in the shallows, he found the sandy bottom with his feet and pulled the boy into his arms, scrambling toward the beach. A small crowd had gathered. When Earl fell to the sand, laying the boy on his back, the crowd closed in around the two.

"Get back," Earl said, his voice a croak, his lungs heaving, out of breath and gasping for air. He looked at the boy, his hair slick to his skull, his clothes clinging to his body, more like a seal than a boy. A spray of freckles marked his forehead. It was the boy from Nahant.

Earl turned the boy over and placed him over his knee. He slapped an open palm between the boy's shoulder blades, waited, and then pounded again.

The boy coughed. Seawater spilled from his mouth. He retched. He drew in a long breath, put a hand to his stomach, and somehow managed to place his knees beneath his chest. He planted a foot on the ground and lunged forward.

"Miss Rose."

He raised an arm and clawed at the air, urging his body back toward the water's edge.

"Rose?" Earl asked.

"She's out there."

"Where?"

"There," the boy said, a tiny hand pointing at the horizon.

Earl was on his feet and back in the water, his eyes on the thin gray line that separated the water from the sky, the line barely discernible. He splashed through the water, going to the right for several yards, and then turned and ran back to the left. Nothing, not a wave and scarcely a ripple between him and the horizon. Earl dove into the water and swam out, his arms pumping again, stopping every few yards to tread water and look around. He looked back toward the shore where the boy stood, held back by an onlooker, but with his arm still pointing out to sea. Earl swam further along the line the boy indicated. He treaded water. He dove below the surface and flailed underwater. The sea surrounded him and slowed his motions. The silt clouded his sight. The ocean slid between his outstretched fingers.

When Earl returned to the shore, he walked over to the boy and looked at his upturned face, wet now with tears. Earl clasped a hand on the boy's back, pulled him close and let him cry against his body.

When Jacob quieted, Earl beckoned to Virginia. "Can you take the boy home? Just up to Nahant. He'll show you where." Virginia nodded and helped Earl pry Jacob from his side. They headed inland, hand in hand. As soon as they were out of sight, Earl turned toward the Tunnel of Love where, moments before, he'd seen two policemen head on a run.

The morning after the incident, Earl arrived at Nahant as the sun was rising. Jacob was waiting for him on the stoop outside his apartment, though neither had spoken a word after Earl had asked Virginia to take him home.

Jacob rose and walked with Earl down Nahant without speaking and without a glance at the empty apartment opposite, the one with the darkened windows on the third floor. They put one foot in front of the other, more like sleepwalkers or condemned criminals on the way to their execution than two people with a purpose. They walked along the beach from the Beachview pavilion to the ballroom at the southern end of the crescent shaped beach and then turned and retraced their steps.

Earl's steps labored against the soft sand. By noon, Earl's legs were weary. He imagined the boy's were the same, though Jacob had not complained. Earl paused at a point across from Shirley Avenue and looked at Jacob. He took the boy's hand in his and turned away from the ocean.

On Nahant, the boy looked up, his eyebrows raised, eyes wide, an expectant look, as if Earl had an answer, a plan, or could somehow undo what had been done. Earl met Jacob's gaze. He moved his head once to the left and then to the right.

Jacob circled his arms around Earl and buried his head in Earl's heavy coat, the warmth of the wool absorbing his tears. When Jacob's sobs subsided, the boy stepped back, turned, and climbed the stone steps. He stopped at the door, glanced back at Earl, wiped his face with his hand, and then opened the door and disappeared inside.

Though the shooting had occurred too late for the morning newspapers, by the time Earl walked uptown, word had spread. The police had instantly recognized the victim and despite the late hour had sent an officer to inform Mrs. Saul Mosko. Someone, most likely an inside man, had passed word to his contact within the Mosko organization. The body had been picked up, but in the confusion, shipped to a morgue affiliated with St. Paul's Catholic Church. From there the news made its way to the Nicolini gang and then through the streets by way of barbers, tailors, green grocers, and pharmacists. So far, no one had identified the shooter. One rumor mentioned a hired killer, another a woman, perhaps a lover.

All morning Earl had forced himself to concentrate on one thing, Rose. He tried to put himself in her state of mind. He went over everything she'd said the last time he'd seen her but had nothing but unanswered questions to show for his efforts.

At two in the afternoon, he made his way to the Imperial Café where, as he suspected, a number of Mosko's men had gathered. He was right, all but one of the tables—the table at the back, the one behind the beaded curtain—were full by the time he walked through the door. Across the café came the sounds of the clink of china and the screech of cutlery across plates. The conversations taking place at each table were in low tones, a hum that played in the background.

Earl found an empty chair and pulled it to a table beside the curtain. Rosenberg sat at the head surrounded by Gene Smilowe, Francis Toomey, and Lenny, Mosko's driver, as well as another of Mosko's men he knew only by sight. Rosenberg's elbow was propped on the table, the fingers of his right hand splayed in the air. He recited a series of names, crooking each finger into his palm as he did so, finishing with his pinky and saying, "My money's on Koiles." Heads nodded all around.

Jack Koiles was Mosko's handpicked successor, his closest associate, though rarely seen in public. Earl had met him once and knew his reputation. He was nothing like Mosko. He lacked the deceased's refinement and subtleties. Koiles had fought his way to the top, from leg-breaker to lieutenant to second in command and, apparently, to boss, without Mosko's connections and head for the business, at least so Earl thought. There would be changes and tough times ahead.

"It's business as usual tomorrow for the funeral, but you can expect some action after that," Rosenberg continued. Heads nodded again. The Koiles gang, if it were to be his, would make a show of force. "Nicolini's already been showing his ugly mug in places he shouldn't be. No respect at all. Koiles will put a stop to that." More nods. No one else had anything to say.

Men came and went all afternoon. Allen Foye sat where Gene had an hour ago and Colin Sakowitz in the seat Rosenberg had occupied. Earl kept to his chair until the crowd thinned. Late in the day, he found himself alone with Lenny. The driver's eyes were downcast and the skin below puffy and red. Like Earl, he'd said little all afternoon.

"The woman," Earl said, fishing.

Lenny nodded. "If I'd have been driving...never would have happened."

"Can't blame yourself."

"He insisted."

"You couldn't say no."

Their conversation continued in half sentences. Earl probed and held back, letting Lenny fill the silence with scraps of information from which Earl pieced together Rose's last weeks and her growing desperation.

Lenny would be discrete, he'd never divulge her name or that the affair had been going on for months, nothing to sully Mosko's name or cause his widow undue suffering. Earl would as well.

Earl mulled over the situation. Rose must have worried someone would make the connection between Mosko, Rose, and Isador Margolin and perhaps try to avenge Mosko's death. That's why she'd extracted the promise from him. But, Earl hoped, with a new boss at the helm, there would be a lot of activity, attentions would turn elsewhere, and the story would fade from the front pages. He might not have to do anything.

Only Earl and the boy from Nahant knew the connection. He'd keep it that way. And he'd abide by his promise to look after Isador. To keep him safe. He'd do that for Rose.

On Friday morning, Earl passed Nahant again on his way to the beach. The stoop in front of the boy's apartment was empty. He hoped Jacob was inside or, better yet, playing ball somewhere with friends. If Rose's body turned up on the beach, it would not be a sight he wanted the boy to see. It wasn't one Earl wanted to see. And though he dreaded finding her, if he did, he wanted to find Rose alone. He wanted to have one moment with her.

Earl did find her after the sea retreated. Her body lay sprawled face down on the rocks where the tide had left her like a seashell, bleached and broken. The chocolate brown outfit she'd worn was thick with sand and, in places, shredded. Her blond hair, still wet and matted, shielded her face from view. He draped his jacket over her head and shoulders and kneeled beside her on the sand.

Earl was there an hour later when the sun broke through the clouds on the horizon. He remained there holding her in his arms until they took her from him.

ABOUT THE AUTHOR

RONA SIMMONS GREW UP IN A MILITARY FAMILY WITH ITS CON-
stant duty rotations denying her the luxury of establishing
roots and the comfort of the familiar, but gaining the invalu-
able opportunity to live abroad and experience diverse cultures.

Rona was determined to pursue a business career and
earned a BA in Economics from Newcomb College and later
an MBA from Georgia State University. She spent thirty years
in corporate America where she honed her skills in analy-
sis and research, never knowing that she'd make use of those
same talents after retiring in unearthing, examining, and con-
structing stories from small kernels of information.

Postcards from Wonderland is her most recent work. Previous
works include *The Quiet Room*, a novel set in Evansville, Indi-
ana, her mother's hometown and based loosely on her grandmother's life, a ghostwritten biography of a prominent Atlanta businessman, a collection of short stories compiled from
interviews of family and friends from the early to mid 1900s,
articles for a local Atlanta magazine and a horticultural journal, and flash fiction broadcast on internet radio.

Rona lives with her husband and (she swears) the last
member of a passel of cats outside Atlanta, Georgia on eight
pine-studded acres. Though her next novel is a work of con-
temporary fiction, Rona insists she's hardly scratched the surface of stories set in the early twentieth century.

* * *

Photographs and other information relevant to *Postcards from Wonderland* are posted on www.ronasimmons.com.

If you enjoyed reading *Postcards from Wonderland*, the author invites you to leave a review on Amazon.com or Goodreads.com. The author also welcomes comments and questions from her readers. To contact Rona Simmons, visit her website or send an email to rona_simmons@bellsouth.net.com.

DISCUSSION

1. The illustrations introducing each section of the book are taken from vintage postcards of Wonderland Park, the now defunct amusement park that once thrilled crowds of visitors at the north end of Revere. By the time Isador and Rose Margolin meet and marry, the park had failed and been demolished, living on only in people's memories. What is the significance of the park, its rise and fall, and the memory of it in the story? How do the specific cards foretell the events of that section?

2. The author tells the story from the perspectives of the four main characters, Rose, Isador, Earl, and Jacob. Did this approach help you understand the characters better? Did you identify with one of the characters more than another? Is the story Rose's, or Isador's or Earl's? How would the story differ if told through the eyes of only one of the four?

3. The characters in the novel are almost exclusively of Jewish descent, even the mobsters. The author has deliberately avoided the more stereotypical portrayal of Italian organized crime. Why do you believe that is? How would the story be different if the characters were Italian or Irish or from any other ethnic background?

4. At the end of the book, Rose takes a very bold action to free herself from the dire circumstances in which she finds her-

self. When do you believe the seeds of that decision were planted? What evidence is there about her plans? What alternatives were available to her?

5. Love and hate, fidelity, and betrayal, and ultimately forgiveness are key themes in the novel. Rose forgives Earl and her request of him seems to indicate she forgives Isador as well. Does she? Could you have done the same?

* * *

The author is delighted to participate in book club discussions of *Postcards from Wonderland* by phone or, where practical, in person. Please contact Rona Simmons through her website (www.ronasimmons.com) or by email (rona_simmons@ bellsouth.net) to arrange a discussion.

ACKNOWLDEDGEMENTS

CONCEIVING, RESEARCHING, WRITING, EDITING, AND PUBLISHING
this story would not have been possible without a great deal
of help from family and friends, to readers, editors, critique
group members, and even complete strangers.

Particular thanks goes to my father who when prodded dug
deep into his past to recall the facts surrounding the arrest and
later release of my great uncle from the Massachusetts State
Penitentiary, an event that, for good reason, had never been
mentioned before but about which he knew enough to spark
the imagination. I also wish to thank my cousin, whose family
resides in Massachusetts, for the family photos and memories
she shared of the "good old days" growing up in Revere and
my sister who once again dared offer her unvarnished opin-
ions and editing advice for the work in progress.

I am indebted to Roland Merullo, author of a number of
novels set in Revere (including in particular *Revere Beach Boulevard* and *The Return*), for his willingness to answer my questions
about the city, the people, especially the gangsters and their
habits and speech patterns and for reading the story in one
of its very early and severely flawed stages. Other sources of
information include Rose Keefe's *The Starker*, Rich Cohen's
Tough Jews: Fathers, Sons, and Gangster Dreams, and Professor Ra-
chel Rubin's *Jewish Gangsters of Modern Literature*.

Further, as any author today knows, the job of recreating
1920s Revere would have been far more difficult and time

consuming without the unsung authors of and contributors to the many websites I consulted, whether of vintage newspapers whose headlines blared the latest gang slayings, period fashion magazines advertising the styles of the day, or the myriad others full of references to Revere Beach, mobsters, Prohibition, and speakeasies. Finally, thanks goes to the collectors of Wonderland Park memorabilia whose postcards, tickets, and stories leant another perspective to my father's memories and brought the sights and sounds of "America's Beach" to life.

As always, my deepest thanks goes to my husband for concealing his impatience as I typed, read aloud, edited, edited, and edited again while dinner languished.

CPSIA information can be obtained at www.ICGtesting.com
Printed in the USA
LVOW11s1333040816

499070LV00006B/203/P